LUBOV LEONOVA

GHOST

A Murder Mystery

FriesenPress

Suite 300 - 990 Fort St
Victoria, BC, V8V 3K2
Canada

www.friesenpress.com

ISBN
978-1-5255-8851-8 (Hardcover)
978-1-5255-8850-1 (Paperback)
978-1-5255-8852-5 (eBook)

1. Fiction, Romance, New Adult

Distributed to the trade by The Ingram Book Company

Table of Contents

Prologue

An old corridor drowned in darkness. Lana sneaked out of the corner and crawled along the stone wall. Her hand held a shining yellow sphere that illuminated her wide hood and revealed her big brown eyes. It was quiet, and the only sound was water droplets falling from the ceiling onto the stone floor. The sound of someone's heavy steps halted her.

Lana stood frozen; the footsteps were close.

"Damn," she whispered.

She clasped her hands, and the Light from the sphere disappeared. Lana hid behind the nearest pillar and held her breath.

A tall guard in a hooded black cloak came out of the end of the corridor. As he approached, the shining red ball of Light in his hands caused the shadows to crawl away and snuggle into the moisture-laden stones. With the Light gleaming on his half-hidden face, the guard looked around. Closing her eyes, Lana turned to the wall, her nails piercing her palms. She couldn't hear anything but the deafening sound of her heart.

Had the guard noticed me?

Several endless seconds passed before Lana dared to open her eyes. The guard walked away, and the shadows behind him writhed back, filling the area the ball of red Light once touched. Lana leaned out from the pillar to see the gleam of torchlights dancing at the far end of the corridor.

Almost there.

She took a deep breath and ran forward.

Lana entered a round hall. The lit torches gleamed on the bars of the dungeon's cells. Nine chambers occupied with prisoners lined the walls. As she removed her hood, the flaxen braids that adorned her head fell to her narrow shoulders.

Someone shuffled in the cell in front of her. A thin face with sad blue eyes looked at her. Approaching the chamber, Lana reached out to touch the cold lattice. The girl in front of her gave her a tired look.

"Rebecca," Lana whispered.

The girl sighed. "What do you want?"

"They told me what happened."

Lana stretched out her hand, but Rebecca leaned back and raised her hand in return. Fresh burns covered her fingertips.

"They took all my magic away," the girl said, looking at her damaged fingers. "I thought you were my friend, Lana, but you're just another deceitful Mercy sister. . . Just admit it—you lied to me."

Lana's heart sank. "I swear, I didn't know. They said the risk of complication—"

"The risk? You promised me it wouldn't happen!" Rebecca's eyes welled; her chin trembled.

"I'll get you out of here—"

Rebecca shook her head. "It's not just me."

Lana's hand squeezed a metal bar. "How many girls have lost their magic?"

"All of us."

Lana stopped breathing. A bed creaked, and in the depths of the chamber, two thin silhouettes arose and walked toward her. Lana had often seen these girls in the corridors of Mercy House—they all used to have harmful Gifts, and she'd personally asked them to go through the procedure of giving their Gifts away. It was hard to believe they had lost all their magic. It wasn't possible, because the risk of complication was exceedingly small. *Wasn't it?*

Lana tried to concentrate. It was too late to turn back now. She'd already stolen a key and almost gotten caught by the guard. Lana took Rebecca's hand, and before Rebecca could say a word, Lana put a small key into her palm.

"The guards change at midnight," Lana whispered. "The corridor will lead you to the back door, and then you'll see how to escape. I'll be waiting for you on the hill."

Rebecca squeezed the key in her hand. Her eyes sparkled, but she didn't say a word.

Lana stepped back. All the other girls were awake now; their eyes glared at her through the darkness of the cells.

Lana looked around. "I didn't know, I swear—"

One of the girls kicked the bars on her left. The clank made Lana flinch.

"Get out of here!" the girl shouted.

"Bitch!" another voice said.

Lana stepped back and stumbled. She fell to her knees on the stone floor, and her blood pulsed in her temples. They continued shouting. They moaned, wailed, and kicked at the metal like furious animals.

If only she could help them all. Lana stood and escaped into the darkness of the corridor.

★ ★ ★

Lana pushed through the heavy entrance door and walked outside. It was night. The rain watered an empty backyard and pelted the garbage bins that stood at the tall fence. Lana looked up, the droplets falling on her face. Cold water mixed with her tears, washing them away.

Lana crossed the yard and climbed up one of the bins, wondering why the silly guards placed it there, giving her a perfect opportunity to escape. Maybe because no Mercy sister had ever run away from this place before?

Lana climbed over the fence and jumped down. Then she ran. The rain became heavier, and her boots slid on the wet grass, but she didn't stop until she reached the hill where she was supposed to meet Rebecca. Here, the forest was dense, and the damp bark of the trees glowed a bright green.

Breathless, Lana leaned on a thick pine tree and glanced back. Pouring rain hit the dark roof and stone walls of Mercy House—a place of hope that was run by liars. When Lana had first come here, she'd just turned twenty one and was eager to help the Mercy sisters who worked with harmful Gifts. How could she have been so naive?

"You will pay for this," Lana said.

Lightning pierced the sky; the flash lit up the walls and empty windows of Mercy House, followed by a deafening sound of thunder. A thin silhouette climbed the hill, closing the distance. Lana squinted through the rain. It was Rebecca. Lana stretched out her hand, and the girl took it.

Rebecca stood in front of her, water droplets sliding down her face. Her clothes were wet, and her shoulders shook.

"I'm so sorry, Becca."

Rebecca narrowed her eyes. "Are you going back now? To the sorority?"

Lana shook her head. "I decided to quit."

"Good choice."

Lana turned toward Mercy House. It stared at her with murky black windows. Lana clenched her teeth. Life was never fair, but how long would this deception last?

"They lied to me, all this time," Lana said. "I thought I was helping, but—"

"You didn't know," Rebecca said. "Lana, I'm not mad anymore. Let's just get the hell out of here."

Lana sighed. "Becca, we have to split up here—"

"No!"

Lana touched Rebecca's shoulders. "They'll start looking for us. We would be taking a huge risk by sticking together. Do you want to make it home?"

Rebecca nodded.

"Listen carefully," Lana continued. "You need to go north; there is a village an hour's walk from here. Steal a horse and then continue riding north. Don't stop until you reach Middle Lake City. It's a huge place and it's easy to get lost."

"Lost, like they won't find me?" Rebecca asked.

"Not for a while. They use magic to find people, but you don't have powers now."

"I see."

"Look for the old theater in the city center. Tell them Lana sent you. They'll help get you home."

"And then?"

"Find your father and mine. Tell them what happened to you when you reach Triville."

"I don't think I can make it." Rebecca's voice trembled.

"I know it's scary, but we need to be brave if we want to stop all this mess happening in Mercy House. Do you understand?"

Rebecca nodded. "I don't want anyone else to suffer."

Lana hugged her tightly. "I'll be in Triville a week from now, and I'll see you there. Together, we'll work this out."

"I'll do my best."

"Me too. I promise."

Lana looked into the girl's scared eyes one more time, then turned and walked away.

Chapter 1. The Gift

Three years later

Fresh green leaves rustled in the spring forest, and the afternoon sun shone through the canopy. Bella walked along a narrow trail. Small birds jumped from branch to branch and twittered, and twigs creaked under her polished red shoes.

Bella stopped and breathed in the sweet smell of the white lilies of the valley that lined the wooded path. Her dress had a bright red flower pattern that matched her shoes perfectly. Bella touched the soft red ribbon in her dark brown hair and adjusted the bow. Her brown eyes looked up at the cloudless blue sky.

"Kyle," she whispered.

Bella smiled. She had been waiting for this day ever since she'd overheard the conversation on the school playground. Kyle spoke with his friend about Sunday, and he was going to hunt with his father in the forest. If Kyle chose this trail on his way back, then he might finally notice her.

Obeying her bodily instincts, Bella picked up a lily of the valley from the forest path and spun around with the bell-shaped flower in her hands. Bella pressed the flower to her chest, her heart beating faster at the thought of *him*.

"Hey, Weirdo!" a chorus of familiar voices interrupted Bella's awkward dance.

She stopped and looked toward the glade. Three girls sat on the lush grass, making flower garlands. All of them were from her literature class. The day suddenly stopped being so nice.

Bella fidgeted with her dress, and the flower fell to the grass.

"Hi," Bella said.

The girl with beautiful golden hair laughed and a flame sparkled in her dark blue eyes. It was Elisa—the beauty of the school, as the boys called her. Bella alluded to her differently, but only when no one could hear.

Bella took a slow step back. "I think I'd better go—"

Elisa stood up, and the two other girls followed her. Bella stopped breathing as the girls approached.

"Well, well, well," Elisa said when she came close. "Just look at this nice dress! She looks like a little princess."

The other girls stood behind Elisa. Rose, a tall girl, with a long pale face and a black braid, never really paid attention to anyone like Bella. The other girl, Julia, had olive skin and warm hazel eyes. In literature class, Julia sat in front of Bella, and she was always kind to her. But not now—Elisa was watching. These girls were all so different. How could they possibly be such good friends?

Julia revealed her charming smile. "It must be a special occasion, Bella. Is it your birthday?"

"Is it?" Elisa gave Bella a sharp look.

Bella looked down at her dress. Her birthday was actually in autumn, and she would turn sixteen, but none of them knew that. Maybe they would be a bit kinder if she had been born today.

Maybe it would be better to pretend.

"Yes, it's today," Bella nodded.

Elisa clasped her hands. "That's another matter, then!"

Rose looked at Bella with her black eyes. "We were making a flower garland for you," she said. Her voice was as listless as her sight.

Bella opened her mouth to explain everything and to excuse herself, but the words stuck in her throat. No, she couldn't tell the truth; the truth would be worse. No one could know about her feelings toward Kyle.

Elisa and Rose approached, and each girl took one of her arms. Bella tried to calm herself down, but like a fish on land, she helplessly inhaled air. Her thoughts twisted with anxiety. *Nothing bad will happen.* She glanced at their enthusiastic faces. *What could these three do to me?*

Once the girls reached the middle of the glade, they released her.

"What are you doing?" Bella asked when her ability to speak returned.

"You'll see," Rose said. Her cold voice sounded like a shard of ice.

Elisa held the garland that was made from lilies of the valley. She looked at Bella and frowned. Then, she approached her and removed the silky red ribbon from Bella's head. Bella watched with wide eyes.

Elisa threaded the red silk around the stems and tied the ends in a nice bow. "Here we go."

Julia took the garland and put it on Bella's head.

The strong aroma of the flowers made Bella wrinkle up her nose, and the girls laughed.

"Little mouse Bella," Rose said.

Great, now they're sharing jokes.

"She is so excited about the garland, she forgot how to speak!" Julia added.

"Ha, ha. Poor little thing!" Elisa said.

Bella patiently watched the girls. She'd learned that this kind of fun would not last forever. She knew the girls were cruel, but she never understood why they enjoyed it. Maybe they had nothing else to do. If they were smarter, they could go home and read books. Then their lives wouldn't be so pathetic.

Bella gave them a scornful look. All she could do now was stand in front of them and wait for their mocking laughter to stop.

Elisa caught her look. "Did you want to say something?"

Bella could say many words she'd learned from adult books, but she was too well brought up to point out others' stupidity. "Thank you," Bella said.

Elisa clasped her hands. "You know what? We have a real present for you!"

Rose smiled with her thin lips.

Julia walked to the edge of the glade and waved her hand, and a young guy walked out of the bushes. It was Kyle, handsome and tall with amazing blue eyes, and now he looked at her with curiosity. Her heart began to pound.

"Oh, my dear! Just look at you two!" Elisa said.

Bella glanced at her but said nothing; her words melted under the pressure. Kyle approached them and Elisa took his hand, pushing him toward Bella. In the middle of the glade, they stood in front of each other, surrounded by the laughing girls.

Bella numbly looked at him through a wall of tears. *Please, don't say anything,* she thought as her lips trembled.

"Now is your chance to confess!" Elisa said.

Bella was completely paralyzed by fear. When had she decided that she deserved a better destiny than being the school freak? Oh, right, it was Kyle who inspired her, and now he was standing in front of her, smiling. *Why would he do this to me?*

Elisa gave her a sharp look. "You know that Kyle is *my* boyfriend, don't you?"

Bella nodded. Everyone in the school knew about them, but she secretly hoped they would break up. She was foolish, thinking Kyle was a better person than this coldhearted selfish doll. *They are just the same.*

Bella hung her head and stared at the ground. Small bugs crawled in between the blades of grass and distracted her from reality. What were their lives like? They probably didn't have to go to school and, of course, they didn't bully each other, which meant that bugs had to be smarter than most humans.

"Come on, deceitful little bitch!" it was Elisa's voice. "We know it's not your birthday."

"You dressed up for *him*!" Rose said.

Bella kept staring at the bugs, her hands gripping the hem of her dress.

"You're in love!" Julia supported.

Someone poked her shoulder. Bella didn't see who it was, and she didn't care. A cold tear slid down her cheek, but she couldn't raise her hand to wipe it. Her body weakened, and her consciousness became concentrated somewhere in the depths of her chest, waiting for the mocking to stop.

"*Love, sweet love*," someone started singing, and the other girls joined.

The girls laughed, then they started skipping around Bella and Kyle like insane frogs.

"*You are my love, sweet love . . .*" they sang.

Bella clenched her teeth. Humans, in general, were cruel. Maybe they thought that humiliating those who were weaker would bring them more respect. Bella had never hated anyone in her life—well, sometimes, she hated herself—but that didn't count. Now they had crossed a line. They were laughing, jumping, singing, and Bella felt a wave of detestation slowly grow from the depths of her soul.

Everything was mixed up. The stinky flowers, Kyle, who was once so kind to her in school, but now stood with them and laughed. The voices of the girls surrounded her; they sang and sang, like nothing could shut them up.

You are the one who changed my world,
You are my sunshine and my hope,
Your charming smile highlights my life,
You are my love, sweet love . . .

Bella closed her eyes. Her mother sang this song to her before she passed away. The memory flashed before Bella's eyes: a cold winter day, frost on a window, her deep cough, and the day she was lost. Life was completely unfair.

How dare they?

The pressure inside of her became unbearable. Bella made herself take a deep breath, then she opened her mouth and screamed as loud as she could, covering her ears. Waves of energy pushed out from her chest. Like an invisible fist, the energy slammed into the girls, and they fell to the ground.

When the energy left her body, Bella stopped screaming. Tiny white pods and wrinkled petals were stuck between her shaking fingers. The girls lay on their backs and looked at the sky with blurred eyes, but Kyle wasn't hurt. He knelt on the grass and stared at her. Bella's heart pounded in her ears.

Kyle ran to Julia and shook her shoulders, but the girl was motionless.

"Come on, wake up!" Kyle shouted.

The sound of his voice made Bella flinch. She stepped back, and a branch cracked under her shoe.

Kyle turned his head and stared at Bella. "What have you done?"

Bella shook her throbbing head. "No," Bella whispered. "I didn't kill them . . ."

Kyle stepped forward. "Fix it, now!" He stared at Bella, and the vein on his neck throbbed.

Bella swung her arms. "I don't know . . . I don't . . . leave me alone!"

She turned around and ran to the forest. Her flower garland fell from her head and landed on the lush grass.

Kyle stayed in the glade, his nostrils inhaling the air. When Bella disappeared into the forest, he approached the garland and moved his hand over the wrinkled flowers. Broken images flashed before his eyes—he saw Bella running through the bushes. She ran to the other side of the creek.

Someone moaned behind him. Kyle looked back—Julia sat on the grass and rubbed her head. Kyle ran to help her stand up. He looked at the other girls. Rose was awake; she stood up and limped to Elisa. Elisa continued to lay on her back with her eyes shut, breathing slowly. Her face was as pale as school chalk, and pieces of grass were stuck in her messy hair.

All three of them approached Elisa and sat around her. Julia took her thin, motionless hand.

"It's Paralyzing magic," Julia concluded. "Unbelievable. I recently wrote an essay about it. It's strong, but its effects are only temporary."

Rose looked at her own palms. "And it feels like crap. I still can't feel my fingers."

Julia sighed. "This power is stronger toward the people she hates. Elisa suffered the most, but she'll be all right."

Kyle shook his head. "Bella. Who knew . . ."

"No one knows what our Gifts will be," Rose said.

Julia looked at Kyle. "You're lucky—her power didn't hurt you. She *really* loves you, Kyle. Oh, poor little thing! What have we done to her?" Julia raised her arms, then she rested them on her chest.

"We did the right thing," Rose said. "She's older than us, and she might end up like the others—in Mercy House."

Julia shook her head. "But we can't leave her alone now! We need to find her."

"Why?" Rose asked.

"She might get lost!"

Rose crossed her arms and moved her gaze to the bushes. "I think we should get out of here."

Kyle looked toward the forest, where the bushes swung in silence among the dark tree trunks. Bella was somewhere out there, alone. Soon, she wouldn't be.

"Kyle, please. Your father is a guardian! He needs to help her!" Julia's warm eyes swirled with numb anxiety.

Kyle put his palm on Julia's shoulder. "Nothing bad will happen. My Gift showed me where she ran. I think she'll find her way back."

"If she wants to come back," Rose added.

Chapter 2. The Favor

Lana approached the old wooden stairs and touched the railing. The house she was looking for was right on the hill, hidden among the tall pine trees. She looked at her map and smiled—the green dots of trees surrounded a blue oval lake, but there was no house drawn on the paper. The man who'd sold her the map hadn't lied—no one knew where the witch lived, even though this house was only a six-hour ride from Triville.

Lana climbed the stairs and walked through the front yard. Guided by a gentle breeze, the daffodils swung toward her like curious children. In front of the house, the bright morning sun fell on luscious green grass and round flower beds framed by river stones.

Lana stopped at the white door and took a deep breath before she knocked three times. She listened carefully, but it was quiet inside.

"Is anybody home?" Lana called out.

There was no reply but the quiet rustle of the grass behind her. Lana turned to the yard. The dirt in the flower beds was wet, and the daffodils had been recently watered, but it had not rained for a couple of days. *The witch must be somewhere nearby*, Lana concluded. She was most likely avoiding unwelcome visitors.

Lana knocked again, louder this time. "I'm not going away, Meredith!"

Quiet footsteps approached. The door opened, revealing a woman not as old as Lana had imagined her to be. White streaks accented her dark hair and nascent wrinkles framed her bright green eyes. She wore a simple beige cotton dress that covered her knees.

"Are you lost, girl?" Meredith asked.

"No. I need your help."

Meredith narrowed her eyes. "I don't know you."

"But I know about you, Meredith."

Meredith sneered. "All right, what do you want?"

Lana clasped the purse hanging on her belt. "To make a deal."

"I don't help strangers." Meredith started closing the door.

"Wait!" Lana put her foot on the threshold.

Meredith raised her hand, and a fireball spell grew in her palm. "Don't mess with me."

Lana raised her arms. "Listen, I'm not asking for myself. I'm only helping my friend."

"Which friend?"

Lana hesitated for a moment. Why would the witch need the name? It didn't matter; she had nothing to hide from her. "Rebecca Turner," she said.

Meredith gave her a suspicious look. "Rebecca died three years ago."

Lana sighed. Even after three years, it wasn't easy to think about Becca's death. But somehow, the witch knew her friend.

"I know, and I'm here to find out why," Lana said.

Meredith clasped her hands together, and the fireball disappeared. "What's your name?"

"I'm Lana."

The witch stepped back. "Come on in, then."

* * *

Lana stepped into a spacious living room; its curtains opened wide to let the daylight in. The walls were lined with shelves holding little glass bottles filled with liquid—probably potions. There were also books, old ones with leather covers. These books had to hold knowledge of the art of magic on their fragile yellow pages. Lana couldn't resist picking up a folder with a smooth green cover and neat golden letters: *The Agreements*. Interesting. Who else had been in the witch's house to sign these papers?

"Don't touch anything!" Meredith said.

Lana flinched, and she almost dropped the folder. She placed it back on the shelf.

Meredith had already put two steaming cups of tea on a round coffee table, so Lana sat on the sofa and took a teacup. The drink smelled of raspberries; it reminded her of the sunny days of her childhood.

"If you want me to help you, you must be completely honest," Meredith said, looming over her like a thundercloud.

Lana took a sip of tea and put the cup on a table. "Of course."

"How did you know Rebecca?"

Lana rested her hands in her lap. "I knew her all my life. Our fathers are guardians who work together in Triville. Three years ago, when I was a sister in Mercy House, Rebecca was brought in. No one there knew of our previous acquaintance."

"What was her Gift?"

"One of the most dangerous ones—she could create flames. As it happens with all new Gifts, Becca couldn't control it properly, and after an accident in school, she was sent to Mercy House."

Meredith scowled. "And you let them take her powers away."

"Of course not!" Lana said. "I mean, I tried to stop the sorority, but I was too late. When I found out they took all of her magic, I helped her escape. I thought that if her father saw her like that, he would do something to shut this facility."

Meredith nodded. "I see."

"On the night of the escape, Becca and I split up, so they wouldn't find us. I told her to be brave, but I was so scared. I was on my way home when I received a letter from my father. He told me about Becca's death." Lana's voice trembled. "He said it was a suicide, but I knew—someone killed her, and after that, I . . . I just couldn't come back home."

Meredith sat down on the sofa next to her. "You did the right thing—you might have been in danger."

"I know."

"Then why did you decide to come back?"

Lana clutched the teacup, chasing the chill from her hands. "Things changed. My father recently became a guardian chief, and he suggested I help him with the archives in Triville. I agreed."

"Hmm, a chief. Why don't you tell your father everything?"

"It's not that easy. I've made a lot of mistakes in the past; he would never believe me. I need solid proof."

The witch widened her eyes in surprise. "Proof?"

"Yes. I started working as a secretary in the archives a week ago, and I figured out that Rebecca's file was hidden. I found it suspicious. Why would the guardians place a suicide case in a secret archive?"

"That's interesting," Meredith said. "Go on."

"The guardians must have the information about the person who killed her, and they don't want anyone to know it. But once I figure it out, they won't be able to hide the truth about Mercy House any longer."

Meredith sneered. "Don't you think your father already knows the truth?"

"My father might be a chief, but he doesn't know everything. Listen, I know him; if he saw injustice, he would stand up against it. But he needs to believe me first."

"Well, I hope you know him well enough. How can I help?"

Lana put her hand in her pocket and pulled out a silver wedding ring. "This ring belongs to my father. I heard you have a rare Gift, and you can extract someone's energy from their personal belongings."

Meredith took the ring and weighed it in her hand. "It would only be a small amount—the size of a pea."

"It's enough. I just need it to open the locker of the secret archive."

Meredith gave her a sly look. "Just a locker . . . I've helped crack many magic locks, but never in a Guardian House. Are you sure you're ready to pay the price?"

Lana took out her purse, but Meredith put her hand on hers. "I'm not talking about the money."

"What, then?"

Meredith turned the ring in her hand and placed it on a coffee table. "Do you know why human energy is called 'Light'?"

Lana shrugged. "Because it shines?"

"Not only that. The word 'light' symbolizes hope, and if it's used in the right way, it can save many lives. Each person's Light is unique—it has a particular color, brightness, and structure. It's a baseline for different spells, and humans have been using these features of Light since the beginning of time. And now, you will be holding someone else's Light in your hands—only you can decide what to do with it. It's a huge responsibility, Lana; many things can go wrong. So, the question is—are you ready for the consequences?"

Lana stared at her. "Yes. Three years ago, I wasn't; I ran away. But I'm ready now."

The witch's eyes gleamed. "I won't take your money. I'll ask you for a favor instead. Not many people know this, but I educate the girls with destructive Gifts."

Lana raised her eyebrows. This is how the witch must have known Becca—she must have come to see Meredith, asking for help. It was too late for Becca, but it wasn't for others.

"Really?" she asked.

"Of course," Meredith said. "Lana, I'm asking you to become my eyes in the Guardian House."

"What do you mean?"

"From time to time, a teenage girl manifests a dangerous Gift, and she ends up in Mercy House. You can check the missing school-girls' files and delay the search until I find the child and hide her from the Gift Hunter."

"The Gift Hunter?"

Meredith nodded. "Yes. There is a special guardian who is exclusively assigned to catch the girls with destructive Gifts. As far as I know, his identity is a secret."

Lana bit her lip, thinking. "What if the girls are really missing?"

"Check the case first to find out whether the child has an active Gift or not."

Lana nodded. "Of course, I'll help. But I've never heard of a spell that shows if a Gift has been manifested."

"I will teach you."

"Okay. It's a deal then."

"Making a deal with a witch involves more than just shaking hands." Meredith took a sharp pin from her hair. "This agreement must be signed in blood. Our deal is in power as long as both of us are alive."

Lana sighed and stretched out her hand. The witch pricked her index finger, causing no pain—just a slight tingle. Meredith stood up and fetched the green folder Lana had found earlier.

The witch pulled a paper out of the folder and put it on the coffee table. "Sign here. If you tell anyone about our deal, you will catch an incurable disease."

Lana looked down at her hand. The red droplet of blood decorated her fingertip like a tiny ruby. When she was looking for Meredith, she was warned the stakes might be high, but she never expected this kind of cost.

"What if I let it slip accidentally?" Lana asked.

Meredith shrugged. "We can change 'a disease' to 'an accident' if you want. Maybe an accident is even better; in that case, you won't suffer."

Lana shook her head. "Please don't. I'll be careful."

She pulled the paper closer and signed the bottom with her blood.

When she finished, Meredith took the ring and smiled. "And now, the real game begins."

* * *

It was late afternoon when Lana walked out of the witch's house. She took the glass sphere out of her pocket. The glass shone in the sun rays, and her father's green Light shimmered inside.

She leaned on the wooden railing. The oval lake was calm below her, and the surface reflected the sun, high above the tree crowns. If she hurried, she would be home before sunset. Her father would not even notice her absence.

There was movement below. A man on a raven-colored horse trotted along the far end of the shore. He wore a black cloak and a hat that shaded his upper face. He stopped, his look piercing her. Lana stepped back. If he was a guardian, she would be in trouble. But what would a guardian be doing here?

What if he followed me?

Lana shook her head. No, she had never seen a guardian who wore a hat. Moreover, the guardians had more important duties than chasing her. He was probably the witch's next visitor, and it would be better for their paths to remain uncrossed. Lana turned back and ran down the stairs.

Chapter 3. The Guardian's Duty

Heavy clouds hung over the city of Santos. The rain had stopped, but the night air remained cool and moist. Fog leaked from between the trees and lulled the dreaming buildings, its gentle gray blanket of mist wrapping homes and silent streets.

The mansion was hidden in the sleeping hills. Far from the city center, the building hid in the shadows. A river of fog slid from the hilltops and covered its gray brick walls, treed yard, and stables. Two guardians in long black cloaks and tall boots stood near its gates, decorated with metal dragons.

One of the guardians took his hood off. Stubble covered Richard's stern face, and his green eyes looked up to the cloudy sky.

"It should be a cold night," he said.

Another guardian turned to him; his yellow beard was covered with water droplets. "Not so cold for you, Laine."

"What do you mean?" Richard asked.

The other guardian turned away and stared at the road. "Nothing."

Richard stepped forward and rubbed his frozen palms. *Rumors.* Everywhere he'd been, everyone enjoyed discussing dirty rumors. In small towns, rumors were the cure to boredom, and big cities were exactly the same. When guardians started talking, it was always a warning sign.

"Rumors are food for gossiping girls—not for men," Richard said.

The guardian gave him a scornful look. Richard shifted his gaze to the sky, where the night was quiet and calm.

"Once, my father noticed that some jam jars had disappeared from our pantry," the guardian said. "He said, 'When there's strong evidence, finding the culprit becomes easy.'"

Richard chuckled. "You stole jam?"

"I'm just happy when people receive their just punishment." The guardian looked forward and up the road, indicating the conversation was over.

Richard shook his head. He returned to his post and took a deep breath. The moist air filled his lungs. People liked rumors, and this silent, yellow-bearded guy might know something about his affair.

The guardians stood in silence for a while, until the sound of heavy steps ruined the stillness of the night. The silhouette of a guardian who carried a yellow Light in his hand slowly approached the gates. It was a tall man in a black cloak. The man took his hood off, revealing a round face.

"Tim!" Richard smiled.

"Hi, Rick," Tim said.

"Anything to report?"

"Things are calm."

Richard knelt on one knee and turned his palm up. Blue energy with silver sparkles started to leak from his fingers, forming into a shining sphere made of his Light.

"My watch has begun," Richard said.

"My watch is over," Tim said. He clasped his hands together, and his yellow Light disappeared.

Richard switched places with Tim and walked through the gate and into the foggy yard. His soft blue Light brightened his way, but he couldn't see anything beyond ten steps ahead. The mist was as thick as milk, and it hid the city streets and few people out walking at this late hour. Many crimes had been committed in this type of weather, and today was no exception.

Richard smiled. "Perfect!"

He stretched out the hand holding his Light, and he whispered a spell. The Light turned about its axis. Richard stretched out his other hand, and pure white energy leaked from his fingertips. It covered the blue ball of Light like a soft blanket. Richard finished the spell and whispered, "Activate!"

White layers of energy around the Light became transparent. Richard shook his hand. The shining blue ball slid from it but stayed hanging in the air.

"Good boy!" Richard said. "And now, *your* watch has begun."

He waved his hand. The ball of Light bounced in the air and slowly floated forward, the blue shine disappearing into the fog. This Hypnotic spell was quite tricky, but almost anything was possible with consistent practice.

Richard looked around and ran to a wall. He had around two hours until the end of his watch, and he had to be quick before anyone noticed that the ball was flying without him. He reached the corner of the building where the ivy rooted and grew lush over gray bricks. The freshly painted white ladder was easily noticeable among the ivy leaves. He touched the metal—it was cold, but not as cold as it used to be in the winter.

Richard climbed up into the fog, adrenaline boiling in his blood. He never knew if he would be able to come back safely. The smell of adventure made him dizzy; it was only in these short moments of danger that he felt alive—when a threat hung over his head, his eyes shone, and his heartbeat went into a crazy rhythm.

Richard climbed higher and higher, until he reached a window on the third floor, where the candlelight shimmered trough the foggy glass. The strong voice of the yellow-bearded guardian roared inside his head: *When there's strong evidence, finding the culprit becomes easy.*

Richard chuckled. No one was as good at hiding evidence as a guardian. He had managed to conceal this affair for several months, and no one suspected him.

Once, the guardian chief who owned this mansion noticed someone had visited. It happened right after the new year. That time, Richard hadn't been meticulous enough, forgetting to close the window, but he hadn't forgotten to remove his energy traces.

After that accident, the chief assigned three guardians to protect his house—two at the gates, and one who did rounds around the mansion. Richard could never have imagined he would have such a great opportunity to be so close to his chief's house. It gave him direct access to his wife's bedroom.

Richard knocked on the glass with his frozen knuckles. The thin glass clattered, and the sound of heels walking on a wooden floor approached the window. The frame slid open.

Camilla was a woman of forty years and as gorgeous as fine wine. Her laughing brown eyes looked straight at him. Camilla's red lips trembled, and her red hair fell on her pale neck. Her purple dress, with a deep neckline, opened a view to her white bosom, speckled with adorable freckles.

Richard climbed on the windowsill and jumped to the floor. He took Camilla's gentle hand and kissed it; her soft skin smelled of roses.

"You're charming today, Lady Camilla," Richard said.

"Glad to see you, Rick," she replied.

His lips kissed her gentle shoulders. She moaned when Richard reached her neck, biting her ear. "I missed you too, my lady," he whispered.

Camilla smiled and put her palm on his chest. Richard could feel her fingers through the thick layer of cloth. She helped him remove his cloak, and it fell to the floor, like a snake that had shed its winter skin. He stretched his hand out to bring her close, but she put her index finger on his lips.

"Take it slowly, my boy," she said.

She stepped back. Richard couldn't take his eyes away from her long dress. Two slits up its sides revealed her hips, ankles, and trimmed black stockings when she moved. It was hard to breathe, and he started unbuttoning his shirt.

Camilla elegantly took a tray of wine and chocolate from the nightstand and laid it on the bed. The glow of the candles illuminated her curves, and her eyes sparkled. She took a piece of chocolate with her fingertips and placed it on her bosom. Her burning look made him sweat.

Richard took his belt off, and his pants fell to the floor. He was ten steps away from Lady Camilla, and he couldn't take his eyes off her. Like a blossoming red rose, she opened beautifully. After all the shy girls who blushed at his jokes, he could not stop himself from being attracted to this woman. He adored her confidence, her grace, her passion. Everything in her made him lose his head and climb up to her bedroom in the middle of the night.

Lady Camilla knew exactly what she wanted, and right now, it was Richard. She crooked her finger, and Richard walked to her; he sat on the bed and leaned his muscular body over his lover. His lips took the chocolate from her bosom, her body trembling under his touch. His mouth was filled with a tart and sweet taste.

He lifted her up and caressed her back. Her dress was too tight, and her breath was heavy in his ear. His fingers found the laces on her back, and he pulled at one of them. Her dress slid down. Richard touched her silky black corset. Beneath his fingers, her heart beat rapidly.

He kissed her alluring body—hands, shoulders, bosom. Her tender fingers held his head, directing him to her sensitive parts. His lips found hers, and they were like two red petals on snow-white skin. He let himself sink into her sensuality, into her tart sweetness.

* * *

They lay on wrinkled sheets, her head on his arm. He touched her silky skin and drew a line on her belly with his fingertip. If he were a sculptor, he would try to duplicate her curves in clay, but he was a guardian, a person who was supposed to protect. Richard sighed. Time ran too fast, even for him. The shimmering light of dying candles was a reminder the end of their game was near. It was time to return to duty.

Camilla gave him a sad look. "I wish we could repeat this."

Richard kissed her forehead. "Some moments of our life should be unique. That's why they are so valuable."

She touched her bosom. "Then I'll keep this night in my heart."

Camilla rose, and Richard lifted himself up on one elbow to watch her. She took a bottle of wine from the tray and filled the glass; the light red liquid sparkled. Only now, Richard realized how thirsty he was.

Again, Camilla anticipated his desire and not because she was a mind reader. Her Gift had limitations—she could not read the thoughts of people she had romantic relations with. But she didn't need to get into his head to know what he wanted, because she knew Richard well, maybe even better than he knew himself. At least, he liked to think so.

Camilla handed the glass to him. Richard took it and drank it down to the bottom. The taste of raspberries filled his mouth, liquid summer in a bottle.

Camilla smiled. "Did you know that each sort of wine has its own characteristics?"

"What about the Roseberry one?"

She moved closer and whispered in his ear. "This one will make you stronger."

"Only troubles make us stronger, not wine. Don't you know that?"

"Of course, I know."

She smiled. Her beautiful face was so close to his, but her cheeks began to blur. Richard wanted to reach his hand out to her, but he couldn't move even a finger. His tongue refused to listen to his commands.

His heart sank. Camilla's mouth opened, but he couldn't understand a word. She slapped his cheeks and shook him, but he couldn't respond. Everything started twirling and he fell to the bed. He narrowed his eyes. Camilla ran out of the room, her nightrobe flapping after her. His eyelids grew heavy, and he closed his eyes.

Richard fell into a foggy dream. In this dream, he walked through the yard of the mansion, but he couldn't find the exit. He stopped and put his hands on his head. His blue Light floated from the fog and moved forward. Richard followed it—he was pretty sure it would lead him to the gates.

Tiredness made his legs heavy, but Richard kept walking forward. Fighting with his weakness, he followed the shine of his Light; it was the only chance he had to get out. Richard gasped. It was a dream, just a dream, but he couldn't make himself wake up. Then he saw his chief. A man with a gray beard and stark yellow eyes stepped into the fog, catching his Light.

Richard moved his heavy tongue. "I can explain."

"No need," the chief said. "Your watch is over."

The chief clasped his hands and Richard's blue Light disappeared; darkness engulfed his consciousness.

Chapter 4. The Night

Bella ran as fast as she could. Wide tree trunks flashed before her eyes, branches scratching against her skin. She stumbled on a root and fell, but she got up and kept running. She didn't feel any pain. Her body obeyed a primeval instinct. She ran like a deer who was escaping a predator. The blood pulsed in her head, and her breath became frequent and heavy. She ran farther and farther into the forest, until she reached the precipice of a hill. She stumbled on a stone and rolled forward, head over heels.

The small stones were sharp as needles. They tore at her skin and scratched her red flower-patterned dress. Bella rolled to the bottom of the ravine, only to land face up, with her back on the cold ground. The metallic taste of blood filled her mouth, her bones and joints aching.

She made an attempt to get up, but her body didn't listen.

Bella took a breath, and a dull pain pierced her ribs. She couldn't run away anymore, but at least she was alive. A creek bubbled nearby, and the canopy of tree branches above rustled like nothing out of the ordinary had happened. The sky was getting dark.

As dark as your heart, her inner voice said.

Bella moaned. She knew this moment would come. She needed to think about what happened, but she didn't know what to think.

"It was me," Bella whispered. She closed her eyes; she remembered the powerful waves of anger rippling from her body, and it was such a relief. Then, her memory drew her a picture of the motionless bodies in the glade, and she opened her eyes.

You hurt them all, the inner voice said. *You might have killed them.*

Her teachers, her favorite books, and even her own parents told her to be a good person and study well, promising that nothing bad would happen if she just complied. They all lied. Now Bella was here—somewhere in the forest, covered with mud and her own blood. The dirty girl with her ugly Gift.

Why? Why does it have to be me? Big tears slid down her flushing cheeks.

She wept uncontrollably, lying on the ground. Bella wished she could stop breathing, but her mouth kept gasping for air.

When she'd cried out all her tears, the sun hung low over the tips of the pine trees. Bella slowly stood up. Her body became heavy, and she could barely take a step. She limped to the creek and fetched some cool water, wiping her swollen face, washing her arms and neck. Her arms and legs were covered with mud and scratches. Some wounds still bled, but at least she hadn't broken any bones. Her clothes looked awful—her best dress was ragged, and her single remaining red shoe was scratched and ugly. The other shoe was probably somewhere in the forest.

Bella sighed. Her father would be mad if she didn't bring her shoes back. He bought them just last week and they were expensive. And Bella had ruined them. . . . like she ruined everything.

"Disgusting girl," Bella said. "People will always hate you."

The inner voice didn't argue.

* * *

Gray dusk fell on the forest. Bella limped through the trees and bushes in search of the trail. She had to tear a piece of cloth from her dress to wind it around her bare foot. Tree branches swung over her head, but the soft light of the night plants soothed her soul.

Despite everything, the nights in Triville forest were beautiful. Pale-green moss glowed on the tree trunks, and night daffodils opened their petals, brightening up the forest with white light. When summer came, the forest looked much brighter from the abundance of flowers, but to her, these innocent shades of spring were special.

Bella approached the open area and stopped. The flowers brightened at the far end of the glade. Her father taught her that plants knew where magic lived; that meant Triville was in that direction. Home was nearby, but her soul was filled with doubts.

What if everyone in town knows about my Gift?

The inner voice awoke: *They do. Kyle told everything to the guardians.*

Bella bit her lip and slowly walked farther in the glade. The daffodils around her glowed with a cold white light. Her heart beat loudly with every step she took.

They'll send you to Mercy House, the inner voice said.

Bella shook her head. "No, it was an accident. I don't even know what really happened, and the girls might be fine."

She walked until she was in the middle of the glade. A sudden gust of cold wind made her shiver.

Exactly, the inner voice said. *Even if they survived, they would not keep this quiet for you.*

Bella took a deep breath and looked up. The stars shimmered in the night sky and only a quiet rustle of leaves broke the silence. Bella remembered a book about the stars she'd read in school, and it said that everything was already decided. She couldn't believe that her destiny was to carry this unbearable Gift.

Bella's memories flashed before her eyes: this afternoon, the glade, and the girls falling back, like puppets. She had to go to Mercy House to get rid of her Gift, but what if the rumors were true? Could they take all her magic away?

All the teachers hated this rumor, and they tried to suppress it, but it made everyone talk even more. Last week, Elisa and Julia discussed it in front of her, just before literature class. They said it was safer to go to the forest witch, because she took in the girls with destructive Gifts and taught them magic. The witch did it illegally, and no one knew exactly where she lived, but the witch responded to the girls who were in trouble. All Bella needed to do was call the witch's name, and hopefully, she would hear it.

Bella sighed. It was time to make a decision—probably, the most important decision of her life. What did she want to become—a powerful witch, or a school freak? Her heart already knew the answer, and she could only follow its voice.

She walked to the thickest tree, with glowing mint-green moss, and put her palm on the tree trunk. "Meredith," she called out.

The sudden loud crack of a branch startled her, and Bella spun around. She could see no one else in the glade, and she put her palm on her chest to calm her racing heart.

"Who is it?" Bella asked.

Her inner voice shut down and hid like a terrified mouse.

"Probably just a squirrel," she said to herself.

One of the bushes swayed. Something with a heavy gaze was hiding there. Bella tried to remember how she'd managed to use her powers earlier.

"I was upset," Bella said. She raised her hands, but the magic didn't come out.

The dark silhouette of a man separated from the tree trunk and slowly walked toward her. Motionless, she stood near the tree, trying to convince herself that he was walking toward something else and not her.

"I see you, brave girl," he said in a soft voice.

Bella stopped breathing.

"You could grow powerful. Too powerful," he said.

His face was hidden under the shadow of his hat, but his eyes were visible. They shone bright green. He approached and touched her shoulder. He smelled of tobacco and fir. Bella put her palm on his, and his inner strength soothed her. He had to have great magical power and this power gave her confidence to speak.

"I thought all the witches were women," Bella said.

He chuckled. "I'm not the witch you're looking for."

"Then, who are you?"

He took his hand away. "I'm the one who can see your future. You have a very important role, girl—because of you, two people will meet."

"How?"

His teeth shone in the moonlight. "They will start investigating a murder."

"Which murder?"

He took a knife from his scabbard; the metal reflected the remaining light of the forest.

"Yours."

Strangely, Bella's heartbeat was calm. She was charmed by his hypnosis, and she wasn't scared anymore. Her inner voice seemed to be in a sweet dream while she stood in front of him.

"You want to kill me," she said.

He raised his arm. "Do you think I ever wanted this? I wish it could be different, but there's far too much at stake."

He struck, and the knife pierced her stomach. Bella looked down. A dark wet spot appeared on her dress, growing bigger and bigger, but she didn't feel any pain. The blood seemed almost black in the soft moonlight. Her fingertips touched her warm pulsing wound.

She wanted to ask him something, but while she tried to remember what it was, her legs buckled, and she fell to the ground. A lonely daffodil bud was torn from its stalk and lay on the muddy grass, its light shining in front of her eyes.

Then, the soft white glow transformed into the face of her mother, and her mother gently patted Bella's head with her soft hands. *You are my love, sweet love*, her voice soothed.

Bella closed her eyes and allowed her consciousness to surrender to the soft voice.

Chapter 5. A Wooden Smile

A small window let in the morning sun's rays. They shone through the thin glass and lit up the cramped room. A compact wooden desk was in the corner. Lana sat at the desk and read, her slim figure hardly noticeable among the piles of books and journals on the table. She held an open folder in her hands, and her eyes slid down the lines as she gently turned a page with her fingertips to prevent any damage.

"*Massive burns led the victim to suicide,*" Lana read out loud. She shook her head. "Bullshit."

She put the folder down. A thick book with a soft leather cover was on a pile nearby. She picked it up. It was covered with a thin layer of dust, but she could still see a bright illustration on it—a white dragon with its wings outspread. A woman sat on the dragon's back, her red hair flowing and her brave green eyes looking straight forward. Lana had read this book at least ten times when she was a child, but now, the fairy tale seemed ridiculous and naive. Children were the biggest dreamers, but she was no longer a child.

Now, she was at a dead end. The witch had warned her it would not be easy, and it was foolish of her to hope that she would find out the truth about the murder in a secret file. She knew they had erased the evidence and hid Becca's file, so no one would ask the hard questions.

But now was not time to give up. All she needed was to find another trace.

Lana wiped the cover of the book with her palm. The light cloud of dust tickled her nose, and she sneezed.

"I should clean this place up," she said, wiping her nose.

A sudden knock made her flinch. Lana sat in silence, waiting for the morning visitor to walk away. The knock repeated, and Lana grabbed the folder with Rebecca's file.

"Just a minute!" she said.

Lana moved the pile of books to the corner of her desk, then she opened the top drawer and hid the folder between some wrinkled sheets of paper.

"Come on in!"

She pushed the drawer closed. The pile at the corner of her desk wobbled, and the books fell to the wooden floor with a deafening noise. Lana stood and started gather them as the door opened.

A short man, with curly dark brown hair and a round nose, walked into the room. A teenage girl with the same hair and sad brown eyes held his hand.

"Please excuse us," the man said. "The guardian on duty was about to leave. He said to come here."

"Of course." Lana put the rest of the books on the top of the pile and stood up. "How can I help you?"

The man frowned. Lana looked down—her black shirt and pants were covered with dust from the books. She dusted it off and smiled at the man. "Please, have a seat."

The man looked around and sat on a chair; it bent under his weight. The room could fit only a single chair for the visitor, so the girl stood near her father.

Lana sat in front of the man. He had dark circles under his eyes. Hopefully, it wasn't anything serious; it would be best to read his thoughts first.

Lana stretched out her hand. "I'm Lana. Lana Morris."

"The chief's daughter?"

"Exactly."

The man sighed and stretched his hand toward Lana. She touched his rough palm and closed her eyes. His consciousness was captivated by fear, and an image of his daughter arose before her sight.

The girl had a red ribbon in her curly hair; she wore a dress with a bright poppy pattern. The girl screamed and ran to the dark forest in the night. She ran through the trees as the branches stretched out their black crooked fingers and scratched her skin. Her eyes were full of tears. The birds screamed overhead. She ran faster and faster, until she stumbled and fell in the darkness.

Lana opened her eyes and released the man's hand. Her heart pounded.

"What's happened?" Lana asked.

"My daughter—she's lost," the man said.

Lana bit her lip. The guardian on duty who sent this man here was either irresponsible, or just dumb, because a missing child case always took top priority. Now, she was the only person who could help.

Lana opened her notebook and took out a short pencil. "When did you last see her?"

"She took her new shoes," the girl with the curly hair said. "And she said she went to pick some flowers. She couldn't go far in those shoes, right?"

"Melissa, please," the man said.

The girl sobbed and put her head on his shoulder.

"Lana, right?"

"Yes."

The man patted his daughter's head and glanced at Lana. "We would like to speak with Chief Bernard Morris. When will he be in?"

"In an hour, or so," Lana replied.

The man's chin trembled.

Lana sighed. When something bad happened to a kid, there was nothing more heinous for a parent than being a victim of their own negligence. Situations like this were rare in Triville, but when they did happen, they left deep scars on the souls of the townspeople. Unfortunately, Lana knew it all too well.

She put her pencil down. "Listen, I know I'm just a secretary, not a guardian. I can try to contact the chief, but it will take time." Lana paused and added, "The sooner we start, the faster we will be able to find your daughter. She might be alone out there in the forest. She is probably hungry and scared, and she is waiting for our help. I'll take down your testimony, and we will start working with the team right away."

The man started talking. He talked so fast that Lana hardly managed to put his words on paper. When he finished, he reached into his pocket and handed over a wooden bracelet.

Lana took it. It was a cheap piece of jewelry, with one strip of white ribbon that connected several round wooden beads. One of the beads had a tiny metal chain attached to a wooden teddy bear, with a wide smile on his chubby face.

"This is her favorite bracelet. A gift from her late mother," the man said.

Lana put the bracelet on the desk and gave the man a suspicious look. "By the way, what is Bella's Gift?"

He shook his head. "She hasn't gotten it yet. She's only fifteen."

"That's the age when it manifests."

He narrowed his eyes. "What do you mean? My daughter would never hurt anyone, and she . . . she would tell me if she had a destructive Gift!"

Lana softened her voice. "Don't worry, please. I just thought it might help us in our search. I'm sure she is a good girl who just needs our help."

The man nodded, his gaze unwavering.

Lana hovered her palm over the bracelet. Yellow energy leaked from her fingers; it wrapped around the wooden beads and the smiling teddy bear. Lana glanced at the man. According to him, Bella hadn't received her Gift yet.

But what if she had?

The witch had asked Lana to warn her if any of the schoolgirls were in trouble. There was only one way to check if this was the case for Bella.

Lana had to check to see if the girl was a mage with a manifested Gift, or just a teenager whose powers were still tucked away. As the witch said, the spell took on a black or white color, depending on the presence of a Gift. Lana whispered a Revealing spell; yellow Light shimmered and went out.

Lana frowned. "Hmm . . . this shouldn't be happening."

The man widened his eyes. "What's wrong?"

"Let me try something else."

Lana hovered her palm over the bracelet, and her yellow energy covered it. She couldn't have screwed up the spell; the witch had made her repeat it at least twenty times to remember it. The failure of a spell like this meant that the girl was weak—if not worse. Lana had to use the bracelet to find her before the connection faded completely.

Lana invoked a Searching spell. The energy took on a blue color and twirled around Bella's memento. The bracelet rose, then fell back on the desk with a heavy, empty sound.

Lana slowly raised her eyes. The man who sat in front of her looked confused. At least he didn't know what it meant, and that was for the best.

Lana grabbed the bracelet with a quick hand movement. "You know, I'm not that good at spells. I'll give it to our team."

* * *

When the man left her office, Lana took her notebook and read the draft:

Missing Child Case

Notes for Report

Bella McAllister, fifteen years old. Five feet tall. Black hair, brown eyes, spot on the left cheek.

Was wearing a dress with red flowers and red shoes.

Last seen on Sunday at 2:20 pm.

Approximate direction—the forest. Note: she went to pick flowers.

Personal belongings taken—a wooden bracelet. Note: Searching spell didn't work.

Written by Lana Morris.

Lana bit her pencil. She read the draft again and again. *To understand someone, you should think like them,* her father had said. He used this technique to investigate local crimes.

Think, Lana. Think.

Lana read the draft until the words disappeared. Between the lines, Bella revealed herself. She didn't come home last night, but why did she go into the forest in the first place? Bella's father said she'd looked happy when she left the house. She didn't have a reason to look for the forest witch. There had to be another reason.

Lana rubbed her temples. Bella wore such a beautiful dress and her best shoes, and she had put a red ribbon in her hair. She hadn't taken the childish bracelet, even though it was her favorite one—she was trying to look serious. But why did she work so hard on her image, only to walk into the forest alone?

Lana stood up. *Because Bella wasn't alone.* This girl definitely knew where she was going and who she expected to meet, but something must have gone wrong.

If Lana were a guardian, she would start the search with the missing girl's closest friends. Lana glanced at the time crystal on her hand—it glowed a dark blue: six thirty. The high school would open soon.

Lana reached the door in two strides, and her fingers touched the cold knob. She froze.

She could open this door and get to the school as fast as possible to figure out what happened to the missing girl, but it wasn't the smartest thing to do. Lana sighed and glanced back. The plaque on her desk shone in the morning sun's rays. *Lana Morris, Secretary,* the inscription said. Last time, her impatience had cost her too much, and she had to act differently now. Lana took her hand off the knob and walked back to her desk.

No, she would be smarter this time. She wouldn't screw up her *real* investigation. Lana took a deep breath. Guardian men were stubborn and impatient creatures; they would be hasty in their search. Their roughness was their biggest weakness, but still . . . she had nothing to do with Bella. It was *their* job.

Outside the window, the dandelions shone in the grass, like little suns. After the long dream of winter, nature awoke, and gentle sun rays poured over the earth. Nature was patient. It didn't rush. It waited for the right time to awaken and then faded away, dropping its dry yellow leaves.

Everything good takes time.

Lana sat on her chair and turned a page of her notebook. Her pencil scratched down the sheet until the report was ready. The sound of heavy steps reached her ears, and she looked out the window. Two pairs of black boots walked across the front yard. One of the boots stepped on a dandelion and pressed it into the ground. Lana took her notebook from the desk and walked out of her office.

Chapter 6. A Baseline

Lana walked along the corridor, the old floor creaking under her feet. This place was saturated with the aroma of raw wood, and the tall walls retained the wisdom of generations of guardians who had protected Triville from evil. Paintings of guardian chiefs hung along the wall. Old-style pictures from the last century in heavy frames started the line of succession, and closer to the end, modern drawings were framed by simple wooden planks.

Lana reached the last picture and stopped. A man with kind brown eyes and a gray mustache looked at her from the portrait. *Chief Bernard Morris,* the inscription read.

"I hope I know what I'm doing," Lana whispered.

The door to his office was ajar. Her father, a man in his fifties, looked at a file with his warm brown eyes. His black jacket hung on the back of his fancy chair, and a pile of folders lay at the corner of his massive wooden desk. Another guardian sat in the chair in front of him.

"Good morning," Lana said.

Her father smiled. "Good morning!"

The other guardian was Lieutenant Charles Braun, the most annoying man Lana knew and the reason she left Triville four years ago. His laughing blue eyes looked at her with interest. His perfect oval face was clean-shaven. Lana had tried not to talk to him since she'd returned, but now, his presence in the same room was unavoidable.

Lana frowned and looked back to her father. "Chief, allow me to speak?"

Her father leaned back in his chair. "Proceed."

"An accident happened last night."

Lana put her notebook on the desk, and he took it in his wide hands. His eyes quickly slid across the lines. His silver mustache moved as he read, but no words slid from his lips. Silence hung in the room until he finished reading. He set the notes on the desk and looked at her.

"Good job, Lana," he said.

Lana smiled. Charles glanced at her and then to the chief.

"So, what happened?" Charles asked.

Her father rose and put his jacket on. "A schoolgirl is lost in the forest."

Charles stood up. "A girl?"

"Yes. Charles, I need you to put a team together. This is a number one priority!"

Charles widened his eyes. "Yes, sir!"

When her father walked out of the room, Charles and Lana stood alone.

Charles narrowed his eyes. "Lana, where were you yesterday?"

Lana's heart pounded; she coughed to adjust her voice to a confident tone. "Firstly, I had the day off. I decided to rent a horse and have a nice ride. And secondly, it's none of your business."

He sneered. "Four years, and you haven't changed."

"What makes you think that?"

He touched her shoulder, and Lana moved back.

He gave her a smile. "The same Lana I remember, with too many things in her head."

Lana crossed her arms. "I'm surprised you're still here. With your ambition, you could be a captain somewhere in a big city."

Charles chuckled. "Maybe I like it here."

"A small town with nothing really going on?"

"You arrived only eight days ago. Look at what has already happened."

Lana shook her head and walked away.

* * *

Outside, Lana stepped onto the wide porch. The Guardian House's black stone building hung over her like a monster, and a metal golden dragon shone on the top of its roof. This place was built here a century ago, with only one purpose—to protect the people of Triville from evil.

Lana sighed. Ironically, the evil she tried to stop was in this very building, and she couldn't wait to start digging for the truth.

But not today. Now there was a more important task—to help the guardians find the missing girl in any way she could.

The Guardian House's yard was busy. The quiet morning became lost in the sounds of impatient horses neighing and men's voices. Stable hands put saddles on horses, and guardians discussed the latest news as they walked across the yard in their gorgeous black uniforms, with golden dragons embroidered on their shoulders.

Two guardians stood under a tree and tried different Searching spells on Bella's wooden bracelet, but none of them worked. Lana drew near. One guardian, with a stern tanned face looked at her and frowned; another one stood with his eyes closed. He squeezed the bracelet in his hand.

"No luck?" Lana asked.

The other guardian opened his eyes and shook his head. His red hair shone in the morning sun's rays. Her father had said this guy was brand new to their team; he was here for summer training. He stretched out his hand and gave the bracelet to Lana.

"This thing is useless," he said.

Lana took the bracelet. "I'll take care of it."

He nodded, and he and the other guardian walked away.

The wooden teddy bear's plump face smiled at her. Bella had met with someone, but with whom? Lana twisted the bracelet in her hand. Something was wrong with this case, and no guardian had the thought to question Bella's friends first—maybe because none of them could think like a woman.

Several years ago, Lana was around Bella's age herself, and all she'd thought about was the new young guardian on her father's team—Charles. Love had made her blind.

"I'll check on you," she whispered to the teddy bear. She looked around and put the bracelet in her pocket.

Lana walked across the yard. Fragile and quiet, she was like a goldfish who was thrown into a pool of piranhas. A horse neighed behind her. Lana flinched and turned back.

Charles sat in a saddle, grinning. The dragons on his shoulders reflected in the sunshine.

"What's up, Dandelion?" Charles asked.

Lana pressed her hand to her chest, and it helped to slow her heartbeat. "Did you see my fath—I mean, the chief?" she asked.

Charles chuckled, and dimples appeared on his cheeks. His black horse moved its ears. Of course, he wouldn't help; there wasn't anything he would gain by being a nice person.

"The chief is discussing a search operation," Charles said, then he leaned his face over Lana. "You know, it's better not to distract a man when he is doing guardian work."

Lana scoffed. "Go do your job, Lieutenant. I'll do mine."

He shook his head. "Playing detective again isn't a good idea."

"Neither was our affair," Lana replied.

"Oh, take it easy. I just want you to be level-headed."

"Then we have at least *something* left in common."

He laughed and pulled the reins. "Don't be silly, Dandelion."

His horse bucked, and Lana stepped back.

Charles turned away and rode to the other guardians, lining up in the middle of the yard.

Lana took a deep breath. Well, his arrogance aside, Charles was right about one thing—she should not be foolish anymore.

Lana shook her head and walked to the corner of the courtyard. Her father stood with the guardian captain, George Turner. He was a tall man in his forties, with pale blue eyes and a thin face. He wore a trimmed gray beard with sharp lines. Their horses shuffled their feet, ready for a good ride. The men discussed something with wide hand gestures, and Lana stood nearby, waiting for them to finish their conversation.

Captain Turner was the right hand of the chief and a good friend of their family. He was also Rebecca's father.

After reading her case file, Lana knew that Captain Turner was the one who found his daughter in the barn. They probably kept him from talking, but how could he keep working here? Lana shook her head. She would never understand men.

When they finished talking, Lana approached them and smiled. "I just wanted to wish you good luck."

Captain Turner smiled. "Thank you, Lana. Sometimes, luck is all we need."

He nodded to the chief and mounted his horse. His gorgeous seal-gray stallion trotted into the glade, where ten guardians stood in line. Turner waved his hand, and half of the guardians followed him to the forest trail. The other half remained in their positions. As they waited for the chief, the horses snickered and waved their tails in impatience.

Lana shifted her eyes to her father. "I know you're in a rush, but I just need your approval to check the school."

Her father mounted his horse. "The school?"

"I thought Bella's classmates might have seen her. It might narrow the search area."

Her father touched his mustache, thinking. "That's actually a good idea."

"Thank you."

"Please, be careful. If you find something useful, don't walk into the forest. Just get back here and wait for us to come back."

Lana nodded. "I won't let you down."

"And if it's urgent, use a Light signal. I'll send some guardians to meet you."

"Sure."

Her father took the reins, and his raven-colored horse galloped to the trail. The guardians rode after him. The train of different colored horse tails shone under the bright morning sun—chestnut, bay, black, dapple gray, painted white—flapping in the wind. These animals were gorgeous creatures, but Lana couldn't say the same about the people who rode them.

Chapter 7. The School

Julia sat at her desk, staring at her open book. The letters blurred before her eyes. Her mind too far away to focus on class, and her stubborn consciousness pulled her back to yesterday, drawing the picture of the spring glade. They had laughed and leapt in a silly dance around Bella and Kyle, and then suddenly, some kind of power threw her and pressed her into the grass. She couldn't even breathe.

Julia inhaled the stale classroom air to make sure her lungs were working properly.

Elisa stood at the window, talking with Rose and two other girls. Morning sunshine highlighted her golden hair, and Elisa looked like an angel in her white school shirt. Julia sighed. Elisa was the one who had suggested the silly prank yesterday, and now she was acting like nothing happened.

Someone told a joke, and Elisa laughed with the other girls. Her laughter sounded like wind chimes. The carousel of events rolled before her eyes again. The laughter, the wave of energy, the smell of earth in her nose.

The school bell rang, and the girls walked to their seats. Elisa sat at her desk next to Julia.

"You're so quiet today," Elisa said.

"I'm just . . . I'm okay," Julia replied, her hands crumpling a piece of paper.

"I see."

Julia glanced at the empty desk behind her and turned to her friend. "She's not here."

Elisa sighed and fixed a lock of golden hair. "It was just a joke. You all agreed when I suggested it, especially Kyle. Poor girl, did you see how she looked at him? So many silly girls are obsessed with him."

Julia gave her a judging look. "This is where your jealousy led us. Did you really think that Bella could steal your boyfriend?"

Elisa shrugged her shoulders. "No. I wanted to see what he was ready to do for me."

Julia widened her eyes. "Are you happy now?"

"Actually, no. I think he is cruel and selfish."

"Right. Selfish. But what about Bella?"

Elisa paused. "What about her?"

Julia raised her voice. "What if something bad happened to her?"

Other girls in the classroom stopped talking and turned their heads toward her.

"Hush...!" Elisa hissed.

Julia nodded and looked back to her book.

Elisa glared at her classmates. "What are you staring at? Don't you have anything else to do?"

They turned their heads back to their desks and grew quiet. Only the rustling of paper broke the silence.

The door of the classroom creaked open, and the literature teacher, Mrs. Sullivan, entered. Mrs. Sullivan was a short chubby woman, with warm yellow eyes and round glasses, and everyone in the class called her Owl. Like all the teachers, she wore a blue gown that rustled behind her back.

She coughed. "Good morning, children!" she said in a ringing voice.

"Good morning, Mrs. Sullivan!" a chorus of voices replied.

The teacher waved her hand, and a piece of chalk flew to the chalkboard, writing three words: *The Dangerous Gift*. She turned her head toward the students.

"Today, we will discuss this story," she said. "Please open your books to Chapter Twelve."

Elisa opened her book and stared at the teacher.

Julia glanced at the board, and a cold hand of panic squeezed her throat. Sometimes, Julia thought the owl-like woman could see through people, and today, that was the last thing she needed.

"This story teaches a very important lesson." Mrs. Sullivan looked around. "Has anyone finished reading it?"

Elisa raised her hand. "I did!"

The teacher smiled. "Good job, Miss Palmer! Do you want to share it with the class?"

"Sure." Elisa stood up and fixed her blouse. "This is a story about a teenage boy, whose Gift poisoned everything he touched. He was scared and ashamed of his Gift, and he decided to hide it from others, until he learned how to control it. He thought he had succeeded, but he accidentally killed his best friend when he touched his shoulder. Thus, this boy was sent to a prison, and he regretted his decision for the rest of his life."

"And what is the lesson here?" Mrs. Sullivan asked, looking around the class. Everyone grew silent.

Julia held her breath. If she knew Elisa as well as she thought she did, this was the calm before the storm.

Elisa put her palm on the book and continued. "This story teaches us that the boy should have confessed and asked his teacher for help. Maybe he could have developed his Gift and become a guardian, but because of his cowardice, someone was killed instead. He could have been helped, like any other man."

"You can sit now, Miss Palmer," the teacher said in a plain tone.

"I'm not finished," Elisa said. She looked at Julia and the other girls in the class. "In my opinion, this story ignores something very important. Not everyone has this kind of choice."

"What do you mean?" Mrs. Sullivan asked. The wrinkle between her eyebrows deepened.

Julia looked out the big window, where young leaves shivered under the sun. A small bird jumped on the windowsill and cocked its head.

"I mean, it's only boys that have a choice—not girls," Elisa said.

The teacher frowned. "That's not true. Everyone has a choice."

Elisa shook her head. "Going to Mercy House isn't a choice. It's the place where they collect all our magic and make us Incapables."

The students turned their faces to Mrs. Sullivan.

An apologetic smile appeared on her face. "Miss Palmer means that you have a choice to sacrifice your Gift for the safety of society. You do it voluntarily, and only in the case that it's dangerous and might hurt others." She breathed heavily as she moved along her desk. "They just take your Gift, not all your magic."

Mrs. Sullivan took her handkerchief and wiped the sweat from her forehead. "Of course, any surgery might have complications," she continued. "A blockage of one's magical channels, for example. But I repeat, this kind of complication is very, very rare—"

"Why are you lying?" Elisa asked, giving her a sharp look.

Mrs. Sullivan flinched. "Excuse me?"

"Why are you lying to us about Mercy House?" Elisa repeated. She shook her head and looked at Julia. "They tell us this bullshit like we're stupid. But they just make us Incapables, taking all our magic and human rights away. And *voila*! We're slaves who serve rich assholes in big cities."

"Miss Palmer, watch your language!"

"As you wish," Elisa replied and sat back in her chair. She turned the page over and pretended she was reading.

Mrs. Sullivan looked across the classroom. The girls stared at her with wide eyes, but no one said a word. In the hanging silence, Julia's heartbeat was loud in her ears. Maybe they were just silly rumors, but what if they weren't? Until today, no one had dared to ask.

It was even harder to repeat the question to herself, but Julia couldn't stop thinking about Elisa's words. *What if it happens to me?*

she thought. Her cheeks burned, and she put her cold palms on her face. It was easier to bury it somewhere at the bottom of her heart, to keep it silent. It was easier for everyone—but not Elisa.

Mrs. Sullivan came to Elisa and took her elbow. She pulled her up with her plump hand. "Get out of class," she said, her voice trembling. "Now!"

Elisa grinned, and her dark blue eyes glittered.

A moving chair sounded behind her. "Then I'll go too," Rose's voice said.

Julia rose. She could hear her own quiet voice: "And me." Somehow, she found the strength to look at Mrs. Sullivan.

Mrs. Sullivan's enormous yellow eyes seemed ready to jump out. Elisa took her books and walked to the door. Julia and Rose followed.

Suddenly, the entrance door flew open, and a small woman slid into the classroom. She wore a black shirt and pants, and she had braided flaxen hair. Her brown eyes looked at the three girls with curiosity. She carried a folder in her thin hands.

"Oh, my dear. Look who's here!" Elisa said.

Mrs. Sullivan opened her mouth, but the woman spoke first.

"Lana Morris, secretary of the Guardian House," the woman said.

The teacher approached the woman. "Is anything the matter, Miss Morris?"

"I've never seen you here before. Are you new?"

"I've been here for three years already," Mrs. Sullivan replied.

Lana came closer to Mrs. Sullivan and whispered something in her ear. Julia instinctively stretched her neck to hear the words they exchanged. She only heard small cuts of phrases: "*Missing . . . morning . . . Bella.*"

Julia's heart sank.

"Is Bella lost?" Elisa asked out loud.

"Yes," Lana said. She frowned, thinking. Then she stepped forward and looked at the class. "Did anyone see Bella yesterday?"

Julia glanced at Elisa, who remained silent. Rose turned her face toward the window. Julia put her hand on her chest to soothe her jumping heart.

Lana stepped forward. "Bella went for a walk yesterday and never came back. She is alone in the forest, and we need your help. Anything you saw might be useful in finding her." Lana looked straight at Julia. "Before it's too late," she added.

Julia sighed and approached Lana. "I hope nothing bad has happened to her."

Lana put a hand on Julia's shoulder, and her eyes sparkled for a second. Then Lana took her hand away and said, "Now, all three of you meet me in the hallway. You can tell me what happened in the glade."

Julia was numb.

"Nice job!" Elisa barked and approached Julia. "She's a mind reader," she whispered.

Lana gave her a sad look and walked out of the classroom. Elisa and Rose followed her. Mrs. Sullivan stayed next to Julia; the teacher's breathing was heavy. Julia rushed to the exit.

Chapter 8. The Past that Unites Us

In the school hallway, Lana went to a window and put her folder on the sill. Outside in the schoolyard, elegant wooden benches rested along the trail in the shade of blossoming trees. White and pink petals danced in the air, twisting as they landed on the grass and covering it like a white blanket.

Lana sighed. The beauty of spring was so frail, and it was too easy to ruin everything with one clumsy step. It was spring back when she'd made the terrible mistake with Charles too. She'd left Triville to leave her past behind, but the past followed her, reminding her of things she wanted to forget.

Lana turned around and examined the girls. Next to her, Julia shuffled her feet. Rose looked at her with frank boredom, and Elisa . . . well, she had grown up since Lana saw her last. She hadn't left her with the best goodbye. Kids usually forgot about bad things—at least, it was easier to think so. Lana licked her lips, trying to find the right words.

She gave Elisa a warm look. "You look beautiful. Exactly like your mother."

Elisa's eyebrows twitched. "You dare to mention her after everything you did?"

Lana clenched her teeth. *Perfect.* She hadn't forgotten. And now she'd made things worse.

Lana softened her voice. "The things that happened to you were terrible, and I'm sorry for your loss."

Elisa snorted with disgust.

"We did everything we could to protect her," Lana said.

"But you screwed up."

"I did." Lana nodded.

Rose looked at Lana with sudden interest.

"But, I've learned from my terrible mistake. I'm going to do my best to find Bella."

Elisa grinned. "Maybe she doesn't want to be found."

"What if she does?"

"I'm pretty sure she doesn't."

Lana sighed, thinking. In small towns, nothing spread faster than rumors, and she bet that these girls knew more about the witch than she did. She took the bracelet out of her pocket. The wooden teddy bear bounced before Elisa's face.

"This belongs to Bella," Lana said.

Elisa narrowed her eyes. "So what?"

"If the witch is hiding the girl, the Searching spell won't work on her personal belongings. But fortunately, I know how to check if Bella has a Gift. The spell didn't work, which means only one thing—she is weak or hurt."

Elisa crossed her arms. "So, you know the witch?"

Lana paused. "It doesn't matter now. We know about Bella's power, and that means she is in danger. She won't be able to hide forever. It's just a question of who will find her first—us, or the guardians. Did you know that they have a Gift Hunter?"

Elisa sneered. "Of course we know that. But why should we trust *you*? You're working for the guardians, aren't you?"

"I do, but I'm not one of them," Lana said.

Elisa and Lana glared at each other, and the air in the corridor became heavy.

Julia glanced at Lana. This woman had come here to find out what happened to Bella, and the present was more important than Elisa's uneasy past.

Julia sighed. "How can we help?"

Lana took her folder from the windowsill and sat on the floor. She unfolded the paper in front of her, and the girls sat across from Lana.

It was a map of Triville. The blue curve of the river crossed the paper, and in the middle, houses were surrounded by green dots of trees. The cathedral was between the town hall and the park, where the Bridge of Wishes crossed the river. North of the park was the yellow roof of the Guardian House.

Lana pointed to the forest on the map. "When the Searching spell didn't work, the guardians rode north. They're searching in this area." Lana looked at the girls. "Show me where the accident happened."

The girls exchanged looks. Elisa scowled, and Rose turned away. Julia touched the picture of the school. It was a U-shaped building; one wing was for the girls, and the other was for the boys. Julia put her index finger on a row of red squares. It was the living area at the East End. Her finger slid over the soft paper, until it reached the forest with bright green circles representing the glades.

"We were here," Julia said.

Lana frowned. "We'd better hurry up, then."

Elisa gave her a surprised look. "*We?*"

"Unless you girls want to go back to class." Lana lowered her voice. "Or, you can come with me; we can try to fix what you've done."

"Of course," Julia said.

Rose nodded. "I'm in. I don't want to go back to class."

Elisa sighed. "I guess I don't have any other choice."

Lana looked at Julia. "I saw a boy in your memory. What's his name?"

"Kyle Turner." Julia pointed to the corridor. "He's in the North Wing."

Lana stifled a gasp. *Turner*—she'd heard the name too often in the last two days. She knew the guardian captain had two kids, but it was still a surprise. After everything that happened to his daughter, Rebecca, he was bringing up his son alone. It was unbelievable, but that little boy was now a senior student—and he might know something important.

"Let's bring him with us," Lana said.

＊ ＊ ＊

Elisa and Rose stood in the corner, discussing something in whispers. Lana sat at the windowsill and stared at her time bracelet—the crystal glowed a pale violet color. It was already nine o'clock. Time flew by too fast, and it always played against victims, but rushing was far worse. This is what she'd learned from life's cruel lessons.

Lana looked around. The school corridor was bright, as usual, and once, long ago, she had studied here. At that time, she believed in the guardian code of justice. Now, she doubted it, but still, she had to do her job.

It was a good plan, and it was easy to do—especially with the help of these teenagers. All she needed was to find Bella before the guardians did.

Chapter 9. The Mystery of Triville Forest

The rustling of the leaves enlivened the forest, and a tender aroma from the lilies of the valley filled the air. The students and Lana reached the glade and stopped. A flower garland with an intertwined red ribbon lay on the grass.

"It happened here, right?" Lana asked.

The girls stood behind her in silence. Lana leaned over and touched the wilted white flowers. The garland was a silent reminder of what they had done to Bella, but it was a good lesson for all of them.

Lana placed her palm over the garland and spread out her energy. The stems were still alive, and they held the energy Bella had released with her Gift. It could work.

Lana whispered a Searching spell, and her yellow Light took on a blue color, twirling across the garland. She let the garland go, and it bounced in the air, floating to the bushes.

Lana followed it. She walked through the bushes, not paying attention to the sharp branches snagging on her shirt. Behind her, Kyle held the branches so Elisa and the other girls could walk freely. Lana sighed. Once, she was in love too, but she wasn't made for relationships. She walked farther, stepping over rocks and tree roots.

Finally, they reached the edge of a precipice. Lana looked down as the garland flew over the edge and landed on the rocky shore of a creek. Running water gleamed under the afternoon sun.

"Why did it stop there?" Kyle asked.

Lana shrugged. "The garland kept the energy of Bella's Gift, but it must have run out here. Something probably happened at this creek."

She sat on the edge, trying to figure out how to get down. Then, she glanced at Kyle. He stood nearby, ready to help. Lana stepped on the gravel. Small rocks moved under her feet, and she started sliding down the slope. Kyle caught her hand.

Lana closed her eyes. Human minds were a foggy maze of secret wishes and suppressed fears, but real memories were always bright. Lana looked into his past, searching for Rebecca's face.

His last memory of her was the night she died. Kyle ran to the barn to the sound of a desperate scream. He opened the wooden door, then he noticed the girl who sat in the corner. *Becca.* The guardian walked to her, and he held a fireball in his hand. The guardian had a black beard, but the image was blurred; Kyle looked only at his sister. Becca's big blue eyes were frozen in fear. Then, she looked straight at Kyle, and her lips mouthed: "Run!"

Kyle turned and ran. Her last scream sounded somewhere behind him. Then it became quiet.

"Are you all right?" Kyle's voice made Lana open her eyes.

Lana blinked. He had the same blue eyes she remembered so well. She looked under her feet. "Yes, thank you. I can handle it."

Kyle scowled. "I see." He helped Lana get down to the shore, then he climbed down after her.

Lana shook the dust from her pants and walked to the garland. She repeated the Searching spell, but this time, the energy twirled across the flowers and disappeared. The spell behaved the same way it had with Bella's bracelet in the morning—not a good sign. Lana shook her head. This went beyond her understanding.

Kyle approached her. "Let me try another Searching spell."

"How do you know it?" Lana asked.

"My father is a guardian. I know some tricks."

Lana stepped back. "Of course. Go ahead."

Kyle lifted his palm and formed a ball of blue Light. Then, he moved his hand over the garland, checking the ground and around the rocks. The energy blinked and disappeared.

"Did you see anything?" Lana asked.

"No," Kyle said. He glanced around and lowered his voice. "It seems like her traces were removed."

Lana walked along the creek before returning to Kyle. "No, trace removal is too complicated. It's also a forbidden spell. Who would do it?"

Kyle shrugged. "I would say the guardians, but as you said, the Searching spell didn't work before any of them knew she was missing."

"Maybe the witch?"

"It's possible, but it's mostly guardians who know this magic. You can remove traces too, right?"

Lana shook her head. "I wish I could."

Kyle sighed. "Anyway, we need to do whatever we can. If there is even a little bit of energy left in this garland, I can use my Gift to see what's happened."

Kyle sat on one knee. He touched the garland, and his eyes shone for a second. He blinked and looked at the burbling creek, like it was telling him the truth.

"She walked along the creek alone, but I didn't get the direction," he said.

The girls stood along the edge of the ravine and looked at them with interest. Lana turned to Kyle. "Here's what we'll do—we'll split into two groups. You go down with Elisa, and I'll take Rose and Julia."

"What if I notice something suspicious?" Kyle asked.

"If you're in serious danger, or you find her, send your Light overhead." Lana sighed. "Please, be careful. It would also be a signal to the other guardians who are searching at the other edge of the forest."

"Got it," Kyle said.

* * *

Lana walked along the shore. The sun was strong, almost causing the lingering shadows to disappear, warming up her face. The girls' steps sounded behind her, and the shore ended in a cliff where the river curved. Lana stopped, thinking. The narrow trail led to the northern part of the forest. The guardians would be in this area soon, and it would be better not to bump into them.

"Why have we stopped?" one of the girls asked.

"Let's just wait a bit," Lana said.

Rose sat on a big stone and stretched her legs. Her skin seemed almost white under the bright sun. Julia approached Lana. Her hazel eyes looked at her with curiosity.

"So, you know Elisa," she said.

"Yes," Lana replied.

Julia raised her eyebrows, waiting for her to continue. Lana looked into the blue cloudless sky. Of course, they all knew what had happened. Rumors were one of the reasons why she'd left Triville, and even after several years, people still remembered. It wasn't good, but at least now she could tell her side of the story.

Lana walked to the river and sat on the rock near Rose. Julia sat on the ground nearby.

"I met Elisa around four years ago," Lana said.

Rose gave her a sharp look. "When you dated a guardian."

Lana flinched. *Well, this won't be easy.* Actually, this story was never easy to remember anyway.

Julia glanced at Rose and then Lana. "Did you love him?"

"Why is that so important?"

Rose moved closer. "Because it would explain everything. That night, when Elisa came to the Guardian House, you were there with him, right?"

Lana sighed. "All right, I was with him. Charles was on duty, and I . . . we were sort of on a date."

Rose's black eyes sparkled. Lana ignored her and continued. "And then, I heard a knock. Charles didn't want to open it, but I did. It was an eleven-year-old girl. She was squeezing a plush toy in her hands—a white teddy bear with traces of blood on it."

"Elisa," Julia said.

Lana nodded. "She said it was proof of her father's crime and asked us to protect her mother."

"But you didn't," Rose concluded.

Lana lowered her eyes. A warm wind touched her blushing face. "For him, that case was just one of many similar ones—an alcoholic husband and a wife with bruises. For me, it was different. I really wanted to help. We decided to visit them and provoke her father—"

"Provoke?" Rose asked.

Lana sighed. "Sometimes, we want to rush our actions, but nothing good happens when we do. It's better to let things develop naturally. But it's also the hardest thing to do."

Julia patted her palm. "I understand."

"Really?" Lana asked.

Julia nodded. "I feel the same about Bella. Oh, I hope we will find her soon."

Rose stood up. "Then we should go."

A loud bang on the opposite side of the shore made them look into the sky, where shimmering blue sparkles melted in the air.

"Kyle," Julia said. "It's his Light."

"And it's not good," Rose added.

"Come on, let's go," Lana said.

They ran along the shore. The river gleamed under the sun; it hissed and streamed forward, like a giant silver snake.

Chapter 10. When Flowers Die

Elisa walked along the creek behind Kyle. The search was a waste of time, but it was better than going back to literature class. *And why was everyone so obsessed with helping Bella?* This girl was not stupid, and she could take care of herself. Even if Lana was right, and Bella really had gotten lost, it was not a good idea to make her meet with Kyle, who was the son of a guardian.

Elisa stopped at the turn in the creek and took a deep breath. Her black school shoes were covered in mud, and her feet were sore. Maybe she hated the idea of helping Lana, but at least she could distract Kyle and buy some time for Bella.

Kyle approached her. "Are you tired?"

"How far could that wretch go?" Elisa asked.

Kyle glanced at the forest. The sun lit up the canopy; it was around noon.

"I don't know, maybe she's close."

Elisa touched a lock of her hair. "Yes, I'm tired." She pointed at the forest trail. "Let's take a break."

They walked into the glade. It was covered with beautiful white flowers—daffodils. She sat on the grass and looked up where the blue, cloudless sky shone above them.

Kyle stopped near her. "I think she's close."

"And what will you do after you find her?"

"I'll release the Light overhead."

Elisa laughed. "Of course."

"I mean, she can't hurt me, so I'll try to convince her to return and speak with the guardians."

"She can hurt *me*," Elisa said.

"I'll protect you."

Elisa looked into his eyes. They were full of pride. "What makes you think that I'm helpless?"

"'Because you're—"

"Weak?" Elisa interrupted him. "Stupid?"

"I mean, you're just a girl."

"So what?" she asked. "You don't know me at all."

"Right, like you know me." Kyle walked around the edge of the glade. The daffodil stalks bent under his feet. This part of the forest didn't have many bushes, and the canopy hardly let any light in. The trail led into the depths of the forest. He came back to Elisa. "Let's go," he said.

Elisa gave him a lazy look, then she took her shoes off and stretched out on the ground. "I think I need more rest."

Kyle glanced back. "But I saw a trail."

"Just a couple more minutes."

Kyle sat next to her, tore a flower out of the ground, and looked at her. She closed her eyes, pretending she was sleeping. Her white blouse was spotless, and her golden hair lay on the grass. She was beautiful—more beautiful than anyone in school. Among the other girls, she shone the brightest, and it was easy to get lost in her light.

Sometimes, she provoked people, and this feature interested him the most, but what interested her? Yes, she was bright and shiny on the outside, but she was rotten and selfish, like an expired melon. That's why the guardians' duty was so important—it gave them power to punish people like her.

Kyle clenched his fist; the flower stem broke in his hand. Interesting—how would *she* like to be provoked? Elisa lay in front of him, fully relaxed. She thought she was smarter than everyone else, but she was wrong.

He took the rest of the flower and touched her neck with the bud. She smiled. Kyle traced the bud up to her cheek, and Elisa opened her eyes. He bent over and kissed her rosy lips, and she responded.

Kyle kissed her with fervor and passion. His hand touched her hip and slid under her skirt.

"Stop it," Elisa said. She tried to rise from the ground.

"You aren't very strong." Kyle kept hold of her.

She tried to push him off, but it made Kyle resist even more. She looked at him with anger.

He grinned. Then she moved her head to his neck and bit him. Her teeth pierced his skin. Kyle screamed and loosened his grip.

It was enough. Elisa jumped up and ran to the bushes in her bare feet. She took several big steps to the middle of the glade, then she stumbled on something soft and lost her balance, falling flat on her face in the grass. His heavy steps and his quick breathing sounded from behind. She closed her eyes tightly, her heart pounding in her chest.

Then he stopped.

Elisa slowly rose and sat up. Kyle's face was pale, like a wall; blood covered his neck where she'd bitten him. His mouth opened helplessly, but no words came out from his throat.

Then, Elisa realized why. A strong smell of blood mixed with mud and rotten flesh throttled her senses. Her blouse was wet and stuck to her body—it wasn't her blood, but it wasn't just Kyle's, either.

"Throw up your Light!" she shouted.

Kyle blinked and started to make a ball of Light in his shaking hands. Elisa looked down and saw everything. The blood covered Elisa's blouse and hands, but that wasn't the worst part. There was so much blood in front of her, she hardly recognized the white dress with the flower pattern.

It was Bella. Dark curls covered a pale, round face. Her lifeless, half-opened eyes looked like two pieces of brown glass.

A sudden memory sprang forth in Elisa's mind—the brown rum bottle that her father drank and her mother's terrified face. Elisa couldn't stop staring at the deep wound on Bella's stomach.

Kyle's hands lifted Elisa from the ground and placed her at the edge of the glade. He talked to her, but she couldn't understand his words.

Then, the guardians came. She saw their black silhouettes, and she heard their resounding voices. They ran around and checked the area with Revealing spells.

Then, Lana was in front of her, speechless.

"I thought she escaped," Elisa said. Her voice trembled with her ragged breathing. "I thought she found her way, but—"

"I know." Lana hugged her. "I know."

Elisa embraced her and burst into tears.

Chapter 11. Crime and Punishment

When Richard opened his eyes, the first thing he saw was a chipped ceiling. Pieces of old plaster fell off the old wooden planks, and now they hung above him. His head was too heavy to lift, and so he stayed still on the stiff bench.

The sharp clanks of metallic pain in his head started to ease. Now, he could recognize the muffled voices of guardians behind the door. His hand touched a rough wall. Richard rose and moaned—all of his muscles hurt. Finally, he managed to put his body into a sitting position, and his bare feet touched the cold floor.

Richard examined himself. He only had a pair of black pants on. A couple of bruises blackened his naked upper body. Someone must have thrown him on this bench. They were either really inaccurate, or mad. A blurry memory of last night arose before his eyes.

He had been caught.

"Unbelievable. Stupid," he whispered.

A small window highlighted the shabby walls and a narrow wooden door. He'd seen this gloomy room before—he used to put suspects in here, but he never imagined he would be in their shoes. He sighed. If he had known, he would have hidden a key under the mattress.

A key turned and the lock clanked, the massive door flying open. Tim walked in, his face fresh and chipper. The guardian held a black piece of clothing in his hand.

Tim smiled. "How was last night?"

Richard frowned. "Guess."

Tim put the clothing on the bench. It was a black button up shirt. Richard took it and started to dress.

"Now you look better," Tim said when Richard finished.

Richard coughed. "So, what the heck is going on?"

Tim shook his head. "Rick, you're in serious trouble."

"Am I?" Richard gave him a sarcastic look.

"Yesterday, I took the shift after you. I was there for almost two hours, and then a carriage arrived."

"Why didn't you warn me?"

"Because, right as the carriage stopped at the gates, Lady Camilla showed up. She screamed for help, and she was half naked. Can you imagine?" Tim giggled. Then, he looked at Richard's strained face, and his smile disappeared.

"And . . . ?"

"And then the chief came out from the carriage and slapped her."

Richard rested a palm on his forehead. "Damn!"

"Exactly!" Tim nodded. "And after all that, the chief broke into the bedroom and found you. At least, I insisted on putting your pants on before they carried you away."

Richard took a deep breath to clear his thoughts. His nightmare had become a reality. He knew that his relationship with Camilla couldn't last long, but it was too hard to stop—even when the risks were extremely high. He flew to the light in her window like a foolish moth.

"Thank you, friend," Richard said.

Tim coughed into his fist. "It's just the first part of the story."

Richard gave him a wary look. "Go on."

"The chief has irrefutable proof of your crime."

"Cheating isn't technically a crime."

"As long as you don't do it on your watch."

Richard stood and punched the wall, a sharp pain piercing his fist. He swore and shook his hand. He'd lost, but this wasn't a game, it was his life. She wasn't just someone's wife—she was *his chief's* wife. It could only mean one thing—the end of his guardian career. At twenty-seven, Richard couldn't imagine doing anything else. Becoming a baker? A carpenter? Nothing could replace good detective work.

Richard sat on the cold floor. The pain pulsed through his fingers, and blood soaked from the new abrasions on his knuckles. They would heal; some things were easier to fix than others.

Richard sighed. "All my life, I've been so afraid to lose this job. Now, I've lost it because of a stupid affair."

"The chief is furious, Rick! He's going to send you to Death Island."

"What?" Richard gasped. "I thought he'd fired me, but . . . isn't that cursed place meant for murderers?"

"Not as a prisoner, Rick, as a warden."

Richard shook his head. "That doesn't sound any better."

Tim raised his hand. "That place isn't cursed; the time-crystal mines create a magnetic anomaly that blocks magical channels—"

"Awesome. Loss of magic is all I ever wanted," Richard concluded.

"The blockage is not pleasant, but it's only temporary."

"But the blockage becomes irreversible after a year of exposure to it. That's how prisoners become Incapables."

"You won't become an Incapable, Richard. You'd have a standard-length contract."

Richard pushed his sore fingers along his scalp, gripping his hair. "For how long?"

"Actually, we were in the process of that discussion. But then we received this." Tim took a folded piece of paper from his pocket.

Richard took it. "What's this?"

"We received it from Triville. Read it."

Richard unfolded the paper. It was a letter from the guardian chief of Triville, a small town not far from Santos. Shaky handwriting told him that this report had been written in a big rush:

A Murder Case #0520-20-345

The victim's name — Bella McAllister

Age — fifteen years old

The approximate time of death — Monday, May 20th. Between midnight and 3 am.

The reason of death — stab wound to the stomach that caused massive blood loss.

Details from the crime scene:

Physical traces — male footprints.

Magic traces — none were found. The magic traces were erased.

Report is written by Bernard Morris, the Chief of Triville Guardian House.

Richard put the letter down. Bella was a teenager at the age when Gifts manifested, and it was such a familiar criminal pattern.

"Ghost," Richard said.

"This is your chance to catch him!"

Richard nodded.

"Rick, sometimes I think you're in an affair with your own luck. This situation is absurd, but you're the best man for this case."

"I am," Richard agreed. "And this time, I won't let him go."

"I'm sure you'll make it right."

"But what about the chief?"

"He agreed to put your issues aside until you find Ghost."

"He did?"

"The chief is not a fool, Rick. He realizes that Ghost is much more important than his personal vendetta."

"Wise."

"Yes, Rick, it's wise to separate your personal life from work."

"Oh, come on! I get it!"

Tim put his hand on Richard's shoulder. "Rick, these mistakes will keep kicking your ass until you start learning from them.

Listen—I just want you to remember—do not mess with guardians. If you do, your career is over."

"I've got it. I promise."

Tim clasped his shoulder. "Good!"

Richard stood up. "I'll be working alone. And I need my horse to get there."

"The horse isn't a problem, but you'll need to work with the local team in Triville. You will help them with this case."

Richard stayed at the open door, scratching his chin. "And what happens after I find the murderer?"

"Six months on the Island, Rick. Just six months. Then you might get a second chance."

"Well, it's not the worst deal."

* * *

The wind and drizzle met Richard on the street. He closed his jacket and put his hood on. The sky above was such a deep gray that he couldn't tell if it was day or evening. A big fountain splashed in the middle of Guardian Square. The time crystal on the fountain shone a dark green, which meant it had just turned four o'clock. Then, it was evening.

A woman sat at the fountain and rubbed her palms. She wore a long red cloak, and a wide hood covered her face, but Richard still recognized her.

He approached. "Camilla?'

She took off her hood and looked at him with her big brown eyes. There was a red mark on her left cheek.

Richard touched her face. "Did he do this to you?"

Camilla took his hand; her palm was cold.

"I'll talk to him!" Richard said.

Camilla sighed. "My poor Ricky! You're such a naive boy."

"Naive?"

"It's over, Ricky. I need to go back to my husband now. He was kind enough to forgive me, and he gave you a second chance."

"I'm so sorry, Camilla."

The shadow of a smile touched her lips. "It's not your fault. Don't blame yourself. When there's strong evidence, finding the culprit becomes easy."

He took her hand. It was so small and cool; he wanted to squeeze it until she became warm. But he couldn't do it anymore; the fire had burned itself out.

"Goodbye, my lady. I will always keep you in my heart."

"Bye, Ricky."

Richard turned away. His heavy boots stepped in dirty puddles. His life was even dirtier. Shame coursed through him as he thought of Tim seeing him lying there, naked. The voice of a yellow-bearded guardian roared in his head: *When there's strong evidence, finding the culprit becomes easy.*

Richard stopped. Shards of memories flashed before his eyes. How did Camilla know what that yellow-bearded guardian had said to him? Unless . . .

She had read him.

Now everything was clear. The wine that she'd given him to drink but had not touched herself. She'd smiled and said it would make him stronger. *If only he had known what she'd meant.*

Richard turned back. Camilla was walking away, and her red coat was clearly visible from the opposite side of the square. He ran after her.

He took her elbow, and Camilla looked at him with hesitation. "Ricky, I said it's over."

He squeezed her elbow. "What was I to you, Camilla? A toy?"

"Can you calm down?"

"You're such a liar! And you keep telling me lies."

Camilla chuckled. "You know why people cheat?"

He narrowed his eyes, silent.

"Because they are too damn scared to be cheated on."

"You poisoned me, didn't you?"

Camilla shrugged. "My husband was a cheater, and all I wanted was to get him back. You could say I attracted his attention."

"By using me? I almost lost my career. My reputation is destroyed!"

She laughed. "Come on, you weren't thinking of your reputation when you were licking chocolate from my body."

"You lied to your husband!"

"Only to tell him the truth in the end. I love him, and I tried to deal with his affairs."

Richard shook his head. "You guys are sick."

"Maybe love is a form of sickness."

Richard stepped back. It started raining, and cold droplets fell on his face. The rain made Camilla's face cold and ugly. He turned around and walked away. He wanted to walk as far as possible from this huge ignorant city, from the wet and the mud. At least he had some time before his punishment started, and it was a chance to solve the case of his life.

I'm coming, Ghost. And this time, nothing will stop me.

Chapter 12. The Light of Our Souls

Heavy gray clouds hung over the cemetery. The shadowy figures of town dwellers slowly moved between the flower beds, gathering near an old orchard. White flowers dropped their pure petals, and they fell on the wet grass and into a fresh grave. There was a small hole in the ground, ten inches in diameter. Bella's father stood near the grave in silence, and her younger sister, Melissa, squeezed a white ceramic vase in her small hands.

Lana checked the time crystal on her bracelet; it was pink—ten in the morning. The ceremony was about to start, but she couldn't find her father among the dull faces and muted clothes.

A rumble rolled through the crowd. People parted, and an old man with a long gray beard emerged. His white gown was decorated with golden stripes: a Temple priest. He walked to the tree and put his wrinkled hand on Melissa's shoulder. The girl sobbed, and tears slid down her cheeks.

The priest turned his face toward the grievers and raised his hand. Everyone went silent.

"Greetings, Triville dwellers," he said in a husky voice. "Thank you for coming here to say goodbye to our dear Bella." The priest moved his gaze across the crowd. "This day fills our hearts with sorrow. It is hard to say goodbye when someone so young passes away."

A loud cry pierced the air.

The priest raised his voice. "It's hard for us—for the people who stay on this earth, only to experience grief. Bella didn't have time to do everything she needed to do, but her path is now over. Her short life was interrupted by cruelty. This child, this pure soul, is in a better place now. She is in Heaven, joining the Great Shine."

Lana looked around—no guardians were present at the ceremony. Only she stood in the front row in her black clothes. Her father still had not arrived to deliver a speech, to calm people down.

"And now," the priest continued, "our brave guardians will give us several words about Bella."

The Priest pointed to Lana, and she held her breath. The priest probably assumed that she could deliver a speech as the chief's daughter. People looked at her, waiting. Lana moved forward on unbalanced feet. She stopped near the priest and stood motionless in front of the huge crowd, not knowing what to say. She only remembered the words her father told her in his office: *You let me down, you forced the teenagers to be involved,* and *poor Elisa will be scarred for the rest of her life.*

Lana found Elisa's face in the crowd. She was in the second row with her classmates. Elisa nodded to her.

The priest looked at her with kind gray eyes. "Just speak from your heart."

His old hand touched her shoulder, and Lana felt his calmness, his pure love of humanity, and his divinity. She turned her face toward the crowd. All eyes were on her now, but there was no judgment in them, only fear.

"Life is a flower," Lana said, and the sound of her voice made her speak with confidence. "When we are born, we are small, like a bud, but we keep growing. The warmth of love makes us stronger, day after day, until our Gifts reveal themselves. Then we start blossoming. In spring, we are beautiful and brave, as we drop our petals of youth and enjoy our lives. We can follow our fate and use our powers to help people."

People looked at her, their eyes filled with hope.

Lana continued. "It breaks our hearts when someone clips us before we can bloom. As you can see, not everyone uses their Gifts the right way. Someone took Bella's life and used his power to hide his crime, but he won't escape his punishment." Lana raised her voice. "I promise you, our guardians will do everything possible to find the murderer. Justice will triumph!"

People started applauding.

Lana smiled and let the priest take her space and start the burial ceremony. Bella's father leaned over the grave and poured in the ashes. Then, Melissa sprinkled some seeds on top, and they covered the grave with earth.

According to the old tradition, the new flower bed would allow the energy of her soul to have peace. The flowers varied, but they always meant something to the person who passed away. Bella's grave was planted with white lilies, the symbol of innocence.

The Temple priest put his hands together. Snow-white energy with golden sparkles twisted in his palms and formed a ball of Light. Lana put her palms up, and her yellow energy leaked from her fingers, until it also took the shape of a sphere. Everyone around her held Light in their hands. There were so many shades—green, blue, yellow. Some with sparkles, others had a pure glow, like her own.

The priest raised his voice. "Let's honor Bella's memory by giving her our energies. Best wishes to the Great Shine!"

His white sparkling Light bounced and floated up into the cloudy sky.

People lifted their hands, and dozens of shining Light balls floated upward, as well. Lana released her yellow Light, and it followed the others. They floated higher and higher, and the beauty of them in the gray sky soothed her beating heart.

Lana put her palm on her chest. *It was one more cold-blooded murder*, she reminded herself. *I will find out who did it.*

She looked around. All eyes looked to the sky, and their faces were peaceful.

A stranger stood behind the crowd; his face looked like an ink spot on white paper. He looked right at her with dark green eyes and grinned.

Lana narrowed her eyes. The stranger put on his hat and turned away. Lana jumped into the crowd toward him, pushing people out of her way. *I can't let him escape.*

Lana stepped on someone's foot and turned to apologize. The woman's eyes were big and yellow through her thick, round glasses.

"Lana, what a beautiful speech," the woman said.

This woman is everywhere.

"Not now, Mrs. Sullivan." Lana pushed her out of the way and ran forward.

When she managed to exit the crowd, the stranger was gone. In the breeze, sacred flowers shifted in their beds, and cherry trees dropped their petals in silence.

Which direction did he take? Lana bit her lip. Her eyes looked right, then left, then right again.

Someone's heavy hand touched her shoulder. Lana yelped and jumped aside. She turned around.

Her father stood in front of her with laughing eyes. "I understand that I'm getting older, but I didn't think I'd become *that* scary."

Lana pointed at the forest. "A stranger was here. I saw him. He ran in there!"

He came closer. "Slow down. What stranger?"

"I saw a man at the ceremony. He wasn't from here!"

Her father frowned.

"He ran into the forest. We should find him!" Lana grabbed his hand and pulled, but she was unable to move him.

"Firstly, the *guardians* will find him," her father said. "And secondly, I'm suspending you until this case is over."

"What?"

He sighed. "Lana, this isn't an ordinary murder. You know that the energy traces were removed with a forbidden and strong spell—no regular mages could have done it. So, I sent a letter to Santos and got a reply from their chief. This murderer . . . It was Ghost."

"A ghost? You don't even believe they exist."

He gave her a sharp look. "No, Lana. Ghost is a serial killer who hunts schoolgirls."

Lana widened her eyes.

"And yes, you might have seen him, which means you're in danger now."

Lana raised her hands. "But father—"

"I said, *you are suspended.* Do *not* go into the forest, and do *not* enter the Guardian House, unless I personally ask you to do so. Until I solve this case, of course. Do you understand?"

Lana nodded. When her father talked to her like this, it was better not to argue.

"Good." He turned around and walked to the orchard.

The crowd started to walk away, leaving Bella's family kneeling on the ground and holding hands. Lana looked back at the forest—the dark silhouettes of the tree trunks stood in silence. Lana shook her head and walked after her father.

Chapter 13. The Suspect

An old tea kettle with a big creeping rust spot rattled and whistled. Julia stood at the kitchen table, with a shabby tablecloth, arranging dishes. Several teacups with cracks hardly fit on the small tray. Julia shook her head. When she suggested Bella's family to help with repast, she had no idea how broken they were.

She approached the window and fixed a dirty curtain with a hole on the edge. A geranium on the windowsill was half dried, and a red cat who slept there lazily dangled his short tail.

Julia petted the cat. "I know. Life is misshapen, buddy."

"Why is the kettle boiling?" a familiar woman's voice asked.

Julia took her eyes from the window and met Mrs. Sullivan's gaze. Today, the teacher looked different in her dark gray dress. Without her school gown, she seemed shorter and older. Mrs. Sullivan walked to the oven and switched it off. It grew quiet in the kitchen, and the voices of the guests who chatted in the living room revealed it.

Julia opened her mouth to say something, but the words stuck in her throat. The last time they spoke, Mrs. Sullivan had been mad at her. Julia still remembered her sharp look.

Was Julia supposed to apologize for her and Elisa's behavior? It would be so weird. The episode in school seemed to have happened years ago, but in reality, only a few days had passed.

Mrs. Sullivan added the leaves in the teacups and waved her hand. The kettle rose and started filling the teacups on the tray. She took one of them and turned to Julia.

"Drink," the teacher said in a soft voice. "It's chamomile and mint. It will soothe you."

Julia took a cup from her hands. The cup had a crack on the rim; she covered it with a fingertip.

Mrs. Sullivan sighed. "Poor Bella. She was just a kid." Her yellow eyes were wet. A tear trembled on one of her round lenses.

Julia took a slow breath. The scene in class wasn't important anymore. It had become one of the small, meaningless things that Julia had worried about last week—like her hairstyle, the color of her dress, or the rumors discussed between classes. Everything that had happened in her life before was distant. No one looked like themselves anymore, and Mrs. Sullivan was no exception.

Julia took a sip from her cup, and the hot tea burned her tongue. She put the cup back on the table. "Mrs. Sullivan, I don't know what to do."

"We will try to get over it," the teacher replied.

"I mean . . . What if it happens to me?"

"You shouldn't think like that. Our guardians will find the murderer."

Julia sighed. She was right. The guardians did their job well, and she was confident in their abilities. But she wasn't so sure about her Gift, which could reveal itself at any moment.

"Mrs. Sullivan?"

"Yes, sweetheart?"

Julia looked into her eyes with caution; she had only one chance to ask. "What Elisa said about Mercy House—is it true?"

"It's just a rumor. I don't know who started it, but I know one thing—when people are afraid, they do desperate things. Like poor Bella, who looked for the witch instead of going home."

Julia flinched. "Bella just got lost, that's all."

Mrs. Sullivan narrowed her eyes. "You should believe us—your teachers and the guardians. The sooner you start telling the truth, the better."

"Of course." Julia lowered her eyes.

Nothing became clear. Maybe nothing would be until her Gift manifested. It was scary. *Oh, Mrs. Sullivan . . .* She was right about one thing—it wasn't good to run from fear. Not with how things ended for poor Bella. She must find a way to overcome this fear, but it was impossible to do in this house, where everyone asked hard questions.

The teacher took the tray in her hands. "Some girls from my class suggested making a memorial board for Bella, so we can hang it in a school corridor. Are you joining us?"

Julia approached the kitchen door that led to the backyard. "Sorry, I don't feel well. I better go outside and get some fresh air."

Mrs. Sullivan smiled. "Of course, sweetheart."

* * *

Julia walked among the blossoming trees. The gray sky hung over the beautiful garden, and the petals fell from branches, circling around her. Rose and Elisa were under the cherry tree, talking in quiet voices. Pink petals gently lay on their heads like tiaras, enlivening their gray dresses and serious faces.

Julia approached the girls.

Elisa smiled. "Look who it is! Where have you been?"

"I helped in the kitchen and talked with Mrs. Sullivan about the rumor."

"And how did it go?"

Julia shrugged.

Elisa chuckled. "Of course. Our fat Owl prefers to hide in a hollow until it's safe. Still bends her narrative about 'the danger of Gift', I guess?"

Julia nodded.

Elisa gave her an intriguing look. "You know what? We can take advantage of it."

"What do you mean?" Julia asked.

Rose looked at her. "We can find out who is monitoring new Gift manifestations."

Julia widened her eyes. "What? Why?"

Elisa softened her voice. "Oh, my dear naive Julia. Don't you think they have their eyes on us? We're about to burst out with our Gifts."

"Why don't you tell the guardians?" Julia asked.

Elisa grinned. "Because they *are* the guardians, Julia. Did you hear what Lana said in school? They have a special Gift Hunter who is spying on us."

Elisa could be a detective, Julia thought. She never stopped digging for the truth. Ironically, Mrs. Sullivan wanted the same thing. But the ugly truth was, none of these women could really help.

"At the creek, Kyle said that only a guardian can erase traces," Rose said.

"We think one of them caught Bella in the forest," Elisa added.

"What are you saying?" Julia asked. "That a guardian killed her?" The sound of her own voice made her shiver.

Elisa nodded. "Finally, you get the point."

"And we can find out which guardian did it," Rose said.

Julia sighed. She didn't like this idea. She didn't like *any* of their ideas, but somehow, she couldn't resist them. "How?" she asked.

Elisa took a thin branch and drew a line on the ground.

"When we were at the creek, something else happened," Elisa said.

"I saw how Kyle's eyes glittered," Rose said.

"Exactly. He might know who the murderer is, but he didn't say so."

"Why?" Julia asked, but she already knew the answer.

Elisa glanced at her and continued her drawing. "When we found the glade where Bella was, he tried to provoke me." She drew several more lines on the ground. Now it was a square. A pink petal twirled and landed on one of the lines.

"Provoke?" Julia asked.

Rose nodded. "Like we provoked Bella. He made her mad."

Elisa looked at Julia. "I tried to buy some time for Bella, but I think he figured it out."

Julia raised her eyebrows. "What did he do?"

"Let's just say, he didn't act like a gentleman."

"He is not what he seems," Rose said.

Julia walked to the cherry tree and took a deep breath. When did everything become so complicated? She pictured Kyle spying on them through the tree branches, and she shook her head. *No, he cannot be like this.*

Elisa drew some lines in the middle of the square. "Kyle might know something about all of us, but I know something about him too. He has a diary, and I bet he keeps it in his bedroom."

Julia looked at the drawing on the ground. Similar squares usually were on the maps of the buildings. Her heart sank. "I won't break into his house," she said.

"You won't," Elisa replied. She pointed at Rose. "*We* will."

Julia stared at them. *Unbelievable.* They were involving her in something. *Again.* When Elisa decided on something, there was no stopping her.

"What should I do?" Julia asked.

"You'll invite him to go for a walk."

Julia paused. "Would he really agree to go with me?"

"Of course." Elisa smiled. "You are perfect for this mission."

"Why?"

"Firstly, you're the calmest person I know. And secondly, you like him."

Julia blushed. "I don't."

"Whatever you say," Elisa said. "You'll be the one to distract him."

"And what if something goes wrong?"

"It's a chance to know who the Gift Hunter is," Rose said.

Elisa's eyes sparkled. "They won't be able to hide it anymore if we find proof and start telling everyone the truth."

Julia looked at them both with wide eyes.

Elisa threw her branch into the bushes and turned to the girls. "Once, my old friend said that no one is here to protect us. We must protect ourselves and stand by each other. I just have one question: Who's with me?"

Rose stepped forward. "I'm always by your side."

Julia nodded. "I'm in."

"Good," Elisa replied. "Let's discuss the plan."

The rustle of a cherry tree muffled their whispers. And when they were gone, pink petals twisted in the moist air and fell on the ground, covering the drawing and their footprints.

Chapter 14. The River of Time

Richard left the dull streets of Santos far behind. The fog and heavy thunderclouds dissipated, and now, the infinite blue sky shone above the tree crowns. Here, in the depths of the forest, the cheerful rustle of leaves whispered about the upcoming summer. A gentle wind tickled green leaves that seemed to laugh under its touch.

Richard stopped his horse and inhaled the smell of fresh grass and flowers. A running river roared nearby. Richard disembarked from the saddle and shook his legs. Coal, his black stallion, put his snout on Richard's shoulder.

Richard patted Coal. "I know, it was a long trip. Tomorrow, we will be in town."

He took the reins and walked to the river shoreline. The main road that he was following ended, and now he had to fully rely on his experience. The most important thing was to go in a single direction. Richard learned that a long time ago when he played hide-and-seek in the forests with his brother.

These small towns were so hard to find. They hid among the forests throughout the entire Kingdom. They were a perfect target for Ghost, who hunted schoolgirls.

Richard walked along the shore and let the horse enjoy some fresh water. He sat on a big rock, feeling a cool breeze touching on his face. A small fish jumped from the water and quickly fell back. Saliva filled his mouth. After three days eating dried food, Richard would kill for a freshly baked trout, but he didn't have any tools to catch it. He couldn't remember the proper spell for fishing, and he wondered if it even existed.

Richard got up and walked along the shore. There were a lot of fish. The trout slid with the river stream; their wide tales teased him. The sound of laughter reached his ears. Richard took several quiet steps to reach the bushes. He moved a branch and saw a family at the shore. A man held a fishing pole, and two kids helped him. A twelve-year-old boy looked at the river, and a small girl placed a fish in a wicker basket. The trout wagged its tail, and its wet scales shone like a rainbow.

Richard emerged from the bush and smiled. "Hello, folks!"

The girl screamed and ran to the fisherman. The boy looked at Richard with wide blue eyes. Sweat droplets shone on his little tanned face.

"Sorry, I didn't mean to scare you." Richard stepped forward.

The fisherman shouted something in a foreign language and took a knife out of his pocket.

"What the heck? I'm a guardian!" Richard pointed at his shoulder with its golden dragon embroidery.

The man pressed the girl to his leg. The boy said something to the fisherman in the language that Richard didn't understand, and they started arguing.

Richard raised his hand, and a silver Paralyzing spell appeared in his palm. "Put the weapon down," he said.

The boy looked at Richard. "My father says that if you want, you can kill him, but please, don't kill me and my sister."

The fisherman held a knife in his shaking hand, dirt wedged under his fingernails. The girl hid her face under her father's hand and sobbed.

Richard frowned. They were a pack of Incapables. He glanced at the basket full of trout. "Okay, tell your father that I'm not going to kill anyone. I just need some food."

The boy said something to his father, then he turned to Richard. "Sorry for his manners. Guardians killed his father, and he is afraid you might kill us. Please take the basket if you want." The boy's tone was flat—in the way people usually read annual reports.

"Boy, what's your name?" Richard asked.

"Eric." The boy fixed the collar of his muddy shirt. "Will you let us go?"

Richard walked to the basket and pulled out two fish by their tails. Two fat trout moved in his hand; they opened their mouths, trying to catch the water droplets from the air. Richard placed the Paralyzing spell on their scales, and the fish stopped moving.

Richard turned to the boy. "Tell your father that I'm sorry, Eric. For everything. Thank you for the fish."

The boy nodded.

Richard walked away along the river shoreline. The scales of the fish in his hand were cold. It was the law of nature—someone had to die to let someone else live. But it was just a fish. A silly piece of fish for his dinner.

* * *

When the sky started getting dark, Richard stopped in a glade. He made a fire and sat near it on the ground, the flame dancing and crackling in front of him. Richard impaled the fish on a stick and placed it above the flame, anticipating a great dinner. He took a sip from his flask, and the smoke teased his nostrils. The Incapables were awful fighters, but at least they were good fishermen.

Communities of Incapables usually hid in small villages in the depths of the forests. These cursed creatures without pride and magic were allowed to leave their territory only with special government permission. They usually performed cheap labor for farmers, miners, and carpenters because the positions only required brute strength. The group he met today probably lived somewhere nearby. Who knew what this strange fisherman had in his dirty head?

GHOST

A branch cracked behind him, and Richard turned his head. He could swear he saw two flashing eyes. He stood and walked to a swaying bush. *Who is it?* In a place like this, it could be anything, anyone—a wild animal who smelled the fish or an Incapable who decided to follow him.

Ghost? No, he wasn't stupid enough to walk right into Richard's hands.

Richard jumped over the bush and stretched out his palm, ready to produce any spell to protect his life.

The boy sat on the ground and looked at him with wide blue eyes. His shirt was covered with mud and grass.

"Eric! What are you doing here?" Richard asked.

"Mr. Guardian, I am so . . . so sorry. Please—"

"I won't kill you, damn it!" Richard gave the boy his hand.

Eric took it and stood up. He wiped the mud off his pants and looked at Richard with interest.

"Don't you think we've met too often for one day?" Richard asked.

"They told me to follow you, just to make sure—"

"I've told you I won't hurt anyone," Richard said in a stiff voice. "Wasn't that clear?"

Eric nodded. He stood motionless, and a silence hung in the air. The boy's stomach rumbled. He must have been chasing Richard ever since they met at the river, but no one had bothered to give the boy even a piece of bread.

Richard sighed. "Okay, let's go. Dinner is almost ready."

* * *

They sat by the fire, and Richard bit into the trout. It had the delicious taste of freedom. He closed his eyes, enjoying to the quiet rustle of the leaves and the calm crackling of the fire. The wildness of nature was beautiful and stark at the same time—priceless.

A loud chomping cut through to his ears, and he opened his eyes. The boy was scarfing down the fish—fat covered his chin and thin fingers. Richard chuckled.

When the boy finished eating, he threw the fish bones in the fire and wiped his face with his sleeves.

Richard smiled. "Eric, you seem like a fine lad."

The boy gave him a curious look. "Can you really do spells?"

Richard nodded. He lifted his palm, and a ball of fire rose in his hand. The boy looked at the fireball with his mouth open. The sparkles reflected in his eyes.

"Do you wanna hold it?" Richard asked.

Eric nodded. He stretched out his hands and took the fireball. He held it in his palms like expensive crystal.

"What do you feel?"

"Warmth," the boy said.

Richard smiled. Did this Incapable boy really need much? He had never seen magic before, and now he was holding a fireball in his hands. He was a stranger from a different world, but he was just a curious boy covered with mud. A boy who dreamed of adventures he could tell his friends about.

"It's getting hot!" the boy said.

"Careful with that thing." Richard took the fireball and threw it into the fire pit. The blaze soared, and the flames ate the branches with greed.

Eric fidgeted. "Do you use these fireballs to . . . I mean, as a weapon?"

"It's forbidden to use it against people. We use this magic mostly for making fires." Richard looked up. The sky was dark, and the fire lit up the bushes around him. He took his time crystal out of his pocket; it had a calm pink light.

"What's that?" the boy asked.

Richard gave him a puzzled look. "A time crystal from Death Island. You should know that."

Eric shook his head.

Richard turned the crystal in his hand. "Death Island is one of our world's wonders. A strong magnetic anomaly transforms the minerals into time crystals. They change color with each passing hour. The crystals turn from red to orange, then yellow, and so on until they're pink at the end of the cycle. Twice a day, the crystals run across the whole light spectrum. Time crystals grow in the darkness of the caves, waiting for people to release them from the rocks."

Eric stretched out his hand and touched the crystal. "Did you release this one?"

"No. It's a job for the prisoners."

Eric narrowed his eyes. "Which prisoners?"

Richard took the crystal back. No one had told the boy that the prisoners were Incapables. Despised by the rest of humanity, they were sent to the Island to work in the mines where they lost their magic. Why did they hide this from the boy? He wasn't a kid, and he deserved to know the truth.

"When someone commits a murder, he or she is sentenced to imprisonment on Death Island," Richard explained. "Prisoners perform heavy labor, like mining, and then they lose their powers because of the Island's magnetic anomaly."

Eric glared at him. "That's why you thought I knew about it? Because I don't have magic?"

"It isn't your fault, boy."

Eric looked at the fire, and the flames gleamed on his face. "My father was born in the village, and he wasn't born with powers. But my mother . . . her magic was taken away from her. The mages burned the magic channels from her fingers and sent her to the community. They forbid her from speaking about it. But one day, my grandfather figured everything out. He tried to spread the truth, and he was killed by the guardians. We had to run. Then we found a village where people hid us and our secret."

Richard shook his head. This story sounded like one of the naive tales his parents told him as a child—a story about poor victims and evil villains. In Eric's reality, the guardians were the villains, which was completely wrong.

"That's sad to hear, Eric. But here is another truth—people tend to lie to hide their past."

The boy gave him a sharp look. His nostrils heavily inhaled the air.

"I'm sorry," Richard said. "We are not as cruel as you've been told."

Eric stood up. "Thank you for the fish."

"It was your fish, pal."

Eric stood in front of the fire, looking at the dark forest before him. "Yes, it was."

Richard arose and touched the boy's shoulder. "Sorry, I didn't mean to upset you."

"I'm not upset." Eric gave him a sharp look. "And I'm not afraid of you."

He turned away and walked into the forest. His slim silhouette disappeared among the glowing tree trunks.

Night wrapped around the glade. Richard put his blanket on the ground to lie down. The air was clear, and the stars appeared in the dark velvet sky. One of the stars blinked and fell. Richard closed his eyes. Most people wished to go back in time and fix their past mistakes, but Richard wasn't one of them. Maybe it would have been easier if he'd said something else and hadn't offended the boy, but easy lessons never taught anyone anything. His only wish was to solve this case and find the Ghost before he chose his next victim

Chapter 15. A Taste of Freedom

Lana walked into her small office. She was suspended, but at least, she could collect her notebooks, so no one could read them in her absence.

The cloudy day's dull light lit up the shelves and the piles of books on the floor she had failed to organize. Once, it was just a filing room. After she started working as a secretary, she'd turned it into her workspace.

Four years ago, she dreamed of becoming a detective, and everything seemed possible back then. She wasn't allowed to become a guardian, but that hadn't stopped her from visiting her father. He let her into this room. Here, Lana read old case files and learned about Gifts and spells. Sometimes, she read only parts of the cases and tried to guess who the criminal was. She became better with time. The basement was empty, and no one interrupted her reading, except for guardians who needed to reference old cases, or just chat with her to kill time when it was quiet.

Lana sighed. Now she was not allowed to even pretend to be a secretary.

Since she'd come back to Triville, everything had become complicated. Her father was right—now was the worst time to continue her investigation. Anyway, it seemed that the new case had nothing to do with Rebecca's murder; she would return to it when the dust settled.

Lana approached her desk and started putting her personal belongings into her backpack. There were several notebooks, and her black jacket hung on the back of the chair. Lana touched the jacket. She sewed it herself several years ago. It was exactly like a guardian uniform except for the missing golden dragon on its shoulder. Lana stood in silence. Her eyes welled. Life was never fair, and she knew it. She'd become used to it, but it was hard to push her investigation aside.

The door flew open. Lana wiped her eyes as a young guardian with red hair walked into the room. He was skinny and pale, and he held a red folder in his long hands—the new guy on their team. Lana met him when the guardians started Bella's search, but she couldn't remember his name.

He smiled. "Hey, Lana! I thought you weren't in today."

Lana nodded in understanding. He was on duty and must not have heard the news about her suspension. "I wasn't," she said. "Just dropped by to take my stuff."

"How was the ceremony?" the guardian asked.

"It was beautiful. Peaceful."

He sighed. "I wish I was there, but someone has to be on duty."

"I know. You can send your Light to her soul."

"I will."

He gave his red folder to Lana, and she read the title. She recognized her father's handwriting: *Ghost—Case Reopened in Triville. Top Secret.*

Lana widened her eyes. Perfect, this guardian was such a rookie, he failed to follow procedure. No one but the chief or a captain could open this folder. Every guardian knew that—except this newbie.

"Where did you get this?" Lana asked.

"Captain Turner left it with me and went out. Now his door is closed, and the chief isn't here. I don't know what I should do with it. I don't want to get in trouble—"

"It's okay," Lana said. "Don't worry. I'll lock it in here and tell the chief. You'll be all right."

He breathed a sigh of relief. "Thank you, Lana. You've saved me."

"No problem."

He smiled and walked away; his steps disappeared down the hall.

Lana stood in front of the open door and held the red folder in her hands. All the muscles in her body went soft. Her mind was captivated with a single wish—to open the damn folder and to read everything to the last word. She had to make an effort to take her eyes off the cover. She put the folder on the shelf, turned away, and walked to the door.

Lana touched the doorknob. The case file beckoned her from behind, whispering its secrets with the rustle of unread pages.

"Damn it!" Lana slammed her hand against the door and stood alone in the filing room. She reached for the shelf in two steps, then took the folder with trembling hands and opened it.

* * *

When Lana closed the folder, the room was bright. The evening sun broke out from the clouds, and its rays warmed the walls. She stood up and put the case file in its place. Her father had managed to collect copies of different reports and pictures of all eleven victims. Now she knew about Ghost. All of his victims were schoolgirls, and as for the witness reports, some of them had disappeared right after their destructive Gifts manifested. However, the main question was still unanswered—*why* had Ghost killed them?

Lana rubbed her temples. Questions. There were too many of them, and she was drowning in uncertainty. When Lana found herself in this condition, she usually took her notebook and started drawing. She sat back down at her desk, allowing her pencil to glide over the smooth paper.

When Lana finished, she put her notebook down and closed her eyes. Everything she knew assembled into a clear picture: Firstly, all the victims were teenagers, at the age when Gifts usually manifested. Several cases of Gift manifestation were reported, but what if all of them had destructive magic? Secondly, as Kyle had said, only an educated mage could remove magic traces—either a guardian or a witch. Witches were mostly women who disobeyed the law and preferred to hide their dislocation, and that's why the guardians had confrontations with them. However, Ghost couldn't be a witch, because it was a man's footprints at the crime scene. An easy conclusion followed—he was a guardian. It explained everything.

Lana stood up. The mysterious murderer whose face no one had ever seen. Once, she heard a rumor about a murderer who killed girls who tried to escape Mercy House. If Ghost had come here to do a cleaning job, he had caught Bella in the forest. He might have been the one who killed Rebecca and staged it as a suicide.

Lana touched her burning cheeks. *Well played, father.* In this deceitful world, truth was a rare treasure. Each time she found out the truth, she met a dead end: from her epic fail with Charles to the rotten sorority of Mercy House and now with this murder investigation. Everything she cared for was justice, but it crashed against the black walls of the cruel system. It always did. Maybe that's why her father wanted her to step away—he'd known everything from the beginning and wanted to protect her from this truth. *If only she could read his thoughts to check it.* Unfortunately, her Gift didn't let her read the thoughts of close blood relatives or people she was in love with.

Lana took the book from her desk. On the cover, the girl riding the dragon looked sad. If Lana could, she would ride into the forest right away to serve justice. Her horse would gallop through the fields and rocky trails, and the wind would hit her face. Lana smiled. *Interesting*—would her father keep silent if Ghost attacked his only daughter?

* * *

Lana approached the stable where the groom cleaned a beautiful palomino horse. The groom was a short man with a bald head and kind brown eyes. His plump hands put set his brush down, and he petted the horse's snout. The horse's sides shone in the evening sun.

"Now you look great, Sunshine!" he said.

Lana smiled. People who loved animals had the best personalities; they were more sincere and kinder than others.

Lana walked up to the groom. "Sunshine. What a beautiful name!"

He smiled and patted the horse. "Yes. She's gorgeous, isn't she?"

Lana nodded.

"She was brought in from the Rocky Kingdom," the groom said. "She's been trained to ride long distances, and she's a great friend."

"I bet she is!" Lana smiled. She touched the horse's face and felt a yellow glow of joy.

Lana opened her eyes. "How much would you take for her?"

He scratched his chin. "Sunshine is unique, so five silver coins would be an honest price."

In her backpack, she found her purse under some maps and notebooks. Two silver and two bronze coins.

Lana sighed. "I'm guessing that Sunshine isn't the only horse you have."

The groom nodded and walked to the stables. Lana followed him.

Gorgeous mares and stallions whinnied at them from their pens. The groom talked about different breeds and their origins. At the very end of the stable, a pretty horse rested her head on the door of her pen. Her eyes were shut.

She pointed to the horse. "What about that one?"

The groom shook his head. "Oh, Mandy . . . she's sick."

Lana walked to the end. She was a chestnut Gidran horse with a white stripe down her face. The horse opened her eyes and gave Lana a tired look. Lana touched the horse's warm snout and closed her eyes. Her consciousness moved through the horse's memories into a tiny, closed room. She choked in desperation. The walls of the stable pressed in on her, and Lana took a deep breath.

The groom touched the pen. "The vet checked her, but nothing seems to be wrong. I mean, physically. Mandy lost her colt this spring, and she's been like this ever since."

Lana took her purse. "How much?"

The groom shrugged. "If no one takes her, she'll die here from depression. I wouldn't ask for any money, but . . . just whatever you can give an old man for horse feed."

Lana gave him her purse. He looked inside the purse, nodded, and opened the pen.

"Nice to meet you, Mandy." Lana petted the horse between her ears. "Let's break these walls together!" she whispered.

The horse nickered and moved her ears.

* * *

Night approached Triville and sprinkled the sky with shimmering stars. Lana rode through the forest trail. Night flowers shone with yellow, blue, and white lights. The moss on the trees glowed a gentle green; summer was close.

Lana stopped the horse at the top of a hill and took a deep breath. Her cloak flapped, and the wind cooled her flushed cheeks. Below, a small town lived its evening life. Lights appeared in the windows. The full moon slowly crawled along the horizon, lightening dark blue roofs and the curve of the running river.

"This is Triville, Mandy. Our town," Lana said.

The horse neighed.

"Beautiful, I know." Lana looked up to where the sky was dark and unknown. One of the stars blinked and fell. Lana followed the star's trace in silence without making a wish. All the wishes she'd ever made had passed her by because they were too unrealistic. A long time ago, she dreamed of solving the case of her life and turning the world upside down. That time had passed, and nothing happened.

That's why she had to take things into her own hands.

Lana was ready to meet Ghost face-to-face, but today, he wasn't interested in chasing her. Lana frowned—she wasn't a teenager. But schoolgirls who had Gifts like Bella might be in danger. Lana clasped the horse's sides and rode down the hill.

Chapter 16. Night Walk

A warm light from the window highlighted the yard. Julia walked the trail with quiet steps. She wore one of her best dresses—made of blue cotton with silver rose embroidery on its hem. A thin woolen shawl covered her frail shoulders. A silver necklace in a shape of a heart decorated her neck. Its single, small diamond shimmered in the moonlight.

Julia tiptoed to the window and looked inside. Kyle sat on a bench and played the piano, reflections from the fireplace dancing on his calm face as his gentle fingers flew over the keys. The sad and charming melody melted her heart.

The currant bush beside her shivered, and Elisa's voice hissed. "Come on, knock on the damn door!"

Julia glanced back. "Just give me a minute!"

The music stopped playing, and Julia took a clumsy step back. The bench slid on the wooden floor, and Kyle's steps approached the door.

Julia froze. She would have run away if the girls were not watching her.

She took a deep breath and approached the black rectangular door.

It was quiet. She held her braid to her chest like it could calm her racing heart. Julia closed her eyes and raised her fist. Her knuckles touched the wooden surface, and she gave it three quiet knocks.

The door creaked and opened. Kyle's face was halved in shadow.

"Julia?" He smiled. "What are you doing here?"

She still had her hand raised; she put it down. The girls were looking at her from the bushes, and it gave her a little more confidence to speak. "Hey!"

"Are you alone?" he asked. His beautiful blue eyes sparkled.

"Am . . ." Julia mumbled. She moved her gaze to the floor. "I was going to ask you to join me on a walk."

"Sure. I'll grab my jacket."

He went inside and closed the door, and she could breathe again.

"Good job, my dear!" the voice whispered from the bushes.

Julia shook her head and stepped out from under the porch. The sky was covered with millions of stars; they blinked and teased her with their magnificent shine. One of them suddenly fell, and Julia closed her eyes to make a silent wish. *Please, let Elisa be wrong about him!*

A rustle of leaves caused by the girls' fussy movements ruined the stillness of the night. It was weird they were there to witness her first date with Kyle. Under different circumstances, she would never have dared come here. He wouldn't look at her twice if she weren't Elisa's friend. She was lucky he'd agreed to come out of the house.

The door's creaking interrupted her thoughts, and Julia turned to face Kyle. In his black jacket, he looked like a real guardian—exactly like his father. Her heart fluttered when Kyle took her hand.

* * *

Two young people slowly walked along the river shoreline, holding hands. A full moon highlighted the water, glistening like a silver chain. Julia almost forgot about the girls back at his house. Kyle told her a story about a guardian who failed his watch by sleeping with his chief's wife.

Julia smiled. "And he always climbed up the ladder to her bedroom?"

"Yes!"

"He must be out of his mind."

"It always happens with law breakers. Sooner or later, they get caught."

Julia's heart skipped a beat. "How exactly did they catch him?"

Kyle smiled, and his white teeth shone in the moonlight. "This is the most interesting part. The two sweethearts decided to celebrate the evening with a good bottle of wine."

"And he got drunk?"

Kyle shook his head. "Sleeping potion. One glass of wine was enough to make him faint."

"But what about her?"

"She didn't touch the wine. Some people say she poisoned him to get revenge on her cheating husband."

Julia sighed. She let go of Kyle's hand and rubbed her palm. "Sometimes I think that people forget how to love. They always lie and mess everything up."

Kyle stopped and touched her shoulder. "Do you trust me?" he asked.

"I really want to," Julia said.

Kyle pointed to an old barn. "Let's go there."

* * *

They approached the forsaken barn. Its cracked red paint seemed black in the moonlight; broken pieces of glass stuck in the window frame. Kyle looked for brushwood, and Julia stayed outside at the fire pit.

She looked around. They went pretty far away from the living area. Only the river ran here, and the silent silhouettes of the trees shifted in front of the starry sky. An owl flew from a branch and screeched. Goosebumps covered her skin, and Julia hugged her shoulders.

Kyle came out from the gates with wooden planks and a bunch of straw. He approached the fire pit and put the straw on the bottom, then he carefully placed the wooden planks on top.

"Do you want to start it?" Kyle asked when he finished assembling the wood.

"No," Julia said. "I mean . . . I can't."

"No worries." Kyle smiled. He took her hands in his, turning her palms toward him. His touch made Julia's hands tremble.

"Just hold your hands like this. It's almost the same as when you release Light. Yes, that's right. Now close your eyes."

Julia relied on Kyle's voice.

"And now," Kyle continued, "relax your muscles. Let the energy flow inside your body before you send it to your hands. Then, imagine fire."

He stepped back. A shard of glass cracked under his shoe.

"What kind of fire?" Julia asked. "A candle?"

"Candles are weak. Imagine something tremendous. Something that makes you sweat."

Julia closed her eyes, immersing herself in the moment when she peered through Kyle's window. The fire gleamed on the ceiling; the wood crackled inside the fireplace. His gentle fingers flew over piano keys, and beautiful piano music filled her heart with warmth.

Julia imagined herself sitting beside the fireplace. Heat waves warmed her body. Her cheeks burned, and the heat filled her belly and chest.

"Now reveal it!" Kyle said.

Julia forwarded the energy to her hands and opened her eyes. Shining orange and red waves left her fingers and formed a ball of fire in her palms.

"See, you're not bad at magic." Kyle smiled.

Julia's fireball reflected in his laughing eyes. Kyle quickly cast a fireball in his own hands, and they both threw their spells into the fire pit. Tongues of flame licked at the straw and ate the wood with greed.

Chapter 17. Dear Diary

Elisa walked out of the bushes and stopped in the backyard. The tall walls of the Turners' house seemed gray at night. She stretched her hand out to the wooden frame of a window.

Rose caught her hand. "There might be a magic trap."

Elisa widened her eyes. "What should we do?"

"Let's be careful. I'll check it first."

"How?"

Rose sighed. "I recently visited my brother in a Guardian Academy, and he showed me. It's an easy Revealing spell; I can do it quickly."

Elisa crossed her arms. "Hurry up, then."

Rose raised her palms to the ledge of the window. Pink energy with red sparkles leaked from her fingers and formed a shining sphere. She touched the frame with the Light and whispered a spell, her face serious with concentration.

Elisa looked around. The night was quiet; only the bushes rustled and witnessed their crime.

"Find anything?" Elisa asked.

Rose lowered her hand. "I don't see any traps. It should be clear."

"I told you so."

Elisa pushed on the frame, and it flew open. White curtains drifted into the depths of the dark room like two ghosts. She jumped and climbed onto the windowsill. The moonlight illuminated a narrow bed under the window.

Elisa jumped down. Her elbow touched a candle holder, and it fell on the wooden floor with a deafening noise. Its candles rolled under the bed.

"Are you okay?" Rose asked.

Elisa sighed. "Let's get on with it!"

She pulled Rose inside and they split up. Elisa formed a Light ball in her palm to see better. Her silver energy with golden sparkles lit up the room, and she walked over to the wide dresser. Her reflection looked at her from the mirror, and she fixed a lock of her hair. She sat down and opened the bottom drawer of the dresser. It was full of unfolded underwear. Elisa snorted in disgust.

"Boys are so sleazy," Rose said, checking the bed with her Light ball. The bed was unmade, and worn clothes were strewn on the wrinkled sheets.

"At least no one will notice we were ever here," Elisa whispered. She wrinkled her nose and put her hand into the pile of underwear to touch the smooth bottom of the drawer.

Rose dropped a book behind Elisa, causing a quiet rustle of papers. Elisa opened the second drawer only to reveal socks, and by the smell, she concluded that half of them were worn.

"Got it!" Rose exclaimed.

Elisa pushed the shelf back and sighed in relief. She approached her friend, who stood at the window with the small brown notebook in her hands.

Elisa took the diary. It was his handwriting.

Unbelievable. It was so easy.

She turned the page and read through the text. Her eyes stopped at a poem that Kyle had read to her once. It was so unusual to see it written on a page. She snickered and turned several pages that had spring dates.

"*School, cricket, hunting with George.*" Elisa kept turning the pages. "Why does he call his father by his first name?"

"Just a typical silly boy!"

"Stop, I saw something." Rose turned the page back over.

"*March 27th,*" Elisa read. "*George said he's going to show me something new today. When will he finally get that I hate hunting?*" She looked at Rose. "So what?"

"Right here." Rose pointed to the bottom of the page. "*George said that I'm an adult now,*" she read aloud, "*and I should follow in his footsteps. I never wanted to be a guardian, but he thinks that he knows me better than I do. He asked me to keep an eye on the schoolgirls. I actually like one, and I would never approach her if it wasn't for my new duty.*"

"Bastard, he's been spying on me!" Elisa gasped.

"On *us.*"

"Whatever. Now we have proof." Elisa slammed the notebook closed.

"And what are we gonna do with it?"

Elisa shrugged. "Show it to Julia, of course."

Rose sighed and leaned on the windowsill. "So, everything is about Julia."

"What do you mean?" Elisa gave her a sharp look.

Rose looked at her with hesitation, then she glanced at the opened window. "You know, the way they look at each other, it's hard to ignore. Just admit that all this time, you've been jealous."

Elisa chuckled. "Are you kidding? Trust me, I don't need that guy. Even if—"

"Not jealous of *him,*" Rose interrupted. "Of *her.*"

Elisa stared at her friend and then turned to face the window. A fresh breeze soothed her burning cheeks. The wind touched the tops of the bushes, and they whispered something; maybe they were trying to remember the secrets they'd heard.

Rose touched her shoulder. "It's okay."

Elisa shifted her gaze at Rose. "Is it that noticeable?"

Rose nodded.

Elisa's heart pounded. Rose was the only person who knew this terrible truth, and she hadn't turned away.

"I didn't realize how much I was into her until I started dating Kyle." Elisa's voice trembled. "All I want is to feel . . . normal. But whenever I'm with him, I wish I was with her."

"Normal?" Rose gave her a sad look. "It's normal to be in love—nothing else matters."

"I wish she was able to feel the same way."

"Why don't you just tell her?"

"It's not that easy."

Rose chuckled. "Yeah, it's much easier to send her away with the guy she likes, then break into his house with your other friend to find proof of his badness."

Elisa's eyes flashed. "He's a jerk, and he'll offend her sooner or later. And when her heart breaks, I'll be there."

Rose glanced at the dark yard. "Honestly, it's not the best plan. Anyway, we got all we needed, so let's get out of here."

"Wait, there might be something else." Elisa opened the notebook. The next pages were marked with April and May dates. The schoolyard. A couple meetings with her.

"We've spent too much time in here. Let's go."

Elisa didn't listen. Instead, she turned several pages. "May 19th. The day Bella went missing."

She put the diary on a windowsill, the white page shining in the moonlight:

. . . the waves of energy. It was like a strong wind, but somehow, her magic didn't hurt me. I fell on my knees and looked at Bella. The anger in her eyes—it seemed that evil power controlled her from inside. I knew that I had to deliver Bella to the Gift Hunter, but at that moment, I didn't think about my duty. Julia was lying on the grass, and I was so scared . . .

Elisa shook her head. "I don't understand. When he dated me, he lied and tried to rape me. But when he writes about Julia, he sounds like a different person."

"He's sick."

"And even more dangerous than we thought." Elisa pointed at the bottom of the page. "Wait, look. Here it is."

"Please, let's read the rest after."

Rose pulled at her elbow, but Elisa could not avert her eyes from the page. *That night, I came to our place. I spoke with . . .* She turned the page. The next few pages were torn out. The girls exchanged glances in silence.

Elisa turned the diary upside down and shook it.

"Stop it!"

"No! This bastard knows the Gift Hunter! He knows everything!"

"Shh," Rose hissed, pointing to the window.

Elisa stopped shaking the notebook.

"Did you hear that?" Rose whispered.

Elisa stood, motionless. Heavy steps approached from the backyard. Her heart sank. Once, she'd asked Kyle why some guardians wore such heavy boots. He replied that their soles were protected. If a guardian entered a magic trap, he could just step over it.

Elisa was trapped; she wished she had magic boots to leave this house unnoticed, but she only had her useless school shoes.

Rose took the diary from her hands and hid it back under the mattress.

"Is anybody home?" asked a man's voice. He was close.

"It might be George," Rose whispered. "Leave through the front door. I'll distract him."

"How?"

Rose glanced at the window. "I'll figure it out. Kyle may have told him about everything, but I have a leverage."

Elisa squeezed her hand. "I won't leave you alone with him."

"Find Julia and warn her," Rose said.

Elisa nodded, then she let go of Rose's hand and ran to the door. She glanced back one more time before leaving. Her friend stood at the window and looked at the man's silhouette; moonlight lit up her beautiful face. Elisa sighed and slid out of the room.

* * *

Elisa ran through the bushes. Sharp branches scratched her hands, but she didn't notice them. She stopped only when she reached the river shoreline. With her palms on her knees, she gasped for breath. Triville's lights shimmered in the west. The inhabitants would soon be slipping into sweet dreams, unaware of what was going on in their own town.

The firelight danced along the bent river. *Of course, this liar, Kyle, chose his favorite place!* It meant that Julia had to be somewhere nearby. Elisa sighed and walked down the road.

A shadow separated itself from the bushes and followed her.

Chapter 18. A Scream in the Night

Sitting beside Kyle, Julia warmed up her hands on the fire. As he looked at the flames, fire gleamed on his tanned face.

"You were here with Elisa too, I guess," Julia said.

"That was different."

"She is so confident. I wish I could be like her."

Kyle stretched out his hand and pushed a piece of hair away from her face. His eyes looked at her with warmth, and Julia's heart pounded somewhere in her belly. "Please don't," he said. "You're much better."

Julia opened her mouth, but no words came out. He was so close, and when he looked at her, she melted under his sight. The bushes rustled behind them in the night air, but when he was close, nothing seemed scary.

"All I want is to protect you," Kyle said.

"From what?"

He sighed. "From everything."

Julia smiled. It was weird to be here with him, but good at the same time. Maybe he'd lied to her, but this moment was beautiful. Maybe that's why people didn't tell ugly truths—to not ruin the beauty of romantic moments.

"I want to be honest with you," Kyle said.

Julia flinched. "What do you mean?"

He put his palms on his head. "I just . . . I've made so many mistakes, and I don't want to make another one."

"Everyone makes mistakes."

"You don't understand, Julia. The things I've done are terrible, and I don't know how to fix them."

She squeezed his hand. "If you realize that, it means you're not hopeless. You can always make better choices."

He gave her a sad smile. "I wish I could, but it's complicated."

Julia sighed. "Elisa told me what happened before you found Bella."

He looked perplexed. "I don't understand. Why did you go out with me, then?"

Julia lowered her eyes. "It's complicated."

A silence hung over them. The fire crackled and shot embers into the night.

"That day," Kyle said, "when you told me Bella went missing, all I wanted was to find her before the guardians. But Elisa was indifferent—even though she was the one who caused everything." Kyle's collar opened, exposing a healing wound on his neck.

Julia leaned closer to the fire, and the flames warmed her palms. "Did you want to punish Elisa?" she asked.

Kyle shook his head. "Maybe. I wanted to provoke her like she provoked Bella."

"And she hurt you."

Kyle rubbed his neck. "Is that all you can say?"

Julia shrugged. "What else should I say?"

"Something like, 'You were wrong.'"

"You know that already. Why should I say it?"

Kyle touched her shoulder. "This is what I like about you."

Julia stood up. "Anyway, you'll find a way to get back together."

"I never wanted to be with her."

Julia raised her eyebrows. "But you date her."

"Not anymore," Kyle lowered his voice. "Yes, I was with her, but what I really wanted was to be closer to you."

"To me? Why?"

Kyle arose and smiled. "Because I *really* like you, Julia." He moved closer and kissed her. His lips were soft and sweet, and she closed her eyes, melting in his gentle embrace.

They stood near the fire, holding hands and looking at each other.

"You're so beautiful," he said.

Julia's heart jumped, ready to burst from her chest. It was weird, but now the girls' plan seemed stupid. The sooner she told him about it, the better.

* * *

Elisa watched them from a tall bush. Kyle had used the same gestures and told her the same words when they'd sat here together a couple of weeks ago.

Elisa shook her head. "Oh, my dear naive Julia. He'll break your heart, sooner than you think."

Julia looked up and Kyle glanced at the bush where Elisa was hiding. She held her breath. It became quiet; only the crackle of the fire broke the silence.

"I should confess too, then," Julia said.

Kyle turned to her, and Elisa breathed out.

"I asked you out because we wanted to find out something about you." Julia's voice trembled.

Kyle narrowed his eyes. "What, exactly?"

"No fucking way," Elisa said. She stepped out.

Someone's hand pushed her back into the bush. Elisa opened her mouth to scream, but a small hand covered her lips. With wide eyes, she stared at the shadow with a big hood.

"Quiet," the shadow whispered.

Elisa nodded.

The shadow removed her hand from Elisa's face and took the hood off. It was Lana.

"What the heck?" Elisa said in the quietest voice she could. "Are you spying on me?"

"Just a little Searching spell." Lana touched her head and showed her a hairpin with three pink pearls.

It was Elisa's. Once, Lana had promised to protect her and her mother, and Elisa gave it to her just in case. Lana had failed, but she never returned it.

Elisa stretched out her hand. "Give it back."

Lana placed the jewelry in her palm. "Now, stay quiet. Seriously."

"You can't use my stuff to spy on me," Elisa whispered.

Lana put her index finger to her mouth, and Elisa stopped talking. By the old barn, two silhouettes hugged beside the fire. It was hard to see Julia; Kyle's back was in front of her.

"We think you work with the Gift Hunter," Julia said. "Is that true?"

The night became silent. Kyle glanced at the bushes and looked back at Julia.

"Yes, I do," he replied. "He made me join him, but I never wanted to. I'm so sorry."

Elisa covered her mouth and looked at Lana.

Lana took a small crystal from her pocket; it was glowing white. She moved the crystal to her mouth and whispered, *"Deactivate."* The crystal blinked and faded.

"Now we really have proof," Elisa said.

"Not really, but it's something I can use."

A desperate scream cut through the silence.

Elisa jumped from the bush and pushed Kyle away from Julia.

Julia looked at her with wide eyes. "Elisa? What are you doing here?"

Elisa hugged her. "Are you all right? Did he hurt you?"

"No," Julia said. "Why did you scream?"

"You screamed." Elisa raised her eyebrows. "Didn't you?"

Julia shook her head.

"I would never hurt her," Kyle said. He approached the girls and put his palm on Julia's shoulder.

Silence hung in the air, and Lana looked around. One of the girls was missing.

"Where is Rose?" Lana asked.

The girls exchanged glances.

Elisa pointed to Kyle. "Ask his father. I left Rose with him."

Kyle crossed his arms. "That's not true. He left town and won't be back until tomorrow."

"Liar!" Elisa exclaimed.

"Are you sure, Elisa?" Lana asked. "Did you see his face?"

Elisa slowly shook her head.

Lana looked up. The black sky hung over them like an abyss, and only the crackling of the fire broke the silence.

"Oh, no," Julia whispered in realization. "Something happened to Rose."

"It didn't," Kyle said. "We'll find her."

Lana looked around. The scream had come from somewhere nearby, and there was no time to waste. "I'm sending a Light signal to the guardians," she said. "Everyone, go home. Now!"

Elisa gave her a sharp look. "No way."

"You are all in danger!" Lana gasped. "Don't you understand?"

All three of them stood before her, the girls holding hands. Their eyes were stubborn, and for a moment, she put herself in her father's shoes, when she'd refused to obey him.

Lana sighed and made a yellow Light ball in her hands. When she raised her eyes, their Lights glowed in their hands as well— Elisa's—silver with yellow sparkles, Julia's—mint green, and Kyle's—shimmering blue. Lana nodded, and they raised their hands. Their Lights shot into the night sky and burst into multicolored pieces.

* * *

Twenty minutes later, Lana stood by Kyle's bedroom window. Two guardians had arrived first, and they were checking the frame and the ground in the backyard with their Lights. She had already checked the area and had found nothing, but maybe they could find a trace.

Kyle approached her. "It's just like last time. All the energy traces have been removed—both inside and outside."

"I don't understand," Lana said. "Why the heck would he come to the house of a guardian captain?"

Kyle shrugged. "He's become bolder."

Lana clenched her fists. "We have to find this bastard."

"Agreed."

The sound of hooves made Lana turn around. Her father arrived on his raven-colored horse. He jumped down and walked toward Lana. He furrowed his eyebrows, and her body shrank under his heavy look. The steps of his heavy boots resonated with her beating heart.

"Chief—" Lana whispered.

"Which part of *you are suspended* was unclear?" he roared.

Lana glanced at Kyle. He looked at the guardian chief with fear.

"I . . . I was just walking around," Lana said.

He fixed his gaze on her. "In the middle of the night in your work clothes?"

Lana lowered her eyes. "Sorry—"

"You think this is a game? Who told you to bring these teenagers?"

Kyle stepped forward. "Mr. Morris—Chief. Lana was here to talk to Elisa. We all were together and came when we heard the scream."

Her father looked at Lana. The vein on his forehead pulsed. "Is this true?"

Lana nodded. "I told them to go home, but they wouldn't listen."

"No one listens here!"

Kyle stepped forward and stood between Lana and her father. "Chief Morris, please. We need to find the murderer and Rose before it's too late. I'll help Lana and follow the girls home."

"No, you'll come with me to the Guardian House and give me your testimony." The chief shifted his gaze to Lana. "I hope you have enough common sense not to follow us. Stay here and keep your eyes on them until Kyle gets back."

She nodded.

* * *

Lana found the two girls into the empty house. They sat at the fire-place, holding hands and staring at the flames, the light revealing their scared faces.

Lana walked into the room and sat on a carpet near them.

"Will you find her?" Elisa asked.

"I'll do my best."

The fire lit up the living room, but it couldn't protect these girls from the monsters living in the darkness. Unfortunately, the most horrible monsters were humans. The guardians didn't bother warning schoolgirls, because they didn't care about prospective victims. They just blindly followed their stupid rules. For once, she was glad she wasn't a guardian.

Lana touched their hands and lowered her voice. "There's a killer in town. You should be careful from now on."

"A killer?" Julia widened her eyes.

"You think he took Rose?" Elisa asked.

Lana sighed. "I don't know for sure, but this person might be connected to the Gift Hunter."

"We don't even have our Gifts yet," Julia said.

"I know, but you three witnessed how Bella released her power. You could be in danger."

The girls exchanged glances.

Lana squeezed their hands. "Listen, I'll do my best to protect you. Don't get into any sort of trouble. Understand?"

Julia nodded.

Elisa sighed. "Lana, you might not remember, but before you left Triville, four years ago, you told me that no one will protect us but ourselves."

Lana's hear sank. "I remember."

"I'll use your advice." Elisa touched her golden locks and removed her hairpin. "I don't know what will happen next, so keep it. Just in case."

Lana took the piece of jewelry. The metal gleamed in the firelight.

"Now, tell us what the heck happened in Mercy House," Elisa said.

Lana glanced at the window. All the guardians had left, and the yard was empty. The moon lit up the windowsill. Outside, large bushes rustled under the quiet wind, and their crooked branches scratched at the windowpane. She looked at Elisa and Julia and started talking. These girls deserved to know about Rebecca's death, so they didn't end up dying too.

Chapter 19. Faster than the Future

A black stallion galloped through a narrow forest trail. Richard squeezed the stallion's sides with his boots. Fast morning rides helped him wake up and organize his thoughts. His stallion loved it too; the rides always invigorated him.

"Come on, Coal!" Richard shouted.

The stallion reached the hill where the trees parted. Richard stopped at the top. The morning in Triville below was calm, and the streets were empty. Gentle pink clouds hugged the town, not ready to release it from dreaming.

"Here we are!" Richard breathed.

He shook the reins, and the stallion trotted down the hill.

* * *

Finding the Guardian House wasn't a hard task—they were always in town centers. Richard stopped in the big green yard. The three-story building loomed over him. It had black stone walls and a golden dragon sitting on its yellow roof. This Guardian House was old—from the time people put up buildings that lasted for centuries.

A young guardian with red hair stood at the entrance and glanced at Richard with curiosity. "Can I help you?"

Richard took the roll of paper from his inner pocket and held it out to the young man. Richard glanced around as the guardian read it. Something was wrong—the yard was empty: no horses, no other guardians.

The guardian finished reading. "Mr. Laine—"

"Lieutenant Laine," Richard corrected him. "I need to speak with Chief Morris. Urgently."

"Sorry, Lieutenant," the young man said with trembling voice. "Another girl went missing last night. The search party left—"

Richard grabbed the young guardian's skinny shoulder. "Damn! Tell me where they went."

* * *

Fallen trees lay on the trail, and Richard had to weave through the bushes with caution. The west side of Triville forest was different. Puffy moss covered the thick tree trunks, and the trail between the hills curved up and down. The young guardian had given him directions, and he followed the path.

Richard stopped near the creek and disembarked from the saddle. Shade covered the stony banks, and the morning air was chilly. Richard took his cloak off and rubbed his palms.

The sound of falling rocks made him look up at the edge of the ravine. A horseman in a black cloak looked at him from above. A wide hood covered the upper part of his face. His chestnut mare had a white stripe on her snout.

Richard waved his hand. "Hey!"

The rider's lips widened in a smile, then he turned around. Horseshoes clattered as the horse galloped into the trees.

"Wait!" Richard shouted, but the horseman didn't stop.

Richard saddled up, and Coal galloped up the hill.

In the forest, they slowed and moved through the trees. A loud bang sounded above his head and Richard looked up. Shards of yellow Light slowly dissipated in the blue sky.

It was close. They trotted to a small glade nearby.

The horseman ran toward him. A silver Paralyzing spell shone in his hand.

Richard widened his eyes. "What the—"

The spell flew at him like an arrow. It was too late to jump from his saddle. He tried to dodge, but the spell hit his shoulder. Richard lost his balance and fell backward.

He landed on the grass, and a branch cracked under his back. Breathless, he tried to move. His left hand refused to obey, but his right one still worked. Using one hand, he sat up. The horseman walked toward him, and his hood fell off.

Her hood. Shining flaxen hair fell to her shoulders. The woman was beautiful. Her cheeks were flushed, and her big brown eyes sparkled.

Richard opened his mouth, but he couldn't move his tongue. *What is a woman doing here?* She wore black guardian clothes, but she was obviously not one of them.

She stepped closer. "You! I saw you at the funeral yesterday."

Richard widened his eyes in recollection. "And?" he asked in a hoarse voice.

"And . . . I've caught you, Ghost!"

Richard raised his free hand and made a Paralyzing spell. She stepped back.

"Guardians will be here soon!" she said, her trembling hands casting a new spell. Her fingers moved too fast; she was unskilled.

Richard grinned. "Sorry to interrupt, but your spell casting is shitty. You have horrible form."

She gave him a scornful look. Richard stood up and came closer. She frowned and raised her hand, ready to shoot him again.

They stood in front of each other in silence. Richard could shoot her right away, but it would be better to find out who this woman was and why she used a Light signal. Maybe she was a witch, maybe just an adventurist. But she definitely was an amateur, which meant she couldn't really hurt him.

The woman narrowed her eyes. "Who the heck are you?"

"No, who the heck are *you*?"

The clatter of hooves reached Richard's ears as someone approached from behind.

"Drop the spells! Put your hands up!" the voice roared.

Richard let the spell slide from his palm. The silver ball fell on the ground, and frost covered the blades of grass under his feet. He put up his hands and turned around.

Guardians surrounded the glade. He counted six people. Five of them sat on their horses, holding Paralyzing spells in their hands. The oldest guardian got off his saddle and walked toward Richard. He was in his fifties with gray hair and a mustache, and his brown eyes shone with anger.

"You must be Chief Morris," Richard said.

The man stopped and frowned. "Suppose I am. Who are you?"

Richard slowly took the roll of paper out of his pocket. "Lieutenant Richard Laine. I came to help with Ghost's case."

The chief took the roll and started reading.

The woman fixed her gaze on Richard.

"I should apologize," Richard said to her. "I came here yesterday to make my observations. Yes, I was at the funeral, but I didn't want to interfere with the investigation too soon. This morning, I came to the Guardian House to meet the team, but then I heard about the other victim."

"Yes, one more girl went missing last night," Chief Morris said. He glanced at the other guardians and waved his hand. They clapped their hands, and their Paralyzing spells disappeared. The woman still held her spell, but when the chief gave her a sharp look, she dropped the silver ball on the grass.

"I'm here now," Richard said. "I'll help you find Ghost."

The chief looked at the woman. "Okay, we're clear. What about you, Lana?"

Lana lowered her eyes in embarrassment, wishing the ground would swallow her up.

But something was wrong. She remembered the look he'd had yesterday and his cold green eyes. She could swear it had been the eyes of a murderer. Maybe it was just a figment of her imagination?

Anyway, whoever he was, he was hiding something. She could recognize liars right away. Maybe she could try to find out where he was last night.

Lana approached Richard and softened her voice. "I must apologize. Strangers attract attention in small towns."

He nodded. "No worries."

"You must be spending last night at Triville Motel."

"Actually, I was in the forest. I like the fresh air."

She stretched out her hand. "I'm Lana."

Richard took her hand and shook it.

His palm was warm and rough. Lana closed her eyes. She saw a fire and Richard eating a fish with an unfamiliar boy in a muddy shirt. He was in the forest—definitely nearby.

"Careful," Charles said behind them. "She's a mind reader."

Richard took his hand away—too quickly. He hesitated for a second, then he returned to his normal condition.

Definitely a liar, Lana concluded. Maybe he was truthful about yesterday, but there had to be something terrible in the depths of his mind.

Her father frowned. "Lana, please."

She looked at her father and lowered her voice. "He shouldn't be here."

"You shouldn't either." Her father narrowed his eyes. "I see you've got yourself a nice horse."

Lana's heart sank. Her father had spent last night in the Guardian House, and he hadn't seen Mandy until now. Lana had completely forgotten that she'd promised him to stay at home—preferably, reading something. Not buying a horse and riding through the forest in a desperate attempt to catch Ghost.

Lana sighed. "Well, since we've figured everything out, I assume I'm not in danger anymore. I'll go home."

Her father put his hand on her shoulder. "You aren't going anywhere."

She widened her eyes. "Why?"

"The real Ghost might be nearby. You'll be safe only with us."

Lana nodded. Guardians chuckled around her, but she didn't care. She was on the case now, and this time, it was quite legal. Maybe she could find something.

Richard stood nearby and looked around like a bloodhound, ready to start searching. "So, where is the search area?"

The chief touched his mustache. "The glades. Ghost placed the last bodies there. I'm guessing he does it to deliver some kind of message."

Richard nodded. "You should also know something. But what I know isn't documented."

"I'm listening."

Richard moved his gaze across the guardians. "Ghost has a Gift of time."

Chief Morris gave him a puzzled look. "Which time Gift?"

"Ghost is an oracle. Yes, it's a very powerful and rare Gift; he can see the future. That's why it was removed from the files—to not stir up panic. But I've been working on this case for a while and I know one trick." Richard took a time crystal from his pocket. The crystal glowed pink. "When someone uses, or is about to use his Gift of time, our time crystals shine white."

Charles raised his eyebrows. "Seriously? How would it help to catch a man who can see the future?"

"The future is uncertain," Lana said.

Richard put his time crystal away. "That's right. The future has several scenarios. He sees the one with the highest probability. We should make the right choices from now on."

The chief nodded. "Then I choose to catch this bastard, and the sooner, the better. Let's go find him!"

The guardians roared, and their horses trotted into the depths of the forest. Lana mounted her saddle and followed them. *An Oracle Gift, then.* She'd heard of it. Oracles were born once every twenty-five years, and this one used his rare and powerful Gift to commit murders. Lana sighed. It was one more mystery, making this case even more confusing, but she had no time to despair.

Chapter 20. GT

The forest trail widened. Richard stopped at the fork of the road, followed by two guardians and Lana. The guardians exchanged glances and took the left side, so he guided his horse to the right. The quiet sound of horse hooves sounded behind him; Lana had followed him.

She turned her face to the roadside, pretending she was interested in the blossoming bushes around them. Richard took a heavy breath. She was definitely waiting for another chance to read him.

He knew about mind readers. They dug deep into people's minds to discover their dirty secrets, and they never cared how their victims felt. Richard had his own methods to get rid of these unwelcome invasions. Lana was young enough to rely on her Gift as absolute, but little did she know how easy it was to turn her own power against her.

Richard slowed his horse down, and Lana walked to his side with a sly look.

Richard grinned. "Not afraid of me anymore?"

"Should I be?"

"Who knows?"

Lana chuckled. "Are you afraid of my Gift?"

"Not really."

Her face became intrigued. "All of us have little secrets, don't we?"

He shifted his gaze to the road. "Some secrets are better left untold."

Lana looked up, thinking. Then she turned her face toward him. "You said you've been investigating Ghost's case for several years."

"Yes."

"Why does he kill only girls with destructive Gifts?"

Richard sighed. "Who knows? Psychopaths have something on their minds—an idea that captivates them. It's hard for us to understand."

Lana paused, then she gave him a sharp look. "Then answer this. How do *you* know about his victims' Gifts?"

Richard bit his tongue. He'd gotten caught on her first question and had told her too much. He paused, finding the proper words, so he wouldn't jeopardize himself further. "In the file—"

"There's no such information in the file. All it says is that *some* of the victims had destructive Gifts. That's it. But the question is—how do *you* know?"

"Guess," he said in a flat tone.

Lana shrugged. "Well, you seem to know him better than anyone."

Richard frowned. *Close. Too close.* "Yes, I do know him. Too much power and too little patience—that's how your Gift can let you down."

Lana moved closer to him. "It's never let me down."

It was time to finish this interrogation and get rid of her. The memory of his night with Camilla rose before him: her silky red hair, curves, and the gentle touches that made the fire inside him blaze. The sweat on their naked bodies made the picture complete.

Richard stretched out and touched her arm.

Lana closed her eyes for a second, then she pulled his hand off and snorted. "Gross!"

He laughed. "You see? Too little patience!"

Lana galloped to the open glade.

Richard smiled. *Well done.* That would stop her from reading him. At least, until he found a better way.

* * *

In the glade, Richard dismounted Coal and walked to the middle of the clearing. Lana was already there.

She turned to him. "There's nothing."

He narrowed his eyes. "Don't you want to look around?"

She shook her head. "He always leaves bodies in the middle of the glades. I read it in his file."

Richard scratched his chin. She paid too much attention to details—even more so than a regular guardian. It was annoying. Somehow, she'd read a top secret file. She was just a chief's daughter, playing a game she didn't understand.

That's why women shouldn't be allowed to do this job. Emotional creatures.

Lana shrugged. "Well, there are many glades to look through—"

"Does your father know that you read a top secret case file?"

Lana scoffed. "Why do you care?"

Richard grinned. "I bet he won't be happy when he figures it out."

Lana narrowed her eyes. "Some secrets are better left untold."

"Exactly. But I know yours now. You still don't know mine."

"I will."

"Will you? Emotions are blinding you, Lana. What would you do if you couldn't rely on your Gift anymore?"

Her breathing became heavy, and her eyes burned with anger. "Go ahead and snitch like a little girl." Lana crossed her arms and glared at him.

Richard was speechless.

A sudden bang interrupted them. A coral Light exploded in the sky over their heads. It was nearby.

"Rose," Lana said. "They found her!"

* * *

When Lana reached the glade, the guardians stood at the edge with somber faces. She walked to the place where Rose lay.

The body on the grass looked dreadful. Lana had to cover her mouth before she could take a closer look. The girl lay on her back, frozen terror still in her wide eyes. A thin line of dried blood crossed her neck. Her clothes were torn, and bloody rags covered her pale skin.

"What animal did this to her?" one of the guardians asked.

Lana shook her head. "The worst animals are human."

"Let me take a look," Richard said from behind her.

The guardians parted, and Richard leaned over the girl's body. He formed a blue Light ball with silver sparkles in his hand and moved it around her head. Richard frowned and removed the rags from the victim's belly, revealing a pale strip of skin and a big stab wound under her chest.

"Look, she was raped," someone whispered.

Richard rose, and the guardians looked at him in silence.

Lana took a breath and pointed to the body. "Check her arm. There's something there!"

Richard hesitated, then he knelt and touched Rose's cold lifeless hand. There were curves of blood on the bottom of her arm. He moved her hand and read two red letters written in blood: *GT.*

"Ghost!" one of the guardians said.

Richard looked at the victim's other hand—there was dry blood on her index finger.

Had she tried to leave a clue? She could not have known about Ghost. The guardians stood in silence; their eyes perplexed. Lana shook her head and walked away.

* * *

When Chief Morris arrived, Lana stood under a tree at the opposite edge of the glade. The chief's forehead wrinkled as he spoke with Richard. This Santos guy was arrogant, but for some reason, her father trusted him. It would be wise to figure out who he was. Not now, of course. When professionals were doing their job, it was best not to interrupt them.

Two guardians covered the body with a long black cloak and carried it away. Lana put her palm on her chest. Like a heavy stone, the new death pressed in on her, not letting her breathe. It was hard to believe she'd just spoken to the girl.

The glade emptied, and bent grass was the only thing that remained of the terrible crime scene. Lana sat on her knees and touched the grass. The murderer had made one mistake, putting the letters on her wrist. Rose didn't know about Ghost. And whoever this murderer was, Richard knew him. The answer lay in his mind, waiting for the day it would be revealed. That day would come whether he wanted it to or not.

Chapter 21. The Fight

Dozens of Light balls soared into the cloudless blue sky. Elisa raised her hands, a silver energy ball with golden sparkles glowing in her palms. The last memory of Rose flashed before her eyes: the night when they read the diary together. Rose was trying to rush her. Rose had a beautiful Light, too—a pink one with red sparkles.

"If I only listened to you, Rose," she whispered. "If we had left just a bit earlier."

Elisa waved her hands. Her Light lifted from her fingertips and floated up to the sky, following the other shining spheres. She looked around. Julia stood next to her and looked up, tears rolling down her cheeks, but she didn't try to wipe them away. Kyle stood at the opposite side of the crowd, looking at the grave where Rose's family had planted tulip bulbs. Kyle noticed her gaze and looked straight at Elisa. He clenched his fists.

Elisa took Julia's cold palm. Julia's face was indifferent; she was deep in thought.

"Let's go," Elisa said.

Julia nodded.

The crowd moved toward the exit. Gray dresses, cloaks, and jackets moved around them, and Elisa followed the flow. At the gates, Elisa looked back. Kyle stood at the grave alone, looking at them.

* * *

Repast started in the afternoon at Rose's house. Elisa sat on the soft green sofa with Julia by her side. Women moved around chaotically from one room to another and talked in quiet voices. In their gray clothes, the guests looked like storm clouds that someone had put into one house as to not ruin the beautiful day outside. Out the window, the May sun shone bright in the blue sky, and sunbeams flooded a beautiful garden's small fountain. Three sparrows sat around the water and twittered. Elisa sighed. Only three days ago, they had talked under the blossoming cherry tree in Bella's garden. Those moments would never happen again, and Elisa felt this realization as suddenly as a thunderstorm.

Back in the dull room, the air was heavy—exactly like the day her mother passed away. The same murky gray clothes surrounded her, and the same fake, sad faces sniffed around, satisfying their curiosity. Nothing had changed.

Rose's mother stood near the window with Mrs. Sullivan, talking.

Elisa patted Julia's shoulder. "I'll be back soon."

Julia shifted her blurred gaze and kept silent.

Elisa approached the women. Mrs. Sullivan's round face blushed. The teacher took her glasses off and started wiping them.

Elisa looked at Rose's mother. "I'm so sorry for your loss, Mrs. Blake."

"It's a loss for all of us," Mrs. Blake replied. She had a pale, thin face and dull black eyes with long eyelashes. The pure light that used to fill her eyes was sunken somewhere in the darkness. It would take a long time for her to overcome the darkness, but one day, she would. She just needed someone who could remind her of the light.

"Rose was my best friend, and I will never forget her," Elisa said.

Mrs. Blake nodded. The shadow of a smile appeared on her lips.

Elisa touched her palm. "Once, I lost my mother, and it was . . . the worst thing that ever happened to me. But her love is still with me. I keep her in my heart and in my memories."

Rose's mother gave her a warm look. "Please, feel free to visit me anytime you want. You and Julia."

"We will," Elisa said.

Mrs. Sullivan put her glasses back on her nose and frowned. "Everyone is talking about that night when Rose went miss—"

Elisa gave her a sharp look. "People talk too much."

"But you were together, weren't you?" the teacher insisted. Her big yellow eyes sparkled as she looked at Mrs. Blake. "Those girls *always* disobey the rules. I wouldn't be surprised if they went off somewhere in the middle of the night and got into trouble."

"Mrs. Sullivan . . ." Elisa said. *Shut up,* she thought.

The teacher gave her indifferent look and turned back to Mrs. Blake. "Like I told you, they got in trouble, and now they don't know how to deal with it. This is how the killer found poor Rose."

Mrs. Blake narrowed her eyes and looked at Elisa.

Elisa shook her head. "Mrs. Sullivan, this isn't the proper place to discuss your concerns. We all knew Rose, and we—"

Mrs. Sullivan swung her arm, her long sleeve drawing a curve in the air. "What should we do with them? How do we save them?"

Elisa clenched her teeth. No one really cared about the mourners. They only cared about themselves. To them, Rose didn't matter. If a girl went missing at night, the first thing that everyone wanted to say was that it was her own fault. It was easier to put the blame on the victim and close the cycle. It was disgusting.

Mrs. Blake faced the window. She was broken. Her daughter had died, and she needed more time to grieve, but the teacher kept moaning and blaming schoolgirls.

Elisa touched Mrs. Blake's shoulder. "I'll be nearby."

When Elisa came back, Julia still sat on the sofa, staring at the bouquet of yellow tulips on the coffee table. Julia rubbed a cup in her hands for warmth, not noticing that the tea had become cold a long time ago. Elisa took the cup from Julia's hands. Her friend blinked as if arousing from a dream.

"Let's go home," Elisa said.

Julia nodded.

* * *

Outside, the hot afternoon sun warmed their faces. They walked along the dusty road, holding hands. A silence hung over them.

Elisa sighed. Rose had known her secret, and she'd taken it to her grave. Maybe it would be easier to tell Julia, but today was the worst day to talk about her feelings.

Julia walked nearby in silence. Her face was pale, and she had dark circles under her eyes. At least it wasn't the worst day to try to reassure her about Kyle.

"There's only two of us left now," Elisa said.

Julia blinked. "I know."

"And no one's here to protect us from the murderer."

Julia stopped and gave her a tired look. "Elisa, please—"

"There's only you and me. Now we know the truth about Ghost and the Gift Hunter, and Lana said that all the murders might be connected. We should steal Kyle's diary and bring the evidence to the Guardian House."

Julia sighed. "That's not a good idea."

"But it's the only way!"

Julia shook her head. "I'm just so tired . . . of everything."

Elisa's gaze pierced her friend. She was like a shark about to attack.

"Please, don't make this worse," Julia moaned.

"Do you think it will suddenly be over?" Elisa asked, raising her voice. "Or are you waiting until one of us dies?"

Julia's eyes flashed. "Why are you shouting at me? You were the one who caused everything!"

"Oh, my dear naive Julia! I know exactly what Kyle told you about me. Now, you're just repeating his words."

"You asked me to date him."

"But I didn't ask you to kiss him." Elisa grinned. "Yes, I *watched* you. You should be more careful when you kiss your friend's boyfriend."

Julia blushed. Her lips trembled, but no words escaped her lips.

Elisa came closer. "He lied to you," she whispered.

"Stop it!"

"I warned you about him. He's not the right person for you."

Julia stepped back. Her dress snagged on a bush, but Julia didn't even notice. "You're crossing a line. You told me that Kyle was a liar, but he was the only one that was honest with me."

Elisa raised her eyebrows. "Really?"

"Yes! Maybe you should find someone else to protect. I'm tired of searching for the dangerous killer who might kill the rest of us."

"And how are you gonna protect yourself?"

Julia clenched her fists and closed her eyes. A wave of anger in her chest rose like a volcano ready to explode. She moved the energy into her hands, and it leaked into her palms. When Julia opened her eyes, a fireball shone in her hand.

Elisa cast a fireball spell as well. She played with it, twisting and moving the flame from one palm to another one. "You're not the only girl who was at that barn." Elisa's voice was as strong as steel. "And you're going to be the next one he's going to try to rape."

"Shut up!"

Julia pushed her hand forward. The fireball flew toward Elisa and left sparkles in the air. Elisa dodged it, missing her shoulder by a hair.

"Never!" Elisa shouted. She threw the spell toward the bush behind Julia, and its dry branches caught flame.

Julia managed to jump away from the bush, but the hem of her dress was stuck between two branches and torc. She lost her balance and fell onto the dirty ground.

She lifted her upper body and looked up. Elisa stood in front of the blazing bush in her long charcoal dress and with a demonic expression on her face. Her golden hair shone in the sun, the fire reflecting in her wide eyes.

"You're out of your mind! Why did I ever think you were my friend?"

"This," Elisa said, pointing to the flames, "is nothing compared to the pain that Kyle will put you in!"

"He wouldn't!" Julia gasped. "And you . . . you . . ."

Elisa sighed. "I'm a better friend than you think. I just want to protect you!"

Julia stood up. Her dress, chin, and hands were covered in dust.

"But who will protect me from *you*?" Julia asked. Then she turned away and walked along the road.

Elisa stood alone on the empty road. Her heart burned, and it was hard to breathe. More than anything, she wanted to run and stop her friend—to hug her and give her every apology she could come up with just to take away the disappointment in her lovely hazel eyes. Elisa sighed. She'd gone too far, and now it was better to leave Julia alone.

Meanwhile, she could solve the problem with Kyle.

Elisa turned and walked in the opposite direction.

Chapter 22. Under a Curtain of Lies

Lana stood at the door of the chief's office. Inside the room, two voices of the guardians danced together. They started with a quiet waltz and moved to an intense samba. Her father's voice shouted, and her heart skipped a beat. Her father never allowed himself to shout. Lana could remember it happening only twice. Once when her mother left him, and the second . . . well, it was right now.

Heavy steps walked toward the door, and Lana stepped back. It was right in time, because Captain Turner walked out of the room. His thin face was red, and his pale blue eyes gave Lana a sharp look.

"Captain." Lana's voice trembled.

He nodded and walked away.

Lana stepped over the threshold.

Thick clouds of blue smoke hung in the room. Her father sat on his chair and looked outside the closed window. He held a cigar in his hand, which was weird to see because he'd quit smoking many years ago. The smell of tobacco filled her lungs, and Lana coughed.

Her father put out his cigar and waved his hands to clear the air. Lana approached the window and opened it, letting the fresh, cool morning wind touch her face. Lana turned back around. Her father's face was pale, and the wrinkles around his eyes were deeper than usual.

"Oh, Father, you really should go home and sleep."

He shook his head. "I wish I could."

She sat on the wide chair in front of him. "What's going on? You called for me."

"Yes, I did. Can you guess why?" His tired eyes pierced her.

Lana bit her tongue. The tongue was a person's worst enemy. Why had she asked Richard about Ghost's case? This guy had definitely told him everything. Trust was so hard to build and so easy to ruin.

Lana licked her dry lips. "Father, I'm so sorry. I read the secret file."

He crossed his arms, waiting for an explanation. At least he didn't fire her right away—that was a good sign.

She lowered her eyes. "I . . . I received it on the day you suspended me. I was scared for my life and wanted to know who I was dealing with."

He coughed into his fist.

"I know I shouldn't have," she said. "I know I lost my faculties. But I promise—I won't do it again."

"Again? You already know everything about this case, don't you?"

Lana sighed. "This guy from Santos knows more. He knows much more than he's telling us."

"Why do you think so?"

"It was him, right? He told you I read the case file!"

Her father chuckled. "Oh, my little Lana, you're so impulsive. Do you want to know how I figured it out?"

Her heart burned, beating fast. She narrowed her eyes. "How?"

He took the red folder from the pile on his desk and put it in front of her. His face was stern. Lana touched a smooth red cover and opened it. She blinked. A hair, long and flaxen, lay on the white page. It could only belong to . . . her. Lana took it with her fingertips and dropped it.

The hair landed on the floor, silently resting on the varnished wooden waves of the planks. Lana wished her heart would stop beating. She didn't want to meet his judging gaze again.

He sighed. "Lana, I was once your age. You might think you know everything, but it's just an illusion. I've made mistakes too. If only I had doubted myself earlier, I might have prevented this murder."

Lana raised her eyes. "Do you trust this Santos guy?"

Her father nodded. "Not only trust—I've verified him. The night Bella was murdered, he was . . . let's say he was dealing with other circumstances in Santos."

"I checked him too. Did he mention that Ghost chooses his victims by their destructive Gifts?"

"Is that just your theory, or do you have proof?"

"I don't have proof, but you can ask Richard and see what he says."

He touched his mustache, thinking. "If I only knew how to convince you to stay away from this case."

"I won't interfere anymore. Honestly."

He sighed. "And why don't I believe you?"

The door opened, and Richard walked into the room. He held a pile of white folders in his hands. He glanced at Lana, frowned, and then looked at the chief.

"Good morning, Chief Morris," Richard said.

"It's morning, but it's not good."

Richard glanced at Lana again. "I'll come back another time."

Her father pointed to the second chair in front of his desk. "Please, have a seat."

Lana started getting up, and her father gave her a sharp look. "And you stay here!"

Lana sat back down. Richard grinned.

Her father pressed his palms together. "So, Lieutenant Laine, how is the investigation going?"

Richard put the folders on the desk, and Lana craned her neck to take a closer look. There was a personnel file of a new guardian on the top, which meant they had investigated him and the other people on the team.

Lana bit her lip. It was unbelievable, but her father had decided to find the murderer . . . by investigating his own team as suspects.

Guardians, victims, Gift Hunters, Ghost, they were all woven in a tightly knitted ball. What if all these murders in Triville were *not* connected with Ghost's case?

Then she was wrong. Lana rubbed her temples. Rose hadn't been found in the middle of a glade; the *real* Ghost would never have made such a clumsy slip. Whoever this murderer was, he had faked the criminal's pattern to hide his crime. It also explained the *GT* on the victim's wrist—it was fake.

Lana looked at her father. "Is one of our guardians an imposter?"
He nodded.

Her head spun. The killer might be someone that she knew, a person she spoke to every day. The solution might be right before her eyes.

Seeing is believing. Lana just saw what she wanted to see. She'd been so blinded by her own investigation; she'd mixed everything up.

Richard took the folder from the top. "As we discussed, the murderer could be one of our local guardians. Captain Turner and I have started investigating them, and now he's assembling everyone for questioning."

Her father touched a red folder. "It could also be Ghost."

Richard nodded. "I won't exclude that possibility. You know what? Let Turner deal with the team, and I'll check the second version personally."

Lana frowned. Only a rookie guardian could have missed such a mismatch in the evidence, but Richard had worked on this case for several years, and he knew it inside and out. Richard was hiding something, and his presence only made everything more confusing. If only she knew of a way to get rid of him.

"Where would you start?" her father asked.

Richard scratched his chin. "Well, Ghost is a maniac, but he's still a human being. He needs to eat and hide somewhere at night.

He came too close to being discovered when Rose went missing, so it would be too dangerous for him to hide in town. I'm guessing he found shelter somewhere in the forest—maybe in a forest man's hut."

Lana's eyes sparkled. "What about a witch's house? I know where one is."

Her father gave her a sharp look. "A witch is illegally residing nearby, and all this time you've known about it? Why didn't you tell me?"

"No one ever asked me," she replied in the most innocent tone she could muster.

He glared at her.

"Technically, she's not in Triville's jurisdiction. There was nothing to report," she added.

Richard stared at her. "You don't know what witches are capable of. They are always in search of lucrative deals. I wouldn't be surprised if she hid the murderer in her house for a piece of silver."

"Then you should go investigate," Lana said.

Her father rubbed his forehead and looked through the open window. Long white curtains rustled in the light wind.

Lana touched the desk's surface with her fingertips. "Chief, I'm not insisting, but I could check the guardians with my Gift."

Richard chuckled. "I wouldn't rely on a mind reader's Gift. They're too easy to fool."

Lana scoffed. "It's never let me down. Not until you came here."

"There's a first time for everything, right?"

Lana clenched her fists. Her nails dug into her palms, but it felt better than speaking to him.

Her father clapped his hands, and they stopped arguing.

"He's right, Lana," her father said. "People can give you false memories or provoke you, especially if they know that you're going to read them."

Richard nodded. His green eyes laughed at her.

Lana took a deep breath and gripped the chair handles. "Okay, so we've clarified that I'm useless. I assume I can go now."

Her father raised his voice. "You aren't going anywhere, young lady!"

He shifted his gaze from her to Richard, then he leaned back in his chair. "You're going to the witch's house together."

Richard and Lana exchanged glances.

"No way!" Lana exclaimed.

"I never thought I would say this, but I agree with her," Richard said.

"It's not a request," her father said, folding his fingers. "Lana, you know where the witch house is; show it to our dear colleague Lieutenant Laine. Also, every guardian here knows you can read their minds—they may be less cautious if you're out of town."

Lana scowled. "So, you just want to get rid of me?"

He continued, "I tried to suspend you, but you don't seem to care. The last thing I need is my daughter chasing a murder by herself."

Lana nodded. "You want me to chase Ghost instead."

"At least, if you meet Ghost in the forest, Richard will be the best guardian to protect you."

Richard raised his hand. "Chief Morris, with all due respect, I am a guardian. Not a babysitter."

"*I* am the chief of Triville Guardian House. You *will* obey my orders!" He dropped his to the desk with a crash. The pile of white folders tumbled to the ground. "Understood?"

They nodded.

"Good. Lana, go to the filing room and prepare. I need Richard here to discuss some other details. He will find you when we're finished. Then, you will discuss a good working plan together. Any questions?"

Lana arose. "No," she said, choking on her anger.

Richard looked at her like a snake ready to jump and start strangling her. "See you later," he grinned.

Lana nodded and walked out of the room, slamming the door behind her.

Chapter 23. Two Steps Back

Lana ran into her office, breathless. Piles of books, folders, and old journals still lay on her small desk. She pushed a pile to the floor with a crash. Who cared about the noise? Her tiny room was in the freaking basement where no one ever walked by.

"Damn Richard!" she shouted. She touched her hot cheeks with her palms and fell to her knees. She lay down, her back touching the cold floor and shivering.

This Santos guy was unbearable. He knew what made her angry, and he was taking advantage of it to hide his stupid secret. And the worst thing was he didn't even realize that he'd managed to ruin everything she'd tried so hard to build. The answer to Rebecca's murder, already a thin thread, was slipping away.

"Think, Lana. Just think." She slowed her breathing after she heard her own voice. Anger clouded her mind. As a mind reader, she knew a lot about people and their emotions. If only she knew how to control her own.

This was exactly what he wanted—Richard had managed to turn everything upside down, and this time, he'd done it in front of her father. Her hands were tied. Her father didn't want her around anymore, and it was all because of him.

Lana sat up and looked around—books and white sheets covered the floor. Richard would be here soon. The best she could do right now was to clean this mess, because if she didn't, it would only show him that his provocation was working.

She was putting the books and notes back when her fingers touched a postcard. It was a picture from Esplendor, the evergreen kingdom. Inside a gorgeous palace decorated with marble floors and tall pillars, couples danced around a ball hall.

Lana pressed the card to her chest; her warm memories of this place soothed her beating heart. She'd bought it in a gift shop, during her long journey to the west coast. Once she got to Esplendor, she fell in love with the ball dances.

She blinked. Her dance teacher had said dancing was like relationships—couples took two steps back and one step forward.

Lana put the postcard back in the folder and rubbed her temples. She had only one option—to journey to the witch's house as soon as possible and return to Triville to continue her investigation. Then, she had to find a way to work with him. The best way to understand a person was to think like them.

When she'd read Richard's mind, he'd taken his hand away so quickly. He played with her emotions like a cat with a ball of yarn, and it pissed her off.

But maybe *he'd* been pissed when she'd read him.

Lana sighed. Maybe she'd moved too fast. He hadn't attacked her—maybe he was trying to protect his personal space. She'd obviously crossed a line and needed to take a couple steps back—or pretend to until she found a better solution.

Lana cleaned up the rest of her documents, sat at her desk, and placed her notebook in front of her. What else did she know about him?

She bit her pencil. Richard had shared an intimate bedroom scene with her on purpose to push her away. But it also meant that he wasn't shy. Interesting, how many women frequented his bed? A lot, probably. Despite all his roughness and insolence, Richard was a handsome young man with beautiful green eyes and wide shoulders.

The pencil cracked in her teeth and broke. Lana placed the two pieces in front of her and bit her lip. Her thoughts had definitely taken a wrong direction. She wouldn't be so stupid, not this time.

The worst thing she could do for this case—and herself—was to make the same mistake twice.

The door flew open, and Richard walked into the room.

Lana threw the pencil pieces in her desk drawer. She smiled. "Please, have a seat."

Richard sat on the chair, looked around, and frowned. There were too many papers in this small space. The shelves pressed in against him, and the air here was moist and stuffy.

"Don't you like my workspace?" she asked.

"I hardly found this teeny tiny room," Richard replied.

A thick book was on the top of Lana's desk. On its bright cover was a woman with flowing red hair, sitting on a dragon. Richard took the book. "I see you like fairy tales," he said.

Lana took the book from his hands. "Don't touch it." She tried to put it in the drawer, but the book was too big; the drawer refused to close.

Richard chuckled. "So, where is the witch's house?"

Lana put her palms together and looked at him with calm eyes. "I'll show you on the map. But before we start working together, I want to clarify some things."

"I'm listening."

"We're working as a team, whether we want to or not."

He nodded. "Mostly not."

"Agreed. But we are, and the most important thing in a team is trust."

"Really?" He raised his eyebrows.

Lana narrowed her eyes. "Yes. So, Richard, I promise not to read your mind. I'll respect your boundaries. I'll also follow all your professional decisions."

He scowled. "What a kind gesture. What do you want from me in exchange?"

"Nothing. I just think it would be the best solution to solve this case."

"How professional of you."

Lana pulled open the drawer and started looking for the map.

Richard looked at her with curiosity. What the heck happened to this woman? She was as calm as a rock. He even missed the sparkles of anger in her eyes and her nice blushing cheeks. Her calmness wasn't a good sign. She'd probably concocted a plan in her small pretty head while he was talking to the chief. It didn't matter; their cooperation would be over soon.

Lana unfolded the map on the table. It was a big sheet of paper, and the forest took up most of the space. He had to look closer to find the small town with the modest inscription *Triville* on it.

She pointed her index finger at the oval lake in the corner of the map. "The witch's house is here—on a hill at the shore."

"Are you sure?"

She nodded. "I was there just once, but I remember the place."

Richard rubbed his palms. Perfect, it was northwest, and his motel was near the forest trail. With his experience of traveling by the local forests, Richard barely needed a map, and now, when he knew the direction of his next destination, he didn't need Lana's help either. But he could not just leave her.

"What did you do there?" Richard asked.

Lana gave him a sharp look. "Can we concentrate on our case?"

He shrugged. "As you wish."

"It's about a six-hour ride."

Richard looked out the window. It was almost dawn.

He put his hand on the map. "If we go at sunrise, we'll get there in the afternoon. Then we can return the same day. What do you think?"

"We better go now."

Richard stared at her. "I know you can't wait for our little journey. But what would the chief say if I brought you into the forest at night?"

Lana crossed her arms. "Sunrise works for me."

Richard stood up. "Then be at my motel at five in the morning, and don't forget the map."

"Sure."

"We could be a great team," he said before he walked out of the room.

When he left, Lana took a deep breath. He was still unbearable, but at least their talk had gone well. She didn't want to trash her room anymore.

Lana folded the map and put it in her backpack. Now she just had to prepare—there was a long trip ahead.

* * *

In the stables, Lana petted Mandy's face. The horse snickered and moved her ears.

The stable groom smiled. "Well, you're good to go. Her new horseshoes will last for at least three months."

Lana checked the belt on the saddle. Everything was ready; she just needed to pack some food and a warm sweater. She gave the groom two bronze coins. "It was nice working with you. Thank you for doing this quickly—we have a big ride tomorrow."

"How far?"

Lana tied her backpack to her belt. "To the lake."

The groom raised his eyebrows. "The forest isn't safe right now. Don't you know that?"

"Don't worry, I'll have a guardian with me."

He nodded. "Just be careful."

"I will." Lana took the reins and looked at Mandy. "Let's go, girl."

She and Mandy trotted slowly down the street. The evening sun hung low in the horizon. Its tired rays touched white clouds and colored their bottoms golden.

Richard's motel was across the road. As her father liked to joke, it was the best and the worst motel in Triville—it was the only one. It was a simple, wooden two-story building with wide windows.

Richard had probably already packed and had gone to bed early. She should do the same thing.

Lana looked at Mandy. "I think I finally found the right approach for this Santos guy."

Mandy neighed.

Lana smiled. "I know, I know. He might be too conceited, but he said we could be a good team. He's a good detective." She looked across the road and widened her eyes in surprise.

Richard walked out from the motel entrance, wearing a backpack and a long black cloak. He stopped to talk with the clerk.

Lana squeezed the reins. "And he's a liar."

She moved down the street out of his sight, crossed the road, and approached him from behind. A second motel worker walked out of the stable with Coal, approached Richard, and bowed.

"Thank you, sir," Richard said, giving him a coin.

She moved closer, until Richard noticed her and flinched.

Lana looked down at him. "Where are you going?"

He narrowed his eyes. "Guess."

Lana shook her head. "We made a deal. What about trusting each other?"

Richard chuckled and mounted his saddle. "I'm not the only one who has problems with trust." He swung the reins, and his black stallion trotted down the street. He turned left at the crossroads.

Lana scoffed. "He's unbearable." She clasped Mandy around her waist, and they followed Richard's waving black cloak to the end of the forest trail. He moved fast, but she was fast too. They galloped after him.

Chapter 24. Storm in a Teacup

The evening sun reflected off the red roof of the Turner household. In the garden, Elisa stood behind a tree, waiting for the moment when the house would become empty. No one was around; the only sound was the rustling of the tree leaves overhead. Elisa fidgeted with the hem of her green silk dress. Hopefully, nobody would notice her in these bushes. *Oh, my poor naive Julia. I will open your eyes to the truth about Kyle.*

The door squeaked, and Elisa peered around the tree trunk. Kyle closed the door and walked down the steps. He fixed his jacket and looked around.

When the sound of his steps disappeared, Elisa walked into to the wide yard.

At the door, she stopped for a moment and took a deep breath. Her heart pounded in her chest. There was no one to watch her back—not anymore. It was hard to do everything on her own, but Elisa knew one thing: as long as she had a choice, she would choose to fight. To be with Julia, she had to find out the truth.

Elisa knocked three times and held her breath. Her quickly made plan wasn't perfect, but it was the only one she had. Quick footsteps approached and the door before it opened.

A tall man in a gray casual shirt with bright blue eyes and a trimmed gray beard smiled. "Elisa! I haven't seen you for a while. How are you?"

Elisa was ready with a fake smile. "Everything is good. How are you, Captain Turner?"

"In the middle of an investigation," he said. "Oh, you probably came to see Kyle."

She nodded and fidgeted with a lock of her hair. "Is he home?"

"He just left. He went to his friend to prepare for exams."

"Of course." Elisa glanced over Captain Turner's shoulder. Inside looked normal—there were two solid wooden chairs at the fireplace, and a plush blanket covered the sofa. A big piano sat at the center of the room. Kyle liked to play, but as she'd figured out, his interests were not limited to music. If only his father knew the games he really played.

"Sorry for my manners," Captain Turner said. "You're welcome to come in."

"Thank you for your invitation, but—"

"I was just making tea. You can tell me about Rose. It might help with the investigation."

"I talked with the guardians already," Elisa said.

"I won't put any pressure on you, I promise." Captain Turner smiled. "I hope you're not afraid of me."

Elisa snorted. She stepped over the threshold and walked into the living room. The kettle whistled in the kitchen.

"I'll make some tea for you too," Captain Turner said.

"Thank you," she replied.

When he left the room, Elisa glanced at the door of Kyle's bedroom. It was too far away; it would be too risky to go there now. She walked to the bookshelves against the wall. A solid layer of dust covered the books and an old, framed family portrait. Elisa took it and wiped away the dust. Four people gazed at her from the old piece of paper. Something was wrong. She took a closer look—no one smiled.

Like four strangers, the people looked at her in silence. Captain Turner's beard was black. The woman by his side had beautiful curly hair, and a ten-year-old boy stood at her left—Kyle. The teenage girl had two thick braids and was squeezing a book in her hands.

Kyle never talked about his mother or sister, but everyone knew about their sad story. Mrs. Turner ran away when her daughter, Rebecca, committed suicide. Captain Turner had to bring up his son alone. People said that Kyle's mother was an airhead, but they liked to gossip to feel smarter and better about themselves. The girl looked at Elisa with sad blue eyes.

"I wish I knew you better, Rebecca Turner," Elisa whispered and put the portrait back on the shelf.

In a cabinet, porcelain cups and beautiful silver tableware shone behind glass. The Turners were not poor, and everyone knew it. Little did they know what the family hid under the sheen of silver. Elisa opened the cabinet and took out a dessert fork. It sparkled in her hand.

Elisa glanced at the kitchen. Captain Turner was still busy, based on the clank of dishes and the murmur of his humming. Elisa put the fork in her décolletage, closed the cabinet, and smiled at her reflection. She had fresh skin, beautiful golden hair streaming down to her chest, and she was wearing a nice green dress. She fixed a lock of her hair before noticing Captain Turner's reflection as he exited the kitchen. Elisa walked to the table, overlaid with a fresh white cloth, and sat in an elegant wooden chair.

Captain Turner had a tray in his hands. He carried two white mugs with forget-me-nots painted on their rims, a big plate with buns, and a pot of honey. He put the tray on the table, then he moved his hand. The kettle poured the tea in a cup on its own. After it was full, the cup rose in the air and landed in front of Elisa; the aroma of peppermint reached her nose. Elisa took the mug, and it pleasantly warmed her palms.

"So, how is it going at school?" Captain Turner asked.

"Everything is okay. Finals are coming up," Elisa replied.

"I heard Rose's funeral was beautiful."

"They planted tulips on her grave. But to me, funerals and death aren't beautiful."

Captain Turner nodded solemnly. "I agree. Unfortunately, some things just happen."

"Yes, when someone commits a murder." Elisa shook her head. "I just can't believe Rose is gone. She was so young. She didn't even get her Gift."

Captain Turner put his cup on the table. "I remember when I was expecting my Gift Revealing. It was like a wrapped gift that I held in my hands." He waved his hand. A bun flew from the big dish and landed on a plate in front of Elisa. Then a silver teaspoon scooped honey from the pot and flew to the bun. A golden stream dribbled on the pastry.

Elisa took the bun and bit into it. The sweet honey and fresh bread melted in her mouth.

Captain Turner looked at her with stern eyes. "It's a wrapped box, but no one knows what's inside."

Elisa swallowed the pastry. "What do you mean?" she asked with hesitation.

Turner placed his palms on the tablecloth. "My daughter had a Gift too. A dangerous one—she could burn people alive."

Elisa raised her eyebrows. "What happened to her?" she asked. According to Lana, he hadn't even tried to find Rebecca's killer.

"I did what I was supposed to do. I sent her to Mercy House."

"And then she became an Incapable," Elisa said.

The man nodded. "My poor girl. We said goodbye, and I sent her far away. Two weeks later, she escaped Mercy House and came back home. She begged me to take her back—to let her live with us even though she was no longer a mage. It was my duty—*my* fucking duty—to get rid of her."

Elisa's breath hitched. "Why are you telling me this?"

He didn't break eye contact. "You're scared, aren't you? Fear makes people do desperate things."

"Like what?" Elisa's voice trembled.

"Like looking for the Gift Hunter."

Captain Turner put his palm on Elisa's hand. It was heavy and hot, but she didn't remove her hand. She just looked at him with wide eyes.

"Or breaking into his house with your best friend."

"Are you . . . ?" Elisa asked. Her tongue was dry and wasn't moving properly.

He laughed. "Yes, it's me. I am the Gift Hunter."

Fear slowly squeezed her throat. She wanted to run, but her body refused to obey.

Sleeping potions have a sweet taste. A sudden memory from her biology class arose in her mind. *And they're easy to hide in sweets.*

His fingers closed her eyelids, and Elisa fell into darkness.

Chapter 25. Ghost's Trail

The forest slowly fell asleep. Black tree crowns shivered up above and opened a view to the navy-blue sky. Night flowers opened their colorful buds and highlighted a narrow trail; the moss on the trees shone with a gentle green light. The road was full of fallen branches and stones, and their horses moved with caution.

Richard looked up. At this rate, they would never make it before sunrise. At least Lana hadn't uttered a single word since they walked into the forest, and he could concentrate on the road.

The mist leaked onto the trail, and yellow lights of the night flowers floated up ahead. Their horses stepped on the wet soft ground, and Richard stopped. There was marshland ahead; he'd taken the wrong direction at the fork. *Awesome.* Now they had to go back. He jumped down from his saddle.

"Lost your way, Richard?" Lana asked.

He gave her a sharp look. "This never happens to me."

She grinned. "There's a first time for everything, right?"

He took a deep breath. He wasn't sure if it was just her nature, or if she was teasing him on purpose, but he had to concentrate on the main goal—to find the path to the lake.

"Just wait here," he said and walked into the bushes. The branches had little yellow flowers that glowed in the mist. The marsh was close.

Somehow, this woman had distracted him from the road, and she'd done it with her silence. She was awkward and stubborn, but not stupid. But at the same time, she was a woman. There had to be something she was afraid of.

Something hissed below his feet, and Richard stopped. He made a Light ball in his hand and leaned over a small green snake that squirmed by his boots. This species wasn't poisonous—nothing to be afraid of. He wasn't scared of snakes, but *she* had to be. Richard grinned and whispered a Hypnotic spell, then he touched the snake with his Light. The energy circled around the creature and became transparent. The snake hissed, crawling onto the trail.

* * *

Alone on the dark forest trail, Lana climbed down from the saddle to stretch her muscles. Richard walked out of the bushes with a wide smile. Lana shook her head and walked toward the forest.

"Where are you going?" he asked.

Lana stopped. "I need to do my business. Just wait for a minute."

"What if I run away?"

"What would the chief say if you left me alone in a night forest?" she asked.

He crossed his arms and stayed silent.

Off the trail, the mist covered the ground. A big oak with crooked branches stood between the bushes. Thick moss covered the trunk of a tree, shining green like sparkling emeralds. This kind of tree had power—its roots took energy from the depths of Mother Earth. All witches knew how to tame the powers of nature to suit their needs, and they could hear messages that were addressed to them.

Lana glanced back and put her palm on the tree bark. Witches and guardians always had confrontations, but in rare cases, they had to work together. Like right now. It was unavoidable, but at least Lana could warn her about Richard.

The bark shone yellow under Lana's palm, and she leaned closer.

"Meredith," she whispered.

The oak shimmered, and the moss's light became dull. Lana clasped the tree, but it kept silent. Ugly tree branches hung over her like dead monsters. Silence was the worst answer.

She stepped back, and something slippery fell on her from above. It touched her neck; Lana screamed, swinging her arms. The snake fell on the grass with a loud hiss.

Lana slowed her breathing and sat on her knees. She stretched her hand out with her yellow Light to see it better. It was a marsh snake. This small creature rolled in a spiral and kept silent. Lana touched the snake's cold and rough skin. She placed her Light on the snake to give it some energy.

"You must be scared to death!" Richard's voice sounded behind her.

Lana petted the snake. "It just fell on me. It might be hurt."

Richard shook his head. "You're as hard as a rock."

"I'm not afraid of animals; it's people who do terrible things." Lana raised her eyes. "Wait, was this your doing?"

Richard smiled. "Guilty."

"How could you use a living creature? You hurt it!"

"It's just stressed." Richard kneeled and touched the snake with his fingertips. The animal quickly crawled away in the grass. "See? It's fine," Richard said. "Let's go. Otherwise, we'll never reach the lake." He stood and stretched out his hand to Lana, but she stayed sitting on the grass.

"Maybe you can finally admit that you've lost your way?" she asked.

Up above, the first star shone in the night sky. "It's hard to see the trail," he said, "but I found a glade to stop for the night."

Lana rose, and they walked to their horses. Little yellow lights shone around them in the mist. This guy was unbearable, but at least the nights here were beautiful.

* * *

Richard threw a Fireball spell into the fire pit. The dry branches ignited and crackled. The flames lit up the surrounding trees, and the fog hid behind the bushes.

GHOST

Lana placed her jacket on the ground and sat near the fire. She opened her backpack and sighed—half a bottle of water, an apple core, and a stinky sandwich that she hadn't eaten at lunch. If only she'd had more time to prepare. Lana glanced at Richard. He was sitting on a fallen tree and was scarfing down food from a glass jar. The smell of jerky and beans reached Lana's nostrils, and her stomach rumbled.

Lana took out the sandwich. The slice of turkey was spoiled, but the bread was still good enough to eat. She threw the meat into the flame and took a thin branch from the ground.

"Are you really gonna eat the rest?" Richard asked.

Lana stabbed the bread with the branch and placed it over the fire. "There's nothing wrong with it," she said.

He chuckled. "Just asking. I won't have time to wait for you tomorrow if you're going to be sitting in the bushes—"

"The fire," Lana interrupted him. "It burns away all the bad smells and makes it taste better."

The slice of bread started to burn, and she twisted the branch. The slice fell on the charcoals, hissing. She sat on her knees and stared at the flame.

Richard looked up at the starry night sky. Compared to this mess, his impending punishment on Death Island didn't seem that bad. He approached Lana and offered her his jar.

She hesitated.

"Come on, don't be so stubborn!"

"Or what?"

"Can you just stop arguing and eat?"

Lana took the jar from his hands. The aroma of beans and spices filled the air. She couldn't resist her hunger anymore.

Chapter 26. A Million Fires

They sat on their jackets and listened to the crackle of burning wood. Richard took the empty jar from her hands and put it on the ground.

"Thank you," Lana said.

Richard opened his flask and inhaled the soothing smell of whiskey. After taking a sip, he offered the flask to Lana. "*This* is what kills bad smells and makes things taste better."

She shook her head.

Richard fidgeted with the flask in his hands. "This would never have happened if you hadn't chased me."

"What do you mean?"

Richard softened his voice. "This morning. We were going to meet—"

"Oh," Lana replied in realization. Her cheeks turned bright pink.

"You were spying on me. I got distracted, and now we're lost."

"I had no idea you were planning to go alone."

Richard narrowed his eyes. "Then how did you find me?"

Lana shrugged. "I just came to the stables to get Mandy. It's not my fault our town is so small."

Richard shifted his gaze to the fire and took another sip of whiskey. "Tomorrow we'll go back to the fork and find the right trail."

"No need." Lana took her backpack and smiled, pulling out a folded sheet of paper. "I have a map."

Richard widened his eyes. "Really, you brought it with you? Why didn't you tell me?"

She shrugged. "You never asked."

Richard forced himself to stay silent. Women never appealed to common sense, and mind readers were the worst.

Lana unfolded the map and put it on the ground. Her index finger quickly found Triville and moved to the Northern Marshes. "The Marshes are nearby, so we should be in this area," she said. "Hmm . . . we made just a little detour. If we leave at sunrise, we should be at the lake before noon."

Richard frowned at her. The fire gleamed on her smooth pretty face, and it was hard to stay mad at her.

He glanced at the red time crystal on her wrist. "It's midnight. We should sleep."

Lana stood up. "I bet you brought a blanket. I'll bring it to you."

"Sure. But you sleep first; I'll stay on watch." Richard mixed the charcoals with a thick branch. He looked up—the stars shone above like a million little fires, layered behind a thin, lazy cloud floating across the sky. The night immersed the forest in a mystic atmosphere; mist wrapped the glowing tree trunks, and nature shone with a pale green light.

At sunrise, the lights would fade, and all the secrecy would disappear. He might never figure out what Lana's secret was, but he was going to try.

Lana laid the blanket on the ground. She put her backpack under her head and rolled into a ball like a kitten. A cute little kitten with a nasty attitude.

"Lana," he called.

She turned to face him. "What?"

"How did you know that Ghost kills girls with new destructive Gifts?"

Lana looked at the sky. "Their ages. They were killed when Gifts usually manifest."

"That's not enough to make such a conclusion."

She sat up. "Of course not. I also checked the circumstances of their deaths and matched them with the witness reports. All the victims disappeared after experiencing an emotional turmoil. Plus, some witnesses saw them releasing their destructive Gifts for the first time, and I assumed it might be the reason why Ghost is killing them."

Richard widened his eyes. "Unbelievable."

Her eyes glittered. "What?"

Her look—Richard knew it all too well; he had the same one when he was investigating crimes. An interesting case was like a narcotic for a detective. It captivated his mind, and he could neither resist nor help himself. It explained a lot.

He threw more wood into the fire, and a heat wave warmed his face. "You sound like a real detective."

Lana shook her head. "I don't want to be a detective. The only thing I want to do is help people as much as I can."

"That's exactly what detectives do."

"Not all of them, unfortunately," she said.

"Yes, that's why I said a *real* detective."

She gave him a sad look. "Of course."

He turned back to the fire, a drop of sweat rolling down his neck.

"What about this Ghost guy?" she asked. "Do you really think it was *him* who killed both girls?"

"I don't know. That's why we need to check it."

"What for? It's clear the murderer was an imposter. He was just trying to confuse you."

"I followed protocol. You saw the letters on the victim's wrist."

Lana stretched her palms toward the fire. "Don't tell me you believed those letters meant 'Ghost.'"

He shrugged. "Why not?"

"Because Rose didn't even know his nickname."

Richard blinked. Damn, she was good.

"I don't know how, but the victim knew something. She wrote his name on her wrist," he said.

"A guardian could have easily done that—they know how to fake evidence."

"It was her, or I'm not a detective."

Lana rolled her eyes. "All right, let's say she did it. But even if that were true, no person in their right mind would write only the first and the last letters of someone's name. I don't know about you, but if I were trying to leave a clue, I would spell out the whole name. No, it has to be something else."

Richard didn't argue. Instead, he stared at the flames, possibilities twisting in his mind. All this time, the answer was right in front of his eyes, and now he saw it clearly. "Two big letters. They're—"

"Initials," Lana said with him.

Richard unbuttoned his collar to breathe easier. Lana had the talents of a detective—she paid more attention to details than most of his colleagues. *But she's just a woman.* "Good catch," he muttered.

Lana pulled at his elbow. "We should tell the chief. We should go—"

"No, we'll stay here and wait," Richard said. He shook her hand away and stood up.

She widened her eyes. "Why are we going farther from town instead of catching the *real* murderer?"

"I'll say why, but you have to answer my question after."

She fidgeted with her blanket until she was comfortable. "Deal," she said, intrigued.

"In cases like this, it's dangerous to wait. But at the same time, rushing can ruin everything."

"What shall we do, then?"

Richard rubbed his palms. "In the beginning, the criminal knows more than you, making him confident. Even if you have a suspect, Lana, you need to be careful—if you're too pushy, the consequences are unpredictable. Your insistence might only scare him, but in the worst case, he might become aggressive. The key is to act when you have just enough proof—that's the art of detective work."

"An art," Lana repeated. Her big brown eyes were bright with excitement.

Richard tried to remember the last time when someone looked at him like this, but nothing came to mind. He smiled. "Exactly. We'll return tomorrow and carefully check all the suspects. Now, it's your turn."

"Mine?" She blinked like she'd forgotten her end of the bargain.

Richard narrowed his eyes. "Yes. You said you wanted to save people. Who are you talking about?"

Lana shifted her gaze to the fire. "It's a long story."

"I have time." He sat down in front of her and prepared to listen.

"Did you know that I used to be a sister at Mercy House?" she asked.

"No."

She sighed. "I worked there for about a month as a psychiatric nurse. They wanted me to help girls get rid of their harmful Gifts."

"You could help. You have a useful Gift."

Lana shook her head. "Not in Mercy House. You know, we had to receive 'official' permission from the patients—to follow protocol—but we didn't tell them the whole truth. Each day, I sat with the girls and convinced them to give up their Gifts to avoid hurting others. We made them feel like monsters who didn't have a place in the world."

"Some Gifts are dangerous," Richard replied.

"Magic becomes dangerous only if you use it to destroy things." Her voice trembled. "They could learn how to control their powers and use them in a good way, but no one wants to teach them."

"I don't understand. These Gifts are too strong for young girls, and sorority just take their Gifts away."

"Just their Gifts?" Lana scoffed. "No. I thought so too, in the beginning. After the procedure, the senior Mercy sisters didn't let us talk with the girls, and they carried the girls away. But then I found out what they were hiding—from all of us. They sent the girls to communities with the other Incapables."

"Sometimes the procedure fails—"

"The procedure works perfectly, Richard," Lana interrupted him. "One night, when everyone fell asleep, I sneaked into the basement. My friend was kept there, like a prisoner. I found *twenty-seven* girls there with burned fingertips. They were *all* Incapables."

Richard stopped breathing. Eric, the Incapable boy he had met on his way to Triville . . . now his story made sense. He had not seen Eric's mother, but the boy had talked about her burned fingertips. That was exactly how military experts took magic away from criminals. They did it only if criminals were too dangerous or at a high risk of escaping on the way to Death Island.

No, no one would do this to a teenage girl. The sorority must have softer procedures.

But no one knew exactly how the process of Gift-taking worked, and until this moment, Richard had never asked this question. Now he had plenty of them. *What really happened to Eric's mother?*

She couldn't be a murderer from Death Island—women were too tender for such heavy labor and were never sent there.

There was only one version of the story left, a true version that perfectly matched Lana's—Eric had told the truth, and his mother was a victim of Mercy House.

Lana hung her head. "They will be Incapables for the rest of their lives. They were just little girls who weren't lucky enough to have "peaceful" Gifts. No one even bothered to teach them how to control their powers. They were sent away from their homes, like they had committed a crime."

"Why didn't you tell anyone?" he asked.

A tear slid down her cheek, and Lana wiped it away with the corner of her sleeve. "I did, but no one cared. My father would never believe me without proof, and that's why I didn't tell him. He would fire me if he knew I had gotten involved."

Silence hung in the air. The flames danced in the fire pit, and the shadows moved among the glowing tree trunks.

Richard put his hand on her shoulder. "If only I had known."

The flames glittered in her wet eyes. "Now you do. Now what?"

Richard took a handkerchief from his pocket and put it in her hand. Lana wiped the corners of her eyes. Her breathing slowed.

"You started to work with the forest witch," he concluded, "to help them escape."

Lana lowered her eyes. "I saw her only once. The rumors about her don't lie. But honestly, she is just a drop in the ocean, and this system ruins more lives than this witch can save."

"Then what are you going to do?" he asked.

She sighed. "I only owed you one answer, right?"

Richard softened his voice. "Someone once said that the most important thing in a team is trust."

Lana scoffed. "Like you care about trust."

"It was before you told me about Mercy House. Lana, this system is too huge and too strong to fight alone. It will break you."

She snorted. "I won't give up."

"I didn't say that. I said it won't be easy, and you'll need all the support you can get."

"I've told you—no guardian would believe me without proof."

"I'll help you."

Lana bit her lip, thinking. Then, she gave him a tired look. "You're right; the system is powerful, but some parts are rotten. When I was in the sorority, I met my friend, Becca. I helped her escape that night. It was too suspicious for us to return to Triville together, and so we split up. She died the day after she came home. The guardians made a big mistake when they killed her and faked her suicide. I managed to figure out it was a guardian who did it, but I didn't see his face. Now, all I need is to find this guardian and prove it to my father."

Richard scratched his chin. "How did you *see* this guardian?"

Her hands gripped the handkerchief. "I read her brother's memory. He was spying when the guardian approached Becca with a fireball in his hand. Then, he ran away. I heard her screaming; it was the night she died."

"When did this happen?"

"A bit more than three years ago," Lana replied.

"Then you should check the people who worked in Triville at that time. The town is small; you have only twelve guardians, and as far as I know, half of them are here because of summer training, so you can exclude them. You need to find the Gift Hunter."

"It's not that easy. His identity is hidden, and as you said, guardians can protect themselves from mind reading."

Richard paused before replying. "I see. That's why you wanted to help the chief find the imposter. Two birds with one stone—you wanted to find the Gift Hunter and get rid of me. But then we were sent to the lake against your wishes."

Lana stood, numb.

He laughed. "You fell into your own trap. Now you see where speedy decisions lead. Honestly, it was a nice try."

She stepped back and crossed her arms. "You're not helping."

Richard kept smiling. "Okay, sorry, it's just . . ."

"Like you've never made a mistake. You're the one who let Ghost go last time."

A smile escaped Richard's face. "I'm trying to fix that," he said.

"I'm trying to fix my mistakes too. I know we're stuck here, but at least we have a new clue to investigate. Maybe it will lead to the right answer. We need to work together if we are going to find the murderer."

Richard moved closer. "Do you believe the real Ghost ever visited the town?"

"Actually, no. But you are right, we need to exclude this version." Lana put her palm on his. "But I know that Ghost is important for you, so I'll help you search the witch's house in case he ever visited her."

"Do you really want to help me, or do you just want to satisfy your curiosity?"

Lana gave him a warm look. "When I say I'm going to help, I mean it, Richard. I tried to shake you because I thought this case might be connected to the Mercy House, but now I see that Ghost has nothing to do with them."

Richard nodded. "Wait, you thought so because his victims—"

"Were the same age and had destructive powers. But it was just a coincidence, and I'll help you prove it."

"I don't believe in coincidences. Everything happens for a reason; we just don't know them yet."

Lana nodded. "Then let's figure it out tomorrow."

"See? We *are* a good team," he said.

Lana smiled back, then she fell onto the blanket.

"Have a good night, Richard," she said gently before she closed her eyes.

"Good night," he replied.

* * *

Richard sat at the fire, until it was almost burnt out. The night air was cool, so he approached Lana and covered her with his jacket. Her breathing was calm, and her bosom slowly rose and fell. A warmth soothed his chest. He leaned over her and kissed her forehead.

Richard walked back to the fire pit. He took a dried branch from the ground and threw it into the dimming charcoals, and the branch hissed. The fire embraced the wood and started kissing it, like a man kissing a beloved woman.

"I'm not sure how to help you, but I know one thing for sure— I'm a liar." Richard sighed. "I'm such a liar."

He sat at the fire until the sky turned gray. In the quiet morning, the night flowers closed their glowing buds and fell asleep, but

Richard didn't want to sleep. The warmth didn't disappear from his chest. If anything, it became stronger.

He got up and walked to the horses. Coal opened his long-lashed black eyes and gave him a puzzled look when Richard took the reins. He glanced at Lana and walked down the trail, his quiet steps disappearing into the dawn.

Chapter 27. Whispers of Wishes

The stars lit up the dark sky over Triville. The river slid through the town park and under an old stone bridge. It had been forged with time crystals set into the metal. In the middle of the night, the bridge shone a gentle green light. Julia touched the cold railing and looked down. The crystals were reflected in the dark running water.

Kyle touched her hand. "So, what happened today? Tell me."

Julia sighed. "Elisa. We had an argument and I . . . I lost control."

Kyle squeezed her palm. "It's okay. Best friends always argue."

"It wasn't only a fight. We almost killed each other."

"I don't believe you could hurt someone."

Julia lowered her voice. "I . . . I threw a fireball at her . . ."

"Did it touch her?"

"It almost hit her shoulder."

Kyle smiled. "It's not good, but you couldn't kill her. To kill someone with a fireball, you need to throw it right into their chest and use a lot of energy. Even if the spell had touched her skin, it would have only left a little burn. It would have easily healed."

Julia lowered her eyes. The river raced underneath them. People said that the water could carry worries away, but today, it didn't help. Kyle's words didn't help either. Nothing had since she walked away from the dusty road. All evening, she thought of it with a heavy heart.

"You two will be all right," Kyle said.

Julia looked at him. "What if she was right?"

Kyle frowned. "About what?"

"I'm in danger, but I haven't done anything about it," Julia said. "Everything around us—all these murders, funerals, and fights . . . it's too much for me!"

Kyle hugged her. Julia sobbed, and her shoulders shook.

"I promise you—we will find the murderer. My father is working on it."

Julia raised her moist eyes. "I don't think it will ever be over."

"It will; of course it will. But now I should bring you home. It's late."

"I don't want to go home."

"What do you want, then?"

"To make a wish," she said.

Julia walked to the middle of the bridge and closed her eyes. The cool night air smelled of fresh water and grass. She could make only one wish, and she decided to make it tonight. The legend said that this bridge had magic powers, and it could make any wish come true. The wish had to be sincere and come from deep inside the wisher's heart; otherwise, it would not come true.

She could only make one wish during her lifetime, and Julia had saved hers. Even when she'd desired something in the past, it had never been important enough. She didn't want to waste such rare magic. If she wasted her wish, she had a feeling that something more important would happen. She was right—life changed too quickly and brought more serious problems with it as it went on. But now, the moment was right, and the words escaped her lips.

"I wish that girls' Gifts and powers weren't being taken away from them."

Julia opened her eyes, but nothing changed. The stars blinked in the sky, and the river rushed through the stone banks. The trees rustled in the night, whispering and laughing at her.

Kyle approached her. "That was beautiful."

"It was silly and so, so naive."

He touched her cheek. "Never say that. People are too selfish these days, but you aren't one of them. That's what I love about you, Julia. You're not afraid to care about others."

Julia blushed. "You don't think so?"

He smiled and leaned toward her. She kissed his warm, sweet lips. His hand gently caressed her hip, sliding lower over her dress. His movements were slow and careful. He was close, closer than anyone had been to her before. He wasn't scary—not a rapist, as Elisa had called him.

Her soft fingers touched the rough scar on his neck.

Kyle's eyes reflected the green light of the time crystals. "Let's go. Unless you have more wishes," he said.

"I've reached my lifetime limit."

"But I haven't."

Julia shook her head. "You only get one."

Kyle nodded. "I know, but you can have it."

She smiled. "That's so sweet, but I can't ask you for it."

Kyle took her hand and kissed it. "I want to do something for you. Just ask me."

"I wish I knew where Elisa was—what she's doing."

"I don't need any magic to tell you that. Elisa was at my house this evening. I saw her when I left."

Julia widened her eyes. "Why didn't you stop her?"

He shrugged. "My father was there. I have something to tell you, Julia. No secrets. Someone tore pages out of my diary, and I bet it was her. Did she tell you everything?"

Julia shook her head. "She told me that you spied on us. When she and Rose found your diary, those pages were already torn out. Kyle, we never found out who the Gift Hunter was."

He raised his eyebrows. "You don't know?"

"No. That's why Elisa went back to your house—to continue her investigation."

Kyle stepped back. "That's not good."

"I know. Sorry, I should have told you before, but—"

"But what?"

Julia lowered her eyes. The silence hung in the air—with one clumsy step, the romance had fallen apart like a flimsy house of cards. "I just want to trust you, Kyle," she said.

"How could you, after everything I've done?"

"Because whatever the truth is, you're not a Gift Hunter. You could never be like that. Yes, you've made mistakes, but you've learned from them, and that makes you different. So, I believe in you." Julia gave him a gentle look; his face shone in the calm light of the time crystals.

Kyle looked up into the sky and closed his eyes. "I wish for Mercy House to burn in hell and to stop Gifts and other magic from being taken away from innocent people."

"You shouldn't have made your wish for me," Julia said after a pause.

"I didn't do it only for you. I did it because this is what I really want. My sister died when I was twelve. You probably heard about it."

Julia put her hand on her chest. "I'm so sorry, Kyle."

"But she didn't commit suicide. He thinks I was just a scared kid who forgot that night, but I remember everything. He shouldn't have taken her life away."

Julia widened her eyes. "Who killed her?"

Kyle sighed. The crystals in the bridge railing turned turquoise, and they lit up her worried face. It was almost dawn, and he had to go home.

Father . . . He couldn't tell her the truth about him—not yet. She would be in danger, and Elisa too. *Elisa had walked into the house. What if she started asking the wrong questions?*

"I promise, I'll tell you everything when I can. I need to go home right now," Kyle said.

"We can go together."

"No, I'll go alone. It's too dangerous."

Julia narrowed her eyes. "At your own home?"

"Yes." Kyle tried to pull his away hand, but she held him tight.

Her heart pounded in her ears. *His sister . . . Mercy House . . . the other girls Lana had told them about . . . She was right.* The Gift Hunter was always nearby, and Rose had been at his house before she went missing. Captain George Turner—Elisa was with him, and Kyle had known it all this time.

Julia released her fingers.

Kyle rubbed his palm. "Julia, I'm sorry, but I have to run." He turned away and started walking down the bridge.

"You're not your father," she said.

Kyle stopped. "I'm sorry."

Julia waved him away. "Stop him!"

He nodded and ran away. His black jacket disappeared in the night.

When Julia stood alone at the bridge, she looked up. "I wish for Elisa not to die." She fell to her knees and dropped her face into her palms, sobbing. It was too late—she'd already wasted her wish on the unknown girls. Now she would give anything to save Elisa's life, but she was helpless.

Her tears slid from her cheeks and fell into the river's running flow. It carried them away to the depths of the forest and to the lake where there was no one left to care.

Chapter 28. Morning in the Forest

The sky brightened. The first birds woke and started jumping from branch to branch, twittering in the rustling leaves and greeting the new day. Lana opened her eyes and touched her shoulders. She was covered with his jacket; it smelled just like him—of whiskey and arrogance.

Lana sat up and looked around. The fire was dead—cold charcoals lay in the fire pit, and a white unfolded map lay on the ground nearby. She was alone at the glade, surrounded by laughing trees and bushes.

Lana jumped and ran to the horses. Mandy was awake, and she chomped at the fresh grass vigorously. Coal was gone.

She touched her burning cheeks. "No fucking way!"

Lana ran to the trail and stopped. She turned left and then right, but couldn't see anything. She clenched her fists. Her nails pierced her palms, but she didn't feel any pain. She stood in the empty trail and breathed heavily, the blood beating in her ears. Richard was gone—again. He'd fooled her, then carried her secret away.

"Good morning, early bird," a voice behind her said.

Lana flinched and turned around. Richard stood in front of her with his stallion and a brown cotton bag in his hands.

Lana breathed out. "You ran away."

He chuckled. "No, I didn't. We just needed breakfast."

"Breakfast?"

"Yes. Someone ate all my food last night. Someone hungry."

Lana put her hand on her chest. If she kept seeing this guy, one day she was going have a heart attack. "Did you shoot a bird? Because if it's a bunny, I won't eat it."

"We wouldn't have time to cook an animal," Richard said. He threw her the bag, and Lana caught it.

She opened the bag. There were some roots covered with dirt inside. She sighed. "At least no bunny suffered."

She closed the bag and walked into the glade after him.

* * *

The fire danced in the pit, licking the roots and sharp branches. Richard took a branch with an impaled root and inhaled the warm, sweet aroma. *She will like it.*

He offered a root to Lana.

She took a bite—and then another one.

Richard smiled. "See? Quick and tasty."

"I've never tried this plant before. What is it?"

"Turnips. They grow underground for the bigger part of the year. Sometimes, I cook them when I travel."

"When you are chasing Ghost?"

"Not only then. Unfortunately, there are too many criminals in this world."

She nodded. "That's true."

Richard ate his portion and took a sip from his flask; the spicy liquid warmed his stomach. The pleasant warmth rolled all over his body, but the whiskey wasn't the only cause.

Lana finished her breakfast and rubbed her palms.

Richard stood up. "Do you know what makes a guardian stronger than all other mages?"

"Male gender," she replied.

Richard raised his hand and cast a Paralyzing spell. The silver ball shone in his palm, and it reflected in her eyes.

"Hours of practice," he said. He threw the spell into a wide tree trunk, and it hit the moss, leaving a circle of frost.

"I can do that spell," Lana said.

Richard grinned. "Oh yes, I remember. But if memory serves, your spell casting is shitty."

Lana got up from the ground. She stretched out her hand, and a silver ball materialized in her palm.

"You move your hands too fast," he said. "That's why you have horrible form."

Lana gave him a sharp look and threw the ball into the same tree trunk. It landed below Richard's spell and left a thin trace of frost on the moss. Richard counted three seconds before her frost disappeared. His ring of frost was still there, melting slowly.

He shook his head. "Try again, but use more energy this time. Intensity is more important than speed."

Lana stretched out her hands, and silver energy formed into a ball again. It was thin and transparent, like morning fog. He put his palms on her warm hands. "Don't rush."

The energy thickened, until it looked like a cloud. Lana threw the ball at the tree. The circle of the frost was wider this time, and it lasted five seconds. It disappeared with his.

"Now, that's better. You just need more practice."

"The magic channels on fingertips become numb after this spell. Why use such a strong spell against criminals?"

"Paralyzing a criminal gives you time to tie him up."

Lana looked at him with curiosity. "Why are you teaching me?"

Richard smiled. "Maybe I just want you to be more skilled."

"Why?" she asked, intrigued.

She was a wonderful woman—maybe a bit emotional, but she was strong and passionate. A sparkle of trust shone in her warm pretty eyes. The key to her heart was in his hands.

But it would be better for it to stay locked. *Rick, these mistakes will keep kicking your ass until you start learning from them.* Tim had told him that, once. Maybe he was right. She was the chief's daughter.

He grinned. "If we meet the murderer face-to-face, I want to make sure you can cover me with something better than crap."

Lana took Richard's jacket from the ground and threw it at him. "Let's go, then. We should get there before noon."

Richard sighed. He squeezed his jacket in his hands and followed her to their horses. They stood close to each other, and Coal nuzzled Mandy's face. Animals were smarter than humans—at least, smarter than most of them. They were free to express themselves. Richard couldn't afford to. Not anymore. He didn't have a choice, but at least he could help Lana's investigation move forward. And now, he would do his best to find Ghost and stay professional.

They mounted their horses, and Lana galloped down the trail.

Richard followed her. The forest enveloped them in its fresh embrace. Gentle shades of the sunrise disappeared in the bright, clear morning sky. Everything below was ready to reveal its mysteries.

Chapter 29. The Marsh of Blood

Elisa raised her heavy eyelids. The dawn lit up the morning forest, and the night flowers around were falling asleep—they slowly closed their buds, their light disappearing.

The branches with fresh green leaves hung over her head. Elisa tried to move, but something constrained her. Her body was tied to the tree trunk, and a rope sliced into her wrists. The rope was soaked with something stinky—*absinthe?* Elisa tried to form a Light ball, moving her numb fingers, but the rope blocked her magical channels.

She tried to scream, but only a wheeze came out. The hem of her silk dress was dirty and ripped. Her arms were scratched like someone had carried her through the bushes.

Then she remembered. *It's him—Captain. Turner. The Gift Hunter.*

"Good morning, Sunshine!" his voice sounded from behind, and she flinched.

The Gift Hunter walked out of the trees. His tired red eyes seemed like two wounds on his puffy face. Manic excitement blazed through them as he grinned and took a sharp knife from his pocket. The polished weapon sparkled in his hand, and a cold tip of the blade touched her cheek.

Elisa clenched her teeth and looked into his eyes.

"Just look at you," he said. "So scared. The sweet innocence of a child!"

Elisa's nostrils flared.

"Don't like to be fooled?" he asked.

"Murderer. You killed your own daughter!"

"Not only her."

Elisa widened her eyes. "It was you. You killed Rose!"

"Indeed. And she deserved it."

Elisa's heart sank.

"And you do not deserve your beauty." He lowered his hand, and the sharp blade slid down her cheek.

Pain pierced the left part of her face. She screamed, and a thin stream of blood leaked down her neck.

He stepped back and laughed.

"You'll pay for this," Elisa said. Her hoarse voice seemed to belong to someone else.

The Gift Hunter removed a wad of paper from his jacket before throwing it at her feet. "A present from your friend," he said. "The bitch who betrayed you."

Elisa looked down. She recognized the handwriting—they were the missing pages from Kyle's diary. The night Rose went missing, they hadn't been able to find them.

Elisa blinked. All the pieces of the puzzle formed into one picture. Rose had found the diary so quickly. She could have easily removed the pages while Elisa was busy checking the drawers.

The last memory of Rose materialized before her eyes—she stood at the window, smiling. *Fear makes people do desperate things*, the Gift Hunter had said.

Rose had lied, but she'd done it because she was afraid. She was as scared as most of the high school girls whose Gifts had not manifested yet, and she wanted to make a deal with a Gift Hunter to save herself from Mercy House.

Elisa raised her gaze. "So, what?"

He kicked the papers. "So, what a silly little bitch!"

Elisa glared at him.

"That's what you were looking for that night. Your friend betrayed you as soon as she figured out who I was!" He came closer and brushed his lips against her ear. "She asked me to give her a chance to escape if she manifested a bad Gift," he whispered.

Elisa hung her head.

"Finally, we've figured it out," he said, touching her chin. "Here is a question for you—what would *you* do for your freedom?"

She looked into his pale, red-tinged eyes and inhaled his stinky tobacco breath. She knew his expression too well; her father had had the same one after he downed a bottle of scotch. It made no sense to talk; words didn't mean anything. He obeyed his instincts now—to prove his rightness, to feel his superiority.

Elisa closed her eyes. This is how her father had broken her mother—a long time before he'd become a murderer. The wound on her cheek stung as warm tears rolled down her face. She fell into the familiar darkness and fear. There was no way to escape.

When he started beating her mother, Elisa hid under her bed. She stayed crouched on the cold floor, motionless and paralyzed with fear. She squeezed her plush bear in her trembling hands until it became quiet. *Mother . . .* her voice was gentle, and her hands were warm.

Pretend you're obeying him. Just pretend! He won't hurt you then. His stinky aftershave and his heavy sticky touches would stay in her memories forever.

One day, Elisa couldn't pretend any longer, and she went to the Guardian House. They had made everything even worse.

Elisa breathed in and out to make her brain work. Yesterday, she'd gazed at Rebecca's portrait. And she'd put a sparkling fork in the front of her dress. Elisa opened her eyes.

The Gift Hunter petted her hair. He must have done the same to Bella, Rose, and even his own daughter.

Elisa wrinkled her nose. He was a guardian—no one could say a word against him. She must stop him.

Elisa took a deep breath. "You're right," she said. "They deserved it."

"What?" He raised his eyebrows.

"I said, Rose deserved it," Elisa repeated. "And all the others."

His eyes sparkled.

"But I'm not a betrayer," Elisa said. "I think trust should be earned, not stolen."

"Really?" He raised his eyebrows.

Elisa's voice softened. "Yes. And I'll do anything you want to earn your trust."

He moved his face to hers. "Anything?" he whispered.

She licked her dry lips. "Yes."

He kissed Elisa, and she had to respond. She closed her eyes to avoid seeing his face. She tried to move her hands, but the ropes held them in place. Finally, he moved his lips away from hers, and he kissed her neck, making disgusting lapping sounds. His shaking fingers untied the knot on the rope.

Elisa held her breath—this was her chance. She would pray, if she believed in the Divine, but she'd never relied on anyone but herself. She listened to his heavy breath and counted the seconds.

The rope fell away. Now, only her wrists were tied. She tried to stand up, but her feet were numb. She stumbled to her knees and fell to the ground.

"Ha-ha. Good girl!" He roared with laughter.

Elisa mustered a smile. What stupidity—she'd just lost her chance to escape.

No. I won't just give up.

"Lie down," Elisa said in a flat tone.

To her surprise, the Gift Hunter stretched out on the ground. Elisa crawled over to him and kissed his lips again, then she sat on his hips and started unbuttoning his shirt. She slowly moved down to his pants and put her hands on his pulsing groin.

His face was fully captivated by lust. His eyes were closed, and his chest went up and down. She carefully took the fork from her décolletage.

"Oh, Captain Turner," Elisa whispered.

He lifted his hips at her words.

She clenched her teeth. Then she squeezed the fork in her hands and stabbed it between his legs.

A loud scream of a wounded predator pierced the air. Elisa jumped to her feet, still weak but usable, and ran toward the bushes. She reached a thick tree and glanced back—the Gift Hunter writhed and wailed on the ground.

Suddenly, he looked at her and moved his hand. A short knife flew at her with a whistle.

She ran.

Reflexes were faster than her thoughts—branches, trees, stones, and bushes fell behind her in a destructive wave, almost touching her back, but she didn't stop. More than anything, she was afraid of falling—that would mean the end. She kept running, not paying attention to the branches that ripped her dress and scratched her skin.

* * *

Elisa didn't know how long she ran. Time stretched and jumbled together. When she stopped hearing the sounds of breaking branches behind her, she slowed down. But she kept walking. The earth under her feet became moist. A light mist leaked over the grass and gently wrapped around her body.

Nature has finally decided to hide me. She laughed at the thought. Her head was spinning, and her right leg hurt.

Elisa looked down—the hilt of the guardian's knife was stuck in her hip. It couldn't be too deep. She wondered how she didn't notice it before and touched it with her fingers.

The sharp pain made her scream, and she fell to the wet ground. She lay on her back, and her tears rolled into her ears. She cried until the wave of pain subsided.

Silence hung in the air; only bugs buzzed over her head. The heavy smell of marshland wrapped around her. Elisa had no idea where she was or which direction she'd come from. She raised her hands—the wet absinthe rope blocked her magic channels. She tried to bite at it, but the sour taste of absinthe filled her mouth, and the rope was too thick. Pain shot up her leg again, and Elisa dropped her hands.

With blurred vision, Elisa looked up into the sky. There, beyond a layer of mist, was a piece of blue sky with floating white clouds.

Is this the end? She knew all people were in this world temporarily, but she couldn't believe that her moment had come. She couldn't feel anything she was supposed to feel—there was no calmness, no peace. Instead, a terrible feeling of loneliness scratched at her soul—worse than the pain in her injured leg. She moaned.

Once, she'd been a little girl who hid under the bed, but nothing had changed since then. She was still a girl who had screwed up after deciding to confront the cruelty of a man. She was always alone. Everyone left her. Her mother, Rose, and even Julia.

She remembered Lana's words: *No one will protect us but ourselves.* Elisa would do anything just to see Lana again. Elisa didn't know where she was—or where Lana was—but she wouldn't die without trying. She had to try. Not just for Julia, but for poor Rose and the girls whose Gifts hadn't manifested yet.

Elisa touched the ground, and her hand found a tough branch. She put it into her mouth and clenched it with her teeth. Then she sat up. Pain shot through her thigh again, making her gasp. She squeezed the knife's hilt with cold hands.

You can do it! One, two, three!

She pulled the knife out; the pain was so intense that she almost fainted. The blood stain on her dress was growing. She spit out the branch and started removing the rope. With the knife, she sawed at the rope in a frenzy, not paying attention to the cuts it was making on her wrists.

"There's no way I'm letting you capture me," she muttered to herself, and the sound of her voice made her feel alive. "Not today, asshole!"

Finally, the rope unraveled, and she was able to release her wrists. Elisa fell on her back and stretched up her hands. Silver Light leaked from her fingers, and it formed into a big bright ball with yellow sparkles. Elisa fed it with more energy to make it bigger. The guardians must have already started looking for her. Hopefully, they would notice her signal from far away.

Releasing the Light took the last of her energy. Elisa's head spun, and the pulsing pain in her hip increased. Her Light ball soared into the white clouds and burst into hundreds of pieces with a loud bang. She smiled and closed her eyes as the mist covered her consciousness.

Chapter 30. The Witch's House

The witch's house was hidden among tall pines on a hill. The wooden building had two floors and a dark gray facade, cracked from time and humidity. Big windows looked at the forest with an indifferent empty gaze.

When their horses stopped at the lakeshore where the trail ended, Lana jumped down to the sand. A long old staircase started where they stood and ended at the house's yard up above.

Lana touched the wooden railing; it was wet and smooth. Nothing had changed since she'd been here last. As she climbed, the stairs creaked under her boots.

But when she reached the yard, it was quiet—too quiet for the daytime. The windows were dusty, and the weeds grew tall in the flower beds. Lana walked to the front porch and stopped. Its white door was ajar, and three red fingerprints covered the surface. Her heart sank.

"Meredith?" Lana called out.

Only a cold breath of wind responded.

"Ghost," Richard said. "He was here."

Lana shook her head. "No. She was . . . she *is* a powerful witch. She would protect herself!"

"I'm sorry."

Lana stepped forward, but Richard took her hand to stop her. Lana hesitated.

"I'll go in alone," he said. "Stay here and cover me."

Lana opened her mouth, but she couldn't find any reason to argue. The murderer might still be inside, and she needed to stay outside in case Ghost tried to escape. It was the right decision. Lana stepped aside and let him walk into the house.

* * *

Lana walked along the perimeter of the property. It was quiet. She glanced at the time crystal on her bracelet. It was bright pink—almost noon. Richard had been inside for twenty minutes already. No one had broken the windows or run away.

The wooden planks squeaked as Richard walked onto the porch. She had never seen him like this—his eyes were dull, and his face was pale. Lana pushed him aside and ran in. He yelled something, but she didn't listen.

A dark hallway met her with silence and the smell of rotten flesh. Lana made a Light ball in her hand and moved forward. Her yellow Light illuminated shards of glass and wood on the dusty floor. An overthrown basket with umbrellas lay in the middle. Lana stepped over the basket and walked into the dark living room.

Thick velvet curtains covered the windows, not letting sunlight in. The witch had closed these curtains when she performed Light extraction rituals. She must have performed one and never opened them again. On the high walls were the black traces of Fireball spells. On a small coffee table, big brown stains covered the white table-cloth. Then Lana raised her eyes.

It was the witch, or what was left of her.

A belt had been tied to a chandelier with broken candle holders, and Meredith's dead body swayed in front of her. The belt was cinched around her thin gray neck, and her lifeless eyes were wide open. Lana put her hand over her mouth. She dropped her Light ball, and it burst into hundreds of sparkles.

Outside, she leaned over the porch railing, and her breakfast left her stomach. Lana wiped her lips with her sleeve and slid down to the wooden floor. Her whole body shivered. She leaned on the railing and closed her eyes.

Fresh air touched her face, and soon she could breathe again. Richard sat in front of her. His face was its normal color again, but she wasn't sure about hers.

"I found a note in there," Richard said. He took a folded piece of paper from his pocket and flapped the sheet to straighten it out. The sheet was torn in half. The letters blurred before her eyes.

Lana gave him a tired look.

"A suicide note," he said.

"Bullshit."

Richard nodded. "I know. You saw the house—there was a fight. He's just teasing us."

"Yesterday I tried to contact her, and I never realized why she didn't respond. I'm such a shitty detective."

He touched her hand. "Don't say that."

Lana sighed. "It's true. I just keep fooling myself; I'll never change anything. Not about Gift hunting, nor about this insane murderer, whoever he is. I'm useless, and I have to admit it and give up. I mean, *really* give up."

"No, Lana, you *are* a good detective; I know what I'm talking about. You noticed details that all the other guardians missed—even me. Like those letters on Rose's wrist. Honestly, I was impressed. You might not believe in yourself now, but you've made me believe in you." Richard didn't smile. Maybe he was lying again.

He squeezed her hand. "Of course, you still need some practice, but one day, you'll be brilliant. We're a good team; we really are."

Lana stared at him. She didn't know what had happened to him in the house, but his face had changed. His eyes were warm and calm, and her heart fluttered when she heard his voice.

Why was he supporting her? *What is the reason for this sudden kindness?*

Lana lowered her eyes. His hand still held her thin palm. She had promised not to use her Gift on him before they had left, but he'd broken his promise first. He was a liar—she knew it for sure; he'd said so last night when she was half asleep. Something had made her wake up when he was on duty, but she couldn't remember what.

Lana closed her eyes and let her Gift connect with his deceitful consciousness. The images of a summer forest blinked before her eyes, and then . . . everything faded in a blinding white light. Warmth covered her mind like the waves of a southern sea. She floated on its spotless waves, directionless.

Lana opened her eyes.

Richard took his hand away and frowned. She opened her mouth, but she couldn't say a word. *Gift blockage.* Only strong emotions could prevent her from using her Gift, but this time, Lana was not angry with him. The last time she'd been blocked like this before was when Charles brought her a bouquet of lilies when her father had invited him over for dinner.

She'd promised herself not to repeat the mistake twice, but now she sat in front of Richard, blinded by the same glare of love.

"Damn," she said.

Richard narrowed his eyes. "What did you see?"

"A . . . a forest?"

"And?"

"And that's it. Sorry."

Richard stood up and walked at the far end of the porch, which had a direct view of the lake. Lana approached him and shaded her eyes. The smooth water surface reflected the forest at the opposite bank. Her hand squeezed the railing.

Stupid. It had been so stupid to read his mind, and now she had no idea how to fix it.

"I didn't see anything, honestly," she said.

He scoffed. "Of course not. Unfortunately, honesty isn't one of your strengths."

"Yours either."

Richard rubbed his chin and looked at Lana. "I just can't believe he's doing it again. But you know what? He will not win this game. I should tell you everything before it's too late—"

A sudden bang interrupted his words. A Light ball burst into pieces above the three crowns at the opposite side of the lake. Silver and yellow sparkles shimmered in a blue sky. Lana recognized the Light right away.

"Elisa!" she shouted.

"It's somewhere at the marshes," Richard said.

"It's a big area."

He gave her a sharp look. "Do you have a better idea?"

Lana pulled a hand through her hair. Her fingers touched a smooth pearl—*Elisa's hairpin*. "I have this!" she said.

Richard gave her a perplexed look. "We don't have time for that!"

Lana didn't have time to explain. She took it out, and a strand of her hair fell to her shoulders. Lana placed the pin on the wooden floor and covered it with her Light. She whispered a Searching spell. Energy twirled around the pin and turned blue. The pin floated, then it moved to the staircase and flew down.

They both ran to the stairs. The pin eagerly awaited them; it circled above their horses by the lakeshore, ready to boost forward to Elisa. They had to hurry before the murderer found Elisa first.

Chapter 31. Everyone Has a Gift

The wet ground sucked at the horses' hooves as they galloped through the marshes. The wind whistled in Lana's ears. Elisa's glowing hairpin flew in front of them, leaving a trace of sparkles in the moist air.

They were fast, but not fast enough.

The Searching spell worked perfectly, but the connection was weakening. Every minute, the light faded, and the blue became almost gray.

Lana clasped Mandy's sides. "You're not going to die!" she screamed. "Not today!"

In this part of the forest, the mist was thick, and Lana had to slow down. The shimmering Searching spell led them through the fog until they reached an open space.

A silhouette in a black cloak was sitting on the ground. The hairpin fell.

Lana stopped her horse. "Elisa?" she called.

The figure stood and turned to them. He had a familiar thin face and pale blue eyes.

Lana widened her eyes. "Captain Turner?"

He took his hood off and stepped aside, limping.

Then, Lana saw Elisa. The girl lay on the grass with her hands crossed on her chest. The cuts on her wrists seemed almost black against her pale skin. A scary smile was frozen on her blue lips, and her cheek was wounded. The hem of her silk dress was ragged, and huge blood spots covered the bright green fabric. The hairpin lay on her chest. The dull light of the spell let Lana know that the girl was still alive.

Lana ran to her. She fell on her knees and pressed her hand to Elisa's cold forehead. Her pulse was weak.

She raised her eyes. "She's lost too much blood, but she's alive."

Both guardians stood in front of her in silence. Their faces were morose.

Then Richard shifted his gaze to Turner. "Captain, how did you get here so fast?"

"I saw the Light signal," he replied.

"From Triville?" Richard moved his hand, and a Paralyzing spell rose from his palm.

Turner raised his hand and cast the same spell; a silver ball sparkled in his hand. "I was fishing at the creek when I saw the Light signal."

Richard narrowed his eyes. "Where are your fishing supplies, then?"

"I left them and ran."

Lana sighed. While the men were arguing, time was passing. She touched Elisa's leg; there was a deep stab wound on her hip. Lana tore some cloth away from the hem of Elisa's dress and started wrapping it around her hip as a bandage.

The men stood five steps apart; their hands held Paralyzing spells, ready to fire.

"So, you won't mind if Lana checks you?" Richard asked.

"She should check you first." Turner shifted his gaze to Lana. "She's known me all her life. She has no reason to doubt me."

Richard looked at her. "You have no idea what secrets people hide."

Turner gave him a sharp look. "*You* are the stranger here. And you're wasting time. What are you hiding?"

Lana shook her head. Something was definitely wrong, but she didn't have time to think about it. The girl was more important now.

Lana pushed her palms forward, and yellow Light released from her fingers. The energy was bright, and it shone in her palms like a little sun. She closed her eyes and whispered a spell she'd learned in the Guardian House library. The ball in her hands blinked and thickened. Lana lowered her hands, and the spell sank into Elisa's chest. Elisa's blue lips became pinker.

Now everything depended on her.

Lana stood up on her weak feet; her head spun.

The men still held silver balls in their hands.

"Captain, what are you waiting for?" she asked. "Send a signal."

"We're too far away," he replied. "No one will notice a signal from here."

"But you noticed it from the creek, Captain," Richard said.

Turner frowned. "We're wasting time. Let's get out of here."

Richard stepped forward, and Turner raised his hand.

Richard raised his hand too. "It's a long walk from Triville creek," he said with a steely tone. "We saw the signal half an hour ago. You couldn't have gotten here so fast without a horse. You were nearby. Admit it, George Turner. Or I should call you *G. T.*?"

Turner scoffed. "Nonsense."

Richard gave him a sharp look. "You checked the personnel files and found nothing because it was *you*. All this time."

Lana shifted her gaze from Richard to Turner. Neither of them could be murderers. Maybe his initials matched, but he was Captain George Turner, a close friend of her family. When she was small, he'd visited their house. She'd climbed on his lap and asked him to tell her stories about the guardians.

Lana shifted her gaze to Richard. Her chest filled with warmth when she looked at him. Yes, she'd had doubts about him in the beginning, but her father had investigated him personally.

But they were acting like children. "Shut up!" Lana shouted with a Paralyzing spell in her hand.

They both looked at her in surprise.

"Drop the spells. Drop them! I don't care who I shoot." Her voice sounded like thunder.

They both lowered their hands, and the balls fell to the wet ground.

"I trust you both. For the sake of common sense, let's go!"

Richard grinned. "Hear that, Captain? Go with Lana. I'll take Elisa."

"I won't let you take the girl, murderer. Want to finish what you started?"

Richard let out an exasperated breath. "Damn it, Lana, he's trying to buy time!"

Lana looked at the captain. "Why don't you take my horse? Richard will carry Elisa."

Turner looked at her with wide eyes. "Do you trust me?"

Lana nodded.

"Then shoot him!" He pointed to Richard.

Lana shook her head. "He's not a murderer."

His pale eyes pierced her. "Really? Oh, *I see.* You always had a weakness for guardians."

Lana raised her eyebrows. "Captain, pull yourself together! Richard and I were together the whole—"

Turner moved his hand, and she stepped back. He raised his voice. "Are you sure? Did you watch him the whole time? Did you sleep last night?"

Lana looked at Richard. "He's right—you left this morning."

"Okay," Richard said. "I don't see any other way. Shoot me."

"What? I can't shoot you!"

Richard gave her a warm look. "Trust me. When I repeat my words, you'll know what to do."

Lana gave him a puzzled look. *What is he talking about?*

He closed his eyes and stretched out his hands to his sides. "Shoot me!" he said.

Lana sighed, then she threw her hand forward. Her spell hit his shoulder, and he fell to his knees.

Fire danced in Captain Turner's eyes. He grinned and raised his hands, then a thick branch tore from a tree and fell on Richard.

Richard tried to jump away, but the branch hit his back, and he fell. He lay on the ground, motionless.

Lana froze, uncomprehending.

Turner stumbled toward her; his breath was heavy. "Little bitch," he said. "I found your traces in the secret filing room the week after you arrived."

Lana moved back, but she bumped into the rough trunk of a fir. "I just wanted to know what happened to your daughter—"

"It's none of your business!" he shouted. "When you pried into this case, I tried to get rid of you. I put a strand of your hair in the file to make your father fire you, but the man is a fool. He always has been."

Lana gasped. "Don't say that!"

He laughed and raised his hand. Another branch started to break above her head. Shards of wood fell on the ground.

"Your daddy will be so upset when he finds your lifeless body near Elisa." He swung his hand. "He'll finally feel my pain."

Lana looked up. The branch tore from the fir tree with a loud crack and started falling. Maybe it was time to pray, but she couldn't remember any prayers. Divine did not matter now; Richard was all she could think of. *If only I trusted him.* Lana raised her hand, touching the fir's sharp needles.

Then time stopped.

She blinked, and the branch was hanging in the air above her. Turner stood in front of her, an ugly smile frozen on his face. Elisa still lay in the grass, motionless.

Richard sat on the ground with his hand outstretched. His eyes shone with bright green Light.

The bracelet on her hand vibrated. Lana's time crystal shone pure white.

A time Gift?

Richard drew a spiral in the air, and everything around them started moving back. First, the branch over her head rose and repaired itself, then Captain Turner took two steps back and raised his hands. Richard rose from the ground and jumped backward, then the branch flew away from him and reattached itself to the broken tree.

When I repeat my words, you will know what to do. The things around her finally arrived at the moment when everything started going downhill. Lana breathed out. Richard was alive, and the power of his Gift had saved them both. It was her move now. This time, she wouldn't be so foolish.

Lana cast the Paralyzing spell in her trembling hands. She added more energy and made the ball thicker this time—hopefully enough to bring this maniac down.

Richard smiled, then he closed his eyes and stretched his arms open, waiting for the spell's embrace. "Shoot me!" he commanded.

Turner had a calm expression on his deceitful face.

"Bastard!" Lana said. She stretched out her hand, and the spell hit his chest.

Captain Turner froze; none of his muscles moved.

"Good job!" Richard cried. He walked toward Turner and closed the man's eyes.

Turner fell to the ground.

Chapter 32. People We Never Forget

Lana sat beside Elisa's head and murmured a complicated spell. Her bright yellow Light floated over the injured girl. Richard approached her and stood nearby, waiting.

"I sent a signal, just in case, and I received a response signal in return," he said when Lana finished the spell. "The guardians are coming, but we can start moving toward them."

She nodded. Her sight was blurry.

"Are you okay?" he asked.

"I'm fine," she said. Her voice was weak. "I just want to make sure she'll survive the trip."

"How will you ride?"

"I won't. You carry Elisa to Triville."

Richard gave her a worried look. "I handcuffed the captain, but he might wake up before the guardians arrive."

"I'll punch him in the face, then."

He chuckled. "I bet you will. We're a good team, huh?"

Lana smiled. "We really are."

Richard stood and took Elisa in his arms; she weighed almost nothing. He mounted Coal and glanced at Lana. "Just be careful."

"If not, can't you turn back time?"

He shook his head. "I can't avert death."

"Don't waste time, then," Lana said. "Go."

Richard nodded and rode away.

Lana crawled toward Turner. The man lay on the grass, and his hands were tied behind his back with magic-blocking cuffs. His cloak was half open, revealing a blood stain on his pants and at the bottom of his gray shirt.

"Good job, girl," Lana whispered and touched the rough, cold skin of his hand. She closed her eyes.

Scenes of his life flashed before her. Elisa smiled and took a sip from a teacup. Then she was tied to the tree trunk, blood streaming down her cheek. Then Lana saw Rose. The girl gave Turner some sheets of paper with trembling hands. Then she lay in the glade, screaming.

Lana moved back into his memories. Rebecca's blue eyes got teary as she shrank into the corner of the barn. She cried, begging him not to send her away from home.

Lana opened her eyes. With her head spinning, she had to lay on her back to keep from fainting. The mist floated above her, and the white puffy clouds turned gray. Her eyelids were heavy, and she closed her eyes for a moment. She couldn't open them again. Lana fought the tiredness until she heard the voices of the guardians and the shrill neighing of their horses.

Her father's strong voice commanded the team. "Split up! Charles, take two men and keep following Richard's traces on the trail. They will lead you to the witch's house."

Charles hesitated. "But Lana . . ."

"She'll be alright." Her father replied in a softer voice. "But Turner killed the witch, and he might have left evidence. Now, go there and investigate the crime scene. Check every damn inch if it's necessary to find proof against this bastard."

"Yes, sir!"

When Charles left, her father approached her. "It's alright. You are safe now."

His hands lifted her from the ground; Lana fell into a gray cloudy nowhere and sank into the fog.

* * *

Richard stood at the big house with the red roof. Evening sunrays warmed its white walls and round flower beds. The entrance door opened, and a woman in a long skirt ran out to the yard. She had wavy blonde hair and warm blue eyes.

With Elisa in his arms, Richard walked to the woman.

She touched Elisa's shoulder. "Lizzy, my dear. You're home now."

Elisa moved her head, and her lips moved. "Julia," she said.

They walked into the bright living room, and Richard placed the girl on the sofa. Her face was pale. The blood stain on her cheek was now dry and brown.

The woman took a wet towel and started wiping Elisa's face.

"Did you call for a doctor?" Richard asked.

The woman nodded. "Yes, I warned him after I saw the guardians. He'll be here soon."

"When did you see the guardians?"

She sighed. "At sunrise. Lizzy didn't come home last night, and I didn't know what to do. Then Kyle and some other guardians came. They told me that Elisa might be in danger."

The woman put the towel down and sobbed. Richard touched her hand, and the woman gave him a worried look. "I gave them her earrings for a Searching spell."

"And it worked," Richard said. "You did a good job, Julia."

The woman shook her head. "No, I'm Rachel, her aunt. Julia is her best friend. She lives across the road."

Elisa's breath was calm. The vein on her forehead was dark blue, which meant she had lost too much blood. Lana shared her life energy with this girl, but it wasn't enough to heal her. Fortunately, magic potions could heal almost every disease, and the doctor must have something.

The door opened, and a short man in his fifties walked into the room. He wore a simple white gown, with an embroidered golden heart over his chest. He carried a small satchel in his plump hand, containing his powders and potions.

"Doctor Fitzgerald," the man introduced himself.

After a brief acquaintance, the man sat by Elisa and examined her with his red Light. His forehead wrinkled. He took Elisa's wrist and felt her weak pulse.

"She just muttered something," Rachel said. "She'll be fine, right?"

The doctor ignored her question and looked at Richard. "Did anyone share their life energy with her?"

"Yes," Richard said. "We created a spell so I could carry her."

"Good," the doctor said. He placed Elisa's hand on her chest. "She has more time, but I'm afraid I have bad news."

Richard gave him a sharp look. "Don't tell me you are out of potions."

The doctor sighed. "That's not it. All potions require good blood circulation, and in her case, the potion will only cause damage to her veins . . . I'm sorry."

Rachel dropped her face into her palms.

Richard put his hand on her shoulder. "We caught the murderer because of Elisa. She won't give up until the end—we should do the same. I'll try to find a solution."

Rachel raised her blurry eyes and nodded.

* * *

Richard walked outside and crossed the road, his steps heavy on the pavement. The evening sunlight illuminated a small house on the opposite side of the road. He was still on duty, and it felt like this day was never-ending. Once, he'd heard that people always remembered the face of the person who delivered tragic news. He had that responsibility now.

He walked onto the porch and knocked three times. The door opened, and a teenage girl with a swollen face and messy hair looked at him with hesitation. Her hazel eyes stopped at the dragon embroidery at his shoulder, and she covered her mouth.

"You must be Julia," he said.

She nodded.

"I'm Lieutenant Richard Laine, and I am investigating the murder case."

Julia looked at him, awaiting the scary news.

If only he could answer her silent question. If only Elisa had a chance.

Richard sighed. "She is alive, but—"

Julia burst into tears and hugged Richard.

"Thank you," Julia whispered. She wiped her tears and shifted her gaze to Elisa's house.

"She is alive, Julia, but she's lost too much blood."

She gave him a puzzled look. "What do you mean? The doctor must heal her."

He sighed. "I hate to say this—I'm so sorry. She has two days, maximum three. Sometimes, all we can do is say goodbye."

Julia pushed him aside. She ran down the porch steps and crossed the road.

When she disappeared behind Elisa's door, Richard walked on the empty street. The trees along the road shivered under the warm wind. The murderer had been caught, but his case had only just begun.

Chapter 33. Naked Truth

Rain droplets hit the yellow roof of the Guardian House and pattered against the windows. Lana sat at the desk in her office, the candlelight lighting up her notebook. She leaned over the papers and wrote the last line of her report.

Lana bit her pencil, read the report one more time, and smiled, satisfied with the result. She glanced at her bracelet—the time crystal was bright blue, and she would see the guardians soon. All of them. Lana's heart fluttered in her chest.

Richard. He was an interesting man and a brilliant detective. For him, she would leave everything behind and embrace the ocean of this endless glare of love.

The rain continued to hit the window, but the dull day couldn't ruin her mood. Her father said he'd carried Lana to Triville, and she'd slept for fifteen hours. Finally, she'd woken up from a long dream filled with fears and doubts. She'd missed the captain's arrest, but she didn't care. They'd finally caught the murderer, and he would pay for all he'd done.

The door opened, and Charles appeared in the doorway, holding a yellow folder. The golden dragon on his shoulder shone. He smiled and walked into the room without waiting for an invitation.

"What do you need?" Lana asked.

Charles sat on a chair in front of her and placed his folder on his lap. He took the wooden nameplate from her desk. "*Secretary Lana Morris,*" he read.

"That's me."

He laughed with his eyes. "Well, I have to admit—you've impressed us all."

Lana took the nameplate from him and put it back. "I was just doing my job."

He nodded. "You caught the real murderer. Who could have known it was Turner?"

"True evil always reveals itself in unexpected ways. The closest people to us are the most dangerous."

"Is it a thorn in my side?"

Lana shrugged. "Put it however you want."

He chuckled. "Oh, come on, Dandelion. I'm not your enemy."

"You're not my friend, either."

Charles placed his folder on her desk and opened it. Turner's file lay on top with his photograph; the captain was young, his hair was dark, and he wore a black beard. His pale eyes looked at her with a calm confidence.

Lana sighed. It was nice to rely on people, but it wasn't safe.

Charles turned the page. "I just want you to clarify some details."

Lana narrowed her eyes. "Which details?"

"I'm responsible for investigating the boy. What's his name . . . ? Kyle, I believe."

"What about him?"

"I just need to check on him—he's not a guardian, but he helped with the case. Oh, you don't know."

Lana shook her head.

Charles smiled. "Of course, Sleeping Beauty. Well, the boy was actually the one who called the guardians. When we came, his home was clean. No energy traces, no evidence that Elisa was ever there. And it was suspicious—Kyle saw her coming into the house. Why would the guardian captain remove her traces?"

"To fake Ghost's steps."

Charles nodded. "Exactly. But he was in a rush and missed something—we found a drop of sleeping potion on a tablecloth. We had to disturb her aunt to take the girl's earring, then I cast a Searching spell. We got lucky—the girl was still alive. We followed the spell and found you."

"Elisa managed to escape," Lana said. "She can be a witness."

"Unfortunately, she cannot give testimony. The doctor said she won't wake up."

Lana's heart sank.

"You did everything right, Lana. We already sent a letter to Santos for a healer, and now we are waiting. Elisa has a chance."

Lana stayed silent.

"Let's concentrate on the investigation now," Charles said. "Yesterday, before we found you and Turner, we met Richard, who reported about the witch's murder. I took two guys from our team to check this crime scene and find the evidence against Turner. We took the blood traces from the witch's door, but it gave us nothing, as it belonged to the witch. No other traces were in the house—the same Erasing spell."

Lana put her palms on the desk. Her head was spinning. Kyle had called the guardians, so he'd known and suspected something. Why hadn't he opened his mouth before?

Lana took the file with Turner's picture. It was hard to believe that someone that close to her could do such terrible things.

"Kyle isn't a bad person," Lana said. "He wanted to protect the girls."

"Then why didn't he?"

Lana shrugged. "Fear, plus a personal connection with the murderer. Maybe in the depths of our souls, we still believe that people can change."

He gave her a warm look. "People change, Lana. Not completely, but we do. For big things if they're worth it."

Lana sighed. It was the same sneaky Charles. He had stolen her heart and put all the blame on her after she'd helped him investigate a domestic violence case.

Well, maybe he was the same, but she was no longer that girl with a crazy dream to become a guardian—a girl who didn't care about the price. He was right; people changed for big things. But while she knew her purpose, she didn't know his.

Lana pulled open her desk drawer and took out a white memory crystal. Yellow sparkles danced inside. The crystal held on to their voices and everything Kyle had said the night Rose went missing.

"That's an expensive thing. Where did you get it?" Charles asked.

"It doesn't matter where it's from. What matters is what's inside. I recorded Kyle when he confessed. I'll give it to you if you answer my question."

He put his palms on the table surface. "Deal. What do you want to know?"

"Why did you change?"

"My career, of course," he replied immediately. "Turner is gone. Now the captain's position is vacant."

Lana twirled the crystal in her fingers. "The king is dead. Long live the king!"

He stretched out his hand. "Your turn."

Lana placed the crystal in his open palm. Charles squeezed it in his hand and listened. Leaves rustled, and the river rushed by. Lana's voice whispered something to Elisa. Kyle talked with Julia in the background.

Charles smiled, and the crystal blinked and faded. "I've missed working with you," he said.

Lana chuckled. "This ship has sailed."

"Maybe not. Listen, four years ago, we were just kids. We were so obsessed with our careers that we hurt each other. But we'll be working together from now on, and I'll support you."

She raised her eyebrows. "You'll what?"

He smiled. "I know it sounds strange, but I put professionalism first now. What I did when we worked on that case was completely wrong. I was a guardian, and I was supposed to take the responsibility."

"Oh, look at you with the late apologies."

"Put it however you want, but I never wanted to hurt you. We were both stupid—blind with ambition."

"That doesn't sound like an apology."

Charles put his hand over hers. "Listen, Lana. You might think that this Richard guy is awesome, but I can see his true face. He's like me—fooling everyone. You don't know the whole truth."

"I don't need it. It's called *trust*."

"I don't want to pry, but I can't stay silent. I can't see how you would want to go through the same shit again."

"He is not you. Richard is different."

"We are all men, Lana, and we are *all* the same."

She crossed her arms over her chest. "Of course. That changes everything."

"Hide behind your sarcasm if you want, but I know you. The *real* you."

"What do you want?"

"You should know something. This Richard . . . do you know that he's been convicted? He'll become a warder on Death Island as soon as this case is closed. He had nothing to lose, and I'm afraid that stealing this case was his bargaining chip."

Lana raised her eyebrows. "And why was he sentenced?"

"He had an affair with his chief's wife."

Lana snorted. "Bullshit."

Charles leaned back in his chair. "Well, I don't blame him—she's a beautiful woman. Big brown eyes, red hair. The red-haired ones are deeply passionate, don't you know?"

Lana bit her lip. The report on her desk blurred in her vision. Red hair and brown eyes—she'd seen this picture already on the day she'd met Richard. She would never forget the day when they stayed alone on the wide trail, and they rode together, talking. Lana had tried to read him, but he pushed her out of his mind with a frank bedroom scene.

She'd never cared about his past, but the fact that the woman was his ex-chief's wife . . . well, it was too much to handle. Lana shifted her gaze back to Charles. "Get out of my office," she said in a flat tone.

Charles raised his eyebrows, then he put the memory crystal in his pocket. "Lana, calm down," he said.

It was too late; she grabbed his yellow folder and threw it at him. Charles caught the folder, but some sheets fell out. He bent to collect them from the floor.

Lana stood up and opened the door. "Get out!"

Charles glanced at her. "I'm sorry, Dande—"

"Out!" she shouted.

He shook his head and walked away.

When Charles stepped over the threshold, Lana slammed the door closed. She walked to her desk and took the book with the white dragon on its cover. The girl who rode the dragon smiled, her red hair flowing behind her and her green eyes laughing. Lana threw the book at the door.

The spine released its dull yellow pages, and they burst out. They slowly glided down and covered the dark wooden floor, like giant ash flakes. This is how dreams always ended, and nothing would ever change it.

Lana took the notebook from her desk and walked out of the room.

* * *

Richard stood at the end of a long corridor in the Guardian House. The chief's door was before him, but he didn't want to walk in there alone. Outside, the street was dull and gray. Dark clouds hung in the sky, ready to burst with rain and lightning. Quick steps sounded from the corridor, and Richard turned his face toward the sound.

Lana ran at him. Her cheeks were red, and her eyes flashed with pure anger. Her thin fingers squeezed a notebook.

Richard stepped back, and his elbow touched the cold glass of the outside window.

"What's happened?" he asked.

"You're a good detective, Lieutenant Laine, but you're a shitty person." Her voice was as cold as a shard of ice.

"Okay, I don't know what happened, but the audition is about to start."

Lana pierced him with her burning gaze.

Richard glanced at the door. "We should give our testimonies to the chief. We can deal with everything else later."

She pressed her notebook to his chest, and he took it. "You can go alone, Richard," she said, her voice dripping with sarcasm. "I can rely on your professionalism."

"I rely on yours too. We'll go in together."

"Tell him everything you need to—how you found the murderer, took control of the operation, and fixed my mistakes. Oh, and don't forget to remind him that I read the confidential case file and made a deal with the forest witch. It could give you some points."

Richard stretched his hand toward her, but Lana stepped back.

"Why would I do that?" he asked.

"Well, I don't really know, Richard. Maybe because you're a liar." She shook her head. "You are such a liar!"

Richard was speechless. That night in the forest, she wasn't fully asleep. *I'm such a liar,* this was what he said, and she must have heard it. *What else did she see?*

Lana sighed and turned away. Her slim black silhouette disappeared into the shade of the corridor. Richard shook his head. Even if she'd heard him, it didn't explain her sudden change in mood.

Lana was an interesting woman, but she was still too young. She was in her early twenties—an age he knew too well. It was a time when childish fears argued with the wisdom of adulthood. He was probably expected to run after her and ask what happened, or maybe she wanted him to calm her down.

Richard stayed where he was. Whatever had happened, it was her fight, not his.

Heavy rain droplets hit the glass behind him. It shivered and clinked in the wind. Lighting tore across the sky and lit up the empty corridor. The report that she'd given him was written in her precise handwriting. Richard walked into the chief's office and closed the door behind him.

Chapter 34. Hope

A cool evening wind brushed against the white curtains in the Guardian House's library. Lana sat on the floor, surrounded by books. The library was filled with information about spells, potions, and herbs. She turned the page and put the book down—there wasn't anything useful in any of the medical handbooks or potion guides.

During the last two days, she'd managed to find recipes for things she'd never thought about: fixing broken bones, healing sepsis, and even connecting torn limbs, but there was nothing about recovering from massive blood loss. It was time to admit the truth—she was at a dead end. All the concoctions relied on blood, and the doctors wouldn't be able to help Elisa. The guardians had sent for a healer, but they hadn't managed to find the one.

Lana closed *The Encyclopedia of Potions* and bit her lip. Another book was near her feet—*The Book of Gifts*. Each Gift had its own limit, and they were all capricious—they refused to manifest when people craved them and revealed themselves in the most improper moments. At the same time, almost anything was possible with the right Gift. Lana opened the book and found the chapter on healers.

In a population of a million people, the Healing Gift manifests in one person, she read. Her eyes slid down.

Healing energy can reverse the process of tissue degeneration. It mends broken bones, stops interior bleeding, and cures inner and external wounds. . . .

If missing, this energy multiplies the useful liquids in a body, including the water in tissues, plasma, and blood. . . .

Healing energy glows a bright pink color; it is warm. It finds the weak places in the sick body, absorbs negative energy, and allows it to leave the body. All that remains after this process is a small scar at the exit point.

The Gift's Limitations: a patient cannot be dead for more than five minutes or be of close blood relation to the healer, and no romantic feelings/sexual attraction can be present between the healer and the patient. The Healing Gift may be applied to the same person only once.

Lana put the book down and rubbed her temples. *Awesome.* It was the only solution for Elisa, but the Healing Gift was *rare.* There were no healers in Triville, and even if someone found a healer in Santos, Elisa could be dead by the time they arrived. Lana's time crystal on her bracelet was purple, which meant that another day was almost gone, and it hadn't brought anything useful.

The door opened, and her father walked into the room. Lana put the book away and stood up. She would read his thoughts if she could avoid asking him about Elisa out loud. But her father knew her too well, and he understood her anxious look.

"Elisa is still asleep," he said.

Lana sighed. "Did they find a healer?"

Her father shook his head.

She lowered her eyes. "I see."

Her father walked across the room and sat on a wide green sofa. He patted the seat next to him, and she sat down.

"Lana, I think you've done enough," he said.

"How do you know?"

"Trust your old father, I know how much is *enough.*"

She stayed silent. There was nothing to argue—he was right. He was always right, even when she wanted to yell and crush the walls. He put his hand on hers, and its warmth calmed her thoughts.

"Lana, you cannot lock yourself in this room forever. These books won't give you all the answers. Some things must run their course."

"Just let it go? Is that your answer?"

He shook his head. "You're very stubborn, Lana, but your stubbornness isn't always helpful."

"What is, then?"

He sighed. "If the doctor is correct, tomorrow is her last day. It's time to say goodbye."

"No way."

"Lana." He squeezed her hand. "I need your Gift now. It's the only way to make Turner pay for everything he's done. The bastard didn't leave any useful evidence. But he might confess to Elisa."

Lana took her hand away. "You want me to read her? No, she's too weak. It could take the last of her energy."

He gave her a tired look. The wrinkles around his eyes were deeper than they had been four years ago, and Lana was the main cause of it. She always had been. How many worries had she brought into his life, already full of daily stresses? She couldn't even count. The least she could do was help the investigation with her Gift. The price was too high, but if she didn't do it, Elisa would die for nothing.

He petted her shoulder. "You'll do it, won't you?"

She nodded. "Tomorrow."

His eyes were warm. "The court hearing is coming up. You'll have to be there."

She widened her eyes. "Me?"

"Yes. Richard said you could give testimony as a mind reader."

Lana snorted.

"You're too strict with him. Don't you think?"

She scoffed. "He's unbearable!"

"So are you." Her father smiled.

Lana shook her head.

"He relied on you, Lana, because you helped us a lot with this case."

"What do you want me to do? Kiss and bless him?"

He laughed. "You could just be . . . a bit kinder."

She bit her lip.

He clasped his hands and arose. "Just think about it, okay?"

Lana sat on the sofa in silence. Her father stood in front of her like a rock. A rock that had always protected her from everything—at least, he tried to. Lana stood and hugged him.

"Are you all right?" he asked.

"Thank you for everything. I'm such a mess."

"This is my job, daughter. To handle the mess."

Lana pushed her face into his shoulder, so he couldn't see her tears. She took a deep breath; his black jacket smelled of tobacco and tiredness.

"You know what's a mess?" he asked. "The post of the captain."

Lana wiped her eyes. "Did you speak with Charles?"

He frowned. "That's the problem. Since Turner was arrested, everyone has been sneaking around. I'm so tired of people trying to influence me."

"You're the chief. Everyone will obey your orders, whether they want to or not. I know you'll make the right choice."

He touched her forehead. "You must have a fever."

Lana pushed his hand away. "I'm fine!"

"Something has happened to you."

Lana shrugged. Many things had happened since this case started; her life had turned upside down. She was questioning everything she believed in. All the romantic feelings she abandoned before now rose and grew like weeds. "It's just been a terrible week," she said.

"That's true."

Lana hugged him again. She couldn't rely on herself, at least not now. Maybe her father would know how to deal with Richard, but she would never dare ask. Not after all the mistakes she'd made.

* * *

When her father left, Lana leaned on the windowsill. Night approached Triville with quiet steps, and windows lit up in houses. She wondered where Richard was and what was he doing. She hadn't seen him at all in two days, buried in library books. Her father had told her that Richard supported her.

Interesting.

Under the window, a rose bush was growing, its small buds closed and not yet ready to blossom. Roses were beautiful and tender like hearts. They grew sharp spikes to protect themselves from enemies.

Somehow, Richard had climbed into her bud despite all of her protection. Now he was comfortably sitting there on the red petals of her soul, drinking from his flask and telling her his sarcastic jokes. What did she need all the spikes for?

What would it be like to kiss him? The image warmed her belly.

She walked to the sofa and lay down. His laughing green eyes flashed amid the carousel of murderers and victims. He had been kind enough to share his case with her, and he'd stayed professional—even when she'd yelled at him. But he'd also slept with his chief's wife.

"Have a good night, Richard," Lana whispered.

She turned her face into the back of the sofa and closed her eyes. An anxious dream hugged her consciousness, and she embraced it.

Chapter 35. Ice and Flame

The small pub was busy, and loud men's voices filled the room—guardians drank and played cards. A strip of evening light fell on the bar where Richard sat alone.

The bartender put an empty glass in front of him. "What are you drinking today?"

Richard raised his eyes. "Whiskey, neat."

The bartender smiled and poured dark brown liquid into his glass. A sunbeam danced in the liquor like the fire that had played in her brown eyes that night. Richard sighed and touched the glass. It was cold—exactly like her. For the last couple of days, he hadn't seen Lana. She'd locked herself in the library, searching for a cure that didn't exist.

Richard twisted the glass in his hand and drank the liquid. There was a chance that this case would bring about justice, but the only witness was in a coma without any hope of survival. The drink warmed his stomach and soothed his anxiety. He'd done everything he could. Now it was time to say goodbye to this town.

Someone's hand touched his shoulder. It was a tall man with bright blue eyes and a wide smile.

"Charles Braun?" Richard asked.

"That's me."

Richard nodded. "I read your report on Turner's case. Good job, Lieutenant."

"You too."

Richard put his glass on the bar and waved his hand. The bartender poured him another portion of whiskey.

Charles gave him a judging look. "Don't get carried away. The court hearing is tomorrow."

"I know, but it's not my case."

"What do you mean?"

Richard shrugged. "I came here to find Ghost. Turner is a different case. So, I'm done here."

Charles nodded. "New adventures ahead, huh?"

"If you can call Death Island an adventure."

Charles waved his hand, and without asking, the bartender brought him the glass with whiskey and a plate with tree nuts.

In small towns like this, everyone knew each other's faces, and no extra words were required. If only it were that easy for him. If only he could find the way to be with Lana.

Charles drank from his glass and exhaled. He moved the nuts closer to Richard. "You seem like a fine man, Laine. I just don't understand one thing."

"What?"

Charles put his glass on the bar and wiped the rim with his index finger. "You found Turner, and you actually caught him. It was brilliant work, and this case was murky. Catching a serial killer, who was a guardian captain, could mean a lot for your career. You had a chance to use it to avoid your punishment—or at least get some slack—but you gave all the credit to a woman you hardly know."

Richard emptied his glass. "All mistakes have a price. I made a mess; I can't run from responsibility anymore."

"You really feel guilty."

Richard shook his head. His mind was filled with different feelings that choked him and squeezed his heart, but a sense of guilt wasn't one of them. Anyway, no one needed to hear about his personal shit.

Richard looked at Charles. The guardian was not an ordinary person—Richard could almost smell his ambition. Maybe he could figure out *his* shit and make this evening a bit more interesting.

"What about you?" Richard asked.

"What about me?"

"The day after we caught Turner, when we all met with the chief, you used the memory crystal as evidence to protect Kyle. Lana gave it to you, but you didn't put it in your account. Instead, you said that *she* gave it to you. Why?"

"Because I'm a professional."

"Really?" Richard grinned. "Come on, buddy, we're never going to see each other again. You seem like a fine man with good strategies. Maybe I can learn from you."

Charles looked around before moving closer to Richard. "I need your word that you won't tell anyone."

Richard lifted his palm. "I give you my Lieutenant's word."

Charles nodded. He turned the empty glass in his hand. "I made a mistake, too. Once, I worked with Lana on a case. At the time, she was helping with paperwork in the Guardian House. She helped me a bit with the case, but after we failed, I put all responsibility on her to save my job."

Richard widened his eyes. "I didn't know that. Why are you kind to her now?"

Charles chuckled. "It's dangerous to underestimate your enemies, but even more so with ex-girlfriends."

"What do you mean?"

Charles threw some nuts in his mouth and made a hand gesture to the bartender before continuing. "The thing is, she's the chief's daughter. She's the best way for me to gain his trust. If we become a couple, I can take Morris's place when he retires."

Richard gave him a sharp look. "You're very ambitious."

"When a piece of pie lands on your table, it's stupid not to take it."

Richard squeezed the empty glass in his hand, his heart pounding. "What about her? Won't she read you right away?"

Charles smiled. "I'm not worried about that part. When we were together, she was in love. Love protects us from using our Gifts."

"She won't forgive you if she finds out."

"As people say, love always finds a way. It's unbelievable how much shit we can leave behind. Everything for the sake of the sweet poison."

Richard narrowed his eyes. "You are *not* in love."

"Love is way overrated. In fact, it's useless. It blinds us and blocks our Gifts. Lana is a good option; I'll have full control over the situation, and she . . . well, she's stubborn—passionate, if you know what I mean." Charles winked.

Richard squeezed his glass harder, and it cracked in his palm. Some of the shards fell on the table. The voices around him quietened. Richard opened his fist and brushed away the rest of the shards. His palm wasn't hurt. There was no pain, no blood. Everything seemed fake—exactly like the man beside him.

Charles smirked. "Take it easy, Laine. You're too drunk."

Richard clenched his fist. "No, I'm finally seeing everything clearly."

Charles opened his mouth, but before he could say a word, Richard rammed his fist into his cheek. Charles's chair swung back, and he fell to the floor with a deafening crash.

Richard stood up from his chair. The surprised guardians around them stopped talking and watched.

Charles pushed himself up on his elbow. "What the fuck, man?"

Richard rubbed his throbbing knuckles. "I wanna ask you the same question."

Charles spat on the floor. His bloody saliva was hardly visible on the dirty wooden floor. "Your word means nothing."

"I won't say anything," Richard said, lifting his hand.

The guardians around them finally rose from their chairs with Paralyzing spells in their hands. In the dark pub, the silver spheres looked like glowing moons.

Richard was surrounded.

Charles stood up and stepped toward him, but two guardians held his arms. "You're a dead man!" he shouted.

A red-haired young guardian glanced at Richard with anxiety. "You better go," he whispered.

Charles glared. "He's right. Get out of our town, before it's too late."

Richard lowered his hand and backed up. The guardians surrounded Charles, asking him questions. Richard turned to the exit and walked out into the dark evening.

Warm wind touched his burning face. Charles was a shitty man, but he was right—it was time to get out of this town. Richard fixed the collar of his jacket and walked along the alley.

Chapter 36. Witness

The bed was too wide for such a thin girl. Elisa's motionless hands had deep scratches, and they lay on top of the soft blanket. Her golden hair had lost its shine and lay on her frail shoulders like pieces of dry, brittle clay. The dying sun rays lit up her pale face, and a bright cut looked burned into her cheek.

Julia sat on a chair near the bed and listened to Elisa's faltering breath. Each time it stopped, Julia's heart skipped a beat. She held Elisa's cold hand with both of hers, but it wasn't enough to warm her up.

"Forgive me," Julia whispered. "Please, don't die!" Tears rolled down her cheeks, but she didn't wipe them away. She clutched Elisa's hand, worried that if she released it, Elisa's spirit would leave her body.

The door creaked open, and quiet steps approached. A woman in a simple white dress stood at the door, her flaxen hair lying on her thin shoulders.

"Lana," Julia said through her tears, hardly recognizing her.

Lana came in and sat by Julia. "Tears won't help," Lana said.

Julia sobbed anyway. Lana took a handkerchief and carefully wiped Julia's puffy face.

"How long have you been here?" Lana asked.

Julia gave her tired look. "I don't know. Since I heard about . . ." She moved her lips, but she couldn't finish the sentence.

Lana looked around the room—a big wooden bed took up most of the space. There was a night table with a nondescript candle holder, and one of the candles was burnt out. A round mirror on a wooden frame hung over the wide dresser. Lana's eyes stopped on a lonely plush teddy bear. A dark spot covered the bear's arm—dried blood. But one piece of evidence was never enough for the guardians. They always waited for more, and it never ended well.

Lana looked at Elisa's still face. "I'm so sorry. I was late. Too late."

"It's not your fault," Julia said.

"If I only had a little more time."

Lana hung her head. The small room pressed in on her. Elisa, this fearless girl, would never open her eyes again. *They were such a deep blue.* Elisa had played her part, and it was Lana's move now. She must do what her father asked, to put a dot in Rebecca's case, even knowing that it would take Elisa's last energy.

Lana put her palm on the blanket by Elisa's hand.

"We should hope for the best," Julia said. "Our guardians are looking for a healer."

"Healing is a very rare Gift; didn't you know that?"

Julia nodded. "One in a million."

Lana sighed and placed her hand back in her lap.

"Lana?"

"Yes?"

Julia lowered her eyes. "Can I ask you something personal?"

"Of course. What do you want to know?"

"How did you get your Gift?"

Lana gave her a sad smile. "Love."

"Love?"

Lana nodded. "Yes, love is a great moving force. Its power can open the beauty of your Gift. But it also doesn't let you hurt the ones who you love—like a shield, it protects them."

"Does it protect you?"

"Yes. I'm not able to read the thoughts of the people I love—or once loved. I can't read my father's thoughts."

Julia smiled. "Maybe that's for the best."

Lana shrugged. "Maybe."

Julia sighed. "Oh, Lana, this week was terrible. The other day, I was so mad at Elisa. Just so mad . . . I'm afraid that one day, I'll release my power and kill someone. I don't want to have a Gift. Maybe it's better not to have one."

Lana petted her shoulder. "It depends on the Gift. If it's destructive, it might manifest when you're angry. But if it's like mine, it will require the opposite feeling."

Julia squirmed in her chair. "If I only knew whether it was love."

"You won't. You'll just feel it or not."

"I'm so afraid. I feel like I'm about to jump off a cliff."

Lana smiled. "I'll tell you what. A bird that is too afraid to fly will sit in its nest until it dies. Yes, love might hurt, and it might be a huge disappointment, but it also brings moments of joy. You can be afraid, but if you stay that way, you'll never see the true beauty of life. Come on, you have two wings! Why not use them? Why not feel the lightness of your body and the wind on your face?"

"The wind on my face," Julia repeated, closing her eyes. A memory of Kyle rose before her: the night on the Bridge of Wishes. Before the tragedy happened. Kyle's gentle fingers touched her skin and played with her hair, then he kissed her. *That's what I love about you, Julia.* The warmth in her chest pulsed with her heart, waiting for release—like a good ruby wine waiting in a barrel, sitting in the dark until its taste deepened. Julia's lips trembled; she was thirsty for it. She let the rich liquor leak from her chest, and she relaxed as the wave of warmth spread. Her hands became light and soft, and energy leaked from her fingers.

"Julia," Lana whispered.

She opened her eyes. She was still holding Elisa's hand. Warm pink energy shone between their palms.

"The energy," Lana said. "I saw it in a book of Gifts. You're *healing* her."

"How?"

"Hush . . . just keep doing it."

Julia squeezed Elisa's thin palm. The pink energy shone brighter, and it twirled around Elisa's hand, climbing up her shoulder and to her neck.

"You're . . . a healer," Lana said.

They both looked at the energy without breathing. Like a pink snake, the energy moved around Elisa's body, until it reached her heart. Then, the energy rolled into a pink ball and sank into her chest. Elisa's breath quickened, and a gentle pink color enlivened her face. Then, a dark pink light shone under the cut on her cheek. The rest of the energy escaped from the cut and evaporated into the air.

Julia released Elisa's hand. Her palms were warm, like she'd just been holding her evening cup of tea.

Elisa's eyelids fluttered. She took a deep breath and opened her eyes.

"Elisa!" Julia jumped on the bed and hugged her friend.

Lana put a hand on her chest. She could breathe again. "Welcome back," she said.

Elisa smiled. "I'm so glad to see you." Then she remembered, and fear filled her eyes.

"I saw your Light signal from the lake," Lana explained.

Elisa raised her eyebrows. "I can't believe you saved my life."

"It wasn't just me." Lana pointed at Julia. "We have a healer here."

Elisa looked at Julia. "You?"

Julia blushed. "I hope you're not angry at me anymore."

Elisa poked her shoulder. "I *knew* you were gonna be a great mage! Oh, my dear, come here!" She pulled Julia in close and hugged her tightly. They both laughed.

Lana smiled. These girls were so similar, but at the same time, so different. Now Elisa held Julia's hands and explored her warm palms in wonder.

Lana coughed, and the girls looked at her. She rose from her chair. "It's time to talk about the case. We'll need your testimony, Elisa."

Julia glanced at Elisa and sighed.

"I'm sorry," Lana said.

"No, it's okay," Julia replied. She shifted her gaze to Elisa. "I'll tell your aunt that you're awake."

Elisa nodded.

* * *

When the door closed, Lana sat on the corner of the bed. She released her notebook and twisted a pencil in her fingers.

"Lana, I'm ready," Elisa said. Her blue eyes shone with confidence, and a thin red line ran down her cheek. Julia's Healing Gift had brought her back to life, but it had left a scar on her pretty face.

Well, magic always has a price to pay. A scar isn't the worst trade-off.

"You sure?" Lana asked. "When I read you, I will see *everything* you thought of in that moment. Not only *what* you did, but *why* you did it. I won't tell your secrets to anyone, of course, but—"

Elisa put her palm on Lana's knee. "I lost a good friend, and I lost my mother because of this stupid system. I almost died when I tried to protect the person I love, and I don't care if you know who it was. Lana, I'll do everything possible to prevent more crimes like this. Yes, I'm 100 percent ready."

Lana glanced at the curtains waving in the window. Only a sliver of the sunset remained. *What else is hiding in the darkness?* The threat was heavy in the dry night air. She didn't know how many threats were in this world—even in her own small town—but at least there would be one less felon. Lana opened her small notebook and wrote, *The George Turner Case: Witness Testimony.*

Chapter 37. The Power of Love

Julia ran down the stairs. She jumped over the last two and stopped in the big living room. It was dark and quiet; only the shimmering candlelight in the kitchen reflected on the wooden floor. Julia walked into the small tidy kitchen.

A woman in a simple green dress and an old apron stood at the window and looked into the dark yard. Her long curly hair was messy, and her face was deep in concentration. She held a sheet of paper in her hand.

Julia approached and touched her arm.

Rachel flinched.

"Sorry, I didn't mean to scare you."

Rachel looked at her with wide eyes. "Elisa. What happened?" Her voice trembled.

Julia smiled. "She woke up. She's all right."

Rachel nodded and stared at the wall behind Julia.

Julia shifted her gaze to the table; an open envelope lay on the white tablecloth. "You're shocked now, but it's true. Lana is talking with her right now."

Rachel walked to the table and sat down. Her hands folded the paper, and she put it back into the envelope.

Julia went to the oven, took the kettle, and filled two mugs with tea. She put them on the table and sat back in front of Rachel.

"Healed, then," Rachel said. She shifted her gaze at Julia. "And you're a healer."

"How did you know?" Julia raised her eyebrows and paused. "Oh, I see," she said. "You watched us, didn't you?"

"It doesn't matter. I'm just glad she's alive." After taking the envelope and hiding it in the wide pocket of her apron, she took a silver teaspoon and mixed her tea.

Julia held her cup with both hands. It warmed her palms. Outside the window, the night was beautiful, and dark leaves trembled in front of the starry sky. "Oh, Rachel, today is the best day ever. Who knew I could have such power?"

Rachel gave her a worried look. "People who can predict the future, I suppose."

Julia took a sip of tea. "I'm so happy I didn't know. It was such a nice surprise."

Rachel sighed. "That's why the Oracle Gift is a curse. You wouldn't feel the same joy if you knew about good things in advance. And you'd feel despair if you knew about the bad things. Deaths you couldn't avert."

Julia widened her eyes. "What makes you think so?"

Rachel looked in her mug. "Just saying."

The sound of quick steps made Julia look at the entrance door. Lana walked into the kitchen and stood at the threshold.

"Can I see her?" Rachel asked.

Lana nodded. "Of course."

Rachel stood and ran to the ladder, the hem of her dress rustling with her quick steps.

Lana sat at the table.

"You were right," Julia said.

"About what?"

Julia put her teacup aside. "I'm so in love," she whispered.

Lana laughed. "You have double the luck, then."

They sat in front of each other at the big window. The night outside was warm and dark. Lana sighed. It would be a good night if she didn't have anxiety squeezing her chest.

Julia put her hand on Lana's. "Why is everyone acting so weird today? Everything is going well. We survived."

Lana sighed. "I just . . . it doesn't matter."

Julia gave her an intrigued look. "Oh, so it's a love matter."

Lana took her hand away. "You're a healer, not a mind reader."

"I saw the guardian from Santos."

"When?"

"He's the one who told me about Elisa."

Lana scoffed and stayed silent.

Julia smiled. "You have this face when I talk about him. Why not . . . How did you say it, 'you have two wings! Why not use them?'"

Lana stared at the tablecloth. Her hand found a napkin and started crumpling it. "Oh, Julia. You're so young. You haven't made as many mistakes as I have. You can love unconditionally, with all your heart, but the truth is ugly—when you grow up, things change."

Julia shook her head. "Here's what I've learned. The truth isn't ugly, cowardice is. You should believe in yourself."

"The problem is that I don't believe in *him*."

"Kyle told me that Richard saved your life."

"It was his job to cover for me."

Julia nodded, then sparkles lit up her eyes. "How did he save you?"

"Everything became a mess. Turner changed at once and started destroying the trees around us. Then Richard reversed time."

Julia narrowed her eyes. "I see. Now tell me—who told you he reversed time?"

"I saw him."

"Why didn't Captain Turner see it?"

Lana shrugged. "Because time was reversed, and so were his memories."

Julia put her elbows on the table and rested her face on her hands. She looked at Lana in silence with her warm eyes, waiting for the epiphany to hit.

Lana shifted her gaze back to the dark window with her heart pounding in her chest. Of *course*—she had been so obsessed with her anger, so sick of his lies, that she hadn't thought about his Gift. Lana rubbed her temples. "I see. His Gift didn't work on me."

Julia's lips widened in a smile. "And . . . ?"

"Oh, Julia. It's not that easy. Some Gifts work with the people we love, but some don't. Telekinesis doesn't have these limits."

Julia smiled wider. "Just ask him."

"Never."

"Then you'll never know."

Lana stood up, determined to finish this awkward conversation. "All right. I need to go home."

"Sure."

Lana walked to the door, but glanced back before leaving. "Congratulations on your Gift, Julia."

* * *

Lana walked out to the dark street where Mandy was waiting for her. Lana took her reins and looked up. The stars covered a velvet sky—just like that night when Richard promised to help her find justice for Rebecca. It was unbelievable, but they caught her murderer together, and Richard even gave her a credit in his report.

Lana sighed and petted Mandy's face. "This Santos guy—let me tell you."

The horse snickered.

"I know you've heard it all already. Oh, if I only knew what to do about him." She adjusted the belt on the saddle. "Father said, I won't find all the answers in a book."

Mandy neighed and pushed her shoulder.

Lana laughed. "Hey, what's up?"

She looked into Mandy's big brown eye. Her own puzzled face reflected back at her. Maybe Julia's theory about Richard's feelings was right, but she couldn't just *ask* him. Maybe she'd forgotten how to trust men, but working with the guardians had taught her to not make moves until she had proof. If only she could read him just once, glance under the curtain of his consciousness, it would be enough.

Lana stopped cold. *Of course—The Book of Gifts.* It listed all the known Gifts, including Time Reversing, and their limitations. Even if he didn't feel the same, at least she could satisfy her curiosity. "Let's go figure it out," she said to Mandy.

She jumped on the saddle, and the horse galloped down the street. Occasional passersby gave her worried looks, but she didn't care. The Guardian House library was so close, and it kept so many secrets. *Not all of them should stay untold.*

Chapter 38. The Book of Gifts

Richard walked along the empty street. Trees around whispered, and the buildings' dark windows gave him curious looks. The warmth of the June night embraced him. He stopped at the crossroads. His motel was on the next street, but he wasn't tired.

Richard walked to the park. During this trip, he'd never been to the Bridge of Wishes. He had to leave tomorrow, but it wouldn't be right to leave without saying goodbye to this cozy town. Maybe he didn't believe that the bridge could make his wish come true, but at least he could do some sightseeing.

He was walking beside the Guardian House when he stepped on a square reflection of light on the pavement. Richard looked up— one of the windows on a top floor was lit by candlelight. The young guardian with red hair had been on duty today and wasn't happy about it; everyone had gone to the bar to celebrate the case's closure. But he'd eventually arrived, which meant that someone had replaced him. *But who?* He could exclude Chief Morris, who had been busy interrogating Turner all day and had gone home early.

Then there was the only option left—*Luna.* The light gleaming on the curtains teased him of her presence. The window was on the third floor, reminding him of Camilla and his impending punishment. He walked to the porch and stopped, thinking.

Walking away was the wisest choice he could make. If his friend Tim were here, he would advise him to turn, walk away, and then try to rebuild his career. But would *she* ever have a choice? No one in his right mind would ever let a woman become a guardian, and it was frustrating. He wished he could see her again and tell her there was hope, but he'd already lied enough. It was better to leave her alone.

Richard glanced at the park; it was so close. The trees rustled in the night air, begging him to use common sense. However, common sense wasn't one of his strengths. Richard sighed and walked inside.

* * *

In the Guardian House's long corridor, Richard's heart beat louder with each slow step. The wooden planks muffled his footsteps. A door to the library was ajar, and light fell on the floor. He opened the door wider and glanced inside.

Lana was sitting on a sofa, her back turned to the door. She wore a white dress and held a huge book in her thin hands, the candlelight playing in her wavy hair. Richard approached her and glanced in the book. *The Gift of Time Reversing*, he read on the top of the page.

"You're a real bookworm," he whispered near her ear.

Lana flinched and slammed the book closed. Her eyes sparkled with pure anger. "What the hell are you doing here?"

Richard smiled. "Nice to see you too."

"You scared the shit out of me!"

He laughed.

"It's not funny!" Her gaze was sharp.

"I'm sorry, I didn't mean to scare you."

"But you did."

He stepped back and gave her a sad look. "Sorry. I'll leave if you want."

She lowered her eyes. "No, please don't."

Richard stood at the threshold, thinking. Then he sat beside her on the sofa.

They sat in silence for a while. The curtains rustled in the wind from the open window. The air was rich with grass and night flowers.

"I'm sorry too," Lana said. "I'm just so wound up with everything."

"We all are."

Lana nodded and put her palms on the closed book. "What an awkward moment," she said. "Can you just reverse time a bit and walk in the room again? You know, like a normal person?"

Richard leaned on a sofa back. "Maybe I don't want to."

Her eyes sparkled. "Why?"

"Why?" He chuckled. "Your face! I won't ever erase it from history!"

Lana pushed his shoulder with her small fist. "Oh, shut up!"

He laughed. "Okay, okay. No more jokes today."

"You're unbearable, Richard."

She held the thick heavy book in her hands: *The Book of Gifts*. If every Gift was in there, hers would be listed too, but he didn't need to read the book to understand how her Gift worked. Among all the women he'd ever met, she was the trickiest. She was like a puzzle that grew more complicated the more he tried to solve it.

Like now—why is she reading about me at such a late hour?

Lana caught his look. "I just wanted to know more about Gifts."

"Which ones?" he asked.

Her eyes shone. "Our witness woke up, Richard! Elisa will tell everything tomorrow at court."

He raised his eyebrows. "Elisa? But the doctor said—"

"Julia," Lana interrupted him. "She . . . she just held her hand, and then . . . Richard, she healed Elisa."

"Julia, the schoolgirl who lives across the street?"

Lana nodded; a smile blossomed on her beautiful face.

"She has a Healing Gift," Richard said.

"Exactly."

Richard smiled. Yes, this town was full of mysteries, and Lana was the biggest one. She looked at him with pure joy, like she'd just discovered what her Light's color was.

He scratched his chin. Solving her captivated his mind, more than formal detective work. Her mood shifted way too fast—from anger to joy—and she didn't confess that she'd read about his Gift.

The memory of the witch's house rose before his eyes, at the moment when she'd held his hand and tried to read him. She hadn't been able to. If she had, she would not be speaking with him right now.

Then what stopped her? He breathed out. Of course, she had a Gift blockage, because of the emotion he hadn't been aware of. But while she liked mind games, he was a good player.

"The Healing Gift is very rare; did you know that?" he asked.

"Yes. Julia will be a great mage. She'll have so many opportunities in life."

"Isn't it as rare as the Time Reversing Gift?"

Lana paused. "I guess so."

He put his hand on hers. Her hand trembled.

"Do you remember our talk at the witch's house, Lana?"

She blushed. "Yes. Why?"

"I promised to tell you everything."

"Yes, you did."

He squeezed her hand. "I want you to read me now."

She widened her eyes. "*Now?*"

He nodded. "Yes, I'm an open book, Lana. Read whatever you need to."

She released her hand. "Maybe I don't want to."

"Why not?"

She rubbed her wrist. The proper excuse refused to come to her mind. He had seen that she read about the Time Reversing Gift. How stupid did he think she was? She was an open book, all right: a tale that he read for pleasure. "Go back to your motel, Richard," she said.

He touched her hot cheek with his fingertips. "There's a problem here."

Lana looked into his dark green eyes. The gleams of candlelight played in them.

"What's that?" She asked.

"If I go, I'll never see you again." He moved closer to her; he smelled of tree nuts and whiskey. She moved her lips to his, and he kissed her.

All the words she wanted to hear from him lost value, and she followed only her desire. There was nothing else left in the world but the two of them.

Melting into his embrace, she kissed him with greed. His lips were not enough. She unbuttoned his shirt and ran her fingers over his back. She touched his strong neck with gentle fingers, slid along his tense muscles. The strength of his fire enveloped her body, and it made her glow from the inside.

Step by step, she discovered him. A flame of torrid desire led her through the sacred corridors of his maze. Her body trembled under his touch, under his loud beating heart. She was eager to touch his roughness and make it malleable.

His hands slid along her body, releasing her from her dress. Her naked skin touched his. He held her tightly in his arms. A blaze of passion lit up the deepest corners of his unknown until she could see his true Light. Like two waves of fire, they merged into one blinding blaze.

Her body writhed under his strong and passionate movements. The blaze enveloped her consciousness, erasing all the boundaries and uncertainty between them. Captured by the fire, she screamed; her voice sank into the stillness of the night.

* * *

When Lana opened her eyes, the sunrise colored the sky in gentle pink shades. Beside her, Richard's eyes were open. She kissed his forehead.

"I wish this night would never end," she said.

"Me too."

Lana put her head on his warm shoulder. "You can reverse time."

He sighed. "Only for a few minutes. My Gift has limits, don't you know?"

"Why would I?"

He glanced at the forsaken book that lay on the floor. "I thought you read about it."

She rose on her elbow. "I didn't get to that point. I was interrupted."

He smiled.

Her index finger drew a curve on his upper body. "I forgot to say thank you. You saved my life."

"You already did. Three times."

She poked his shoulder and laughed. "You're unbearable!"

He caressed her matted hair. "Everything good goes away," he said.

"Do you have to go?"

Richard glanced at the time crystal; it was turquoise.

"We both need to go soon," he replied. "I won't attend the hearing, but I'll be in the court building. I need to tell you everything."

Lana kissed his unshaven cheek. "Of course."

She put her head back on his shoulder, and the sound of his heartbeat soothed her. Where did he come from, and where would he go after all this? She might never know. He was right; everything good went away. These rare moments of happiness just showed up in life, and then they disappeared into the daylight of reality. Time was merciless. But until the sun rose, she could hide from it here in his arms.

Chapter 39. A Row of Knives

The sun warmed the old gray walls of the court building. Bright rays pierced the big, tall windows of the study room, lighting up the tables and wooden benches. Lana sat alone at the table. Two folders lay in front of her: a yellow one containing Turner's case and a red one with *Ghost* written on it.

Lana opened the red folder. An empty square was where the picture of Ghost was supposed to be. The guardians also called him the Mystery Killer, as no one had ever seen him face-to-face. If Lana were a criminal, she would probably view his elusiveness as a good opportunity to disguise her crimes. That's exactly what Turner had done.

However, one discrepancy still disturbed her—neither the guardians nor the chief had ever heard about Ghost until the first murder happened. According to the interrogation report, Turner had decided to fake the Ghost's steps only when he killed Rose. He swore he hadn't killed Bella, but no one believed him.

So many unanswered questions twisted in her head. There were too many discrepancies in this case, like the death of the witch. Lana's father had been surprised when she told him about the witch's house—no one else had known where her house was until the day they found her body. The report said she was killed approximately ten hours earlier than Bella.

Lana shook her head. It didn't make any sense—Turner was a Gift Hunter; if he found the witch, he could have killed her legally. There was no reason to fake a suicide note. And why did he kill Bella, instead of sending her to Mercy House?

Lana placed several pictures of the crime scenes in front of her. There were eleven victims—all teenage girls with dangerous Gifts. The row of pictures spread to the full length of the desk. All of them looked the same—the victims lay in the middle of glades with their lifeless eyes open. She took a closer look—their eyes were calm. Lana had seen this relaxed expression when she studied hypnosis in Mercy House.

Lana opened the yellow folder and found the pictures of the last two victims—Bella and Rose. She placed them at the end of the row.

Bella fit the other pictures—she had the same wound on her belly and the same peaceful face. But Rose, she looked different—she was under a tree at the side of the glade, and her face . . . the fear stood out, frozen in her eyes. And the blood—there was too much of it. The report said Rose was raped, but there was no such record for Bella nor Ghost's other victims.

Lana gasped. Turner had disguised Rose's murder, but he hadn't done it well. Why hadn't he made the same mistake with Bella's?

She leaned back in her chair. Twelve of the murders had been done with the same hand, and as an oracle, Ghost had seen their future. But Rose . . . Turner had killed her for a different purpose— to hide his other crime. He was a rapist, and after Ghost appeared in Triville, maybe Turner thought he could take advantage of Ghost's cover. His greatest advantage was being able to discuss the latest news with other guardians.

Her head throbbed. So many guardians, including her own father, could not have overlooked this. The only reason for their negligence was convenience. In their minds, it was easier *not* to announce the appearance of a serial killer, *not* to create panic in town, and *not* to write long reports. They were too scared to admit that the *real* Ghost killed Bella and the witch. The system was as rotten as the people in it. This wasn't right. It was so wrong that she wanted to scream. Lana clenched her fists and walked to the exit.

The door flew open, and Richard stepped in the room. His smile faded when he saw her.

"Are you okay?" he asked.

Lana stepped forward. "Not now. I need to speak with the chief."

Richard caught her hand and gently pushed her back into the room. "You should speak with me first."

She tried to push him away, but he was like a rock. "There were *two* Ghosts, Richard. I mean, two murderers—the *real* Ghost and Turner, and all this time, my father knew it."

"I know," he said.

She widened her eyes, at a loss for words.

Richard closed the door and locked it. "I'll tell you everything, Lana."

"What the hell, Richard? Don't tell me you're a part of this."

He nodded.

She walked to the table with the case files. "Damn."

He approached her. "In the very beginning, I noticed a difference between the two murders. The chief and I agreed that no one was supposed to know except him and me."

"And now, you're gonna blame a man for a crime he didn't commit? What about the real killer? Oh, yeah, just let him walk freely into another town and kill someone else. It would be too hard to catch him."

Richard crossed his arms. "Are you finished?"

She took a breath and nodded.

Richard glanced at the row of the pictures on the desk. "Firstly, Turner isn't innocent. He would be sentenced to Death Island for life if he had murdered only one of the girls. And secondly, we did this to catch the real killer."

Lana stared at him. "This is why I'll never understand the guardians. You ask people like me to obey the rules, but instead of protecting, you take advantage of us."

"Is that what it means for you—to be a guardian?" he asked. "To wear a uniform and follow some set of rules?"

Lana paused. "Actually, I don't know. Before, I thought I could help innocent people and catch the criminals. But it seems like no one really does it here."

"Have you ever read a guardian code?" Richard asked.

Lana nodded. "Once."

"Yes, we have an oath to help existing systems," Richard said, "but this code also says we must do 'everything possible to help people who suffer from cruelty and injustice.' Unfortunately, sometimes systems don't work properly, and the guardian has to do what's right, even if it breaks the rules and puts his career at risk. Everyone can blindly follow the rules, but not all of us have enough guts to fight with the system that brings harm to people."

"What do you do, then?"

"Like you, I chose to fight. Do you remember what you told me that night in the forest? *The system is powerful, but some parts are rotten.* The only way to break this system was to bring proof to the guardians. Now, you have this proof—Rebecca's case can change everything."

Lana sighed. "Do you think it will make a change?"

"Why not?"

Lana shrugged her shoulders. "Even if Mercy House is shut down, what would they do about destructive Gifts in women?"

He gave her a sly look. "I spoke with the chief about this problem. Don't worry about it, he is already looking for a solution."

"Which solution?"

"Nothing is decided yet," Richard said, "but if it works, the Mercy House problem will be solved."

She moved closer. "At least, give me a clue."

He smiled. "Curiosity killed the cat, Lana. Can you just wait until tomorrow?"

Lana looked at him with impatience, but Richard kept silent.

238

"Fine, I'll wait." Lana said.

Richard walked to the window and sat on a bench. "Now, the question is, how badly do you want to help me catch Ghost?"

Lana sat next to him. "What do I need to do?" she asked.

He rolled a piece of paper in his palms. "The chief knows about the discrepancy, but there's one thing I didn't tell him."

"I'm listening."

Richard sighed. "I've never told this to anyone. Ever."

Lana touched his hand; his heart was beating fast. "Whatever it is, it'll stay between us," she said.

He nodded, twirling the roll of paper. "Lana, if I tell you this, it'll be just the two of us from now on. No one else can know the truth; otherwise, we'll never catch him."

"We're a team," she replied.

"When we were at the witch's house, I found a note. Do you remember?"

She nodded.

"It was just half of the message. Ghost made her write the first part. But he also wrote a message for me on the bottom of the page. I had to tear it off; otherwise, the chief wouldn't let me continue with the case."

"Why would he do that?"

"I'm not working on this case by coincidence, Lana. I've known Ghost all my life. I tried to stop him several years ago, but I couldn't, for one very simple reason." Richard took a deep breath and lowered his eyes. "He's my brother."

Lana was speechless. The bright windows blurred before her eyes, and the ceiling twisted over her head.

Of course. It explained everything. Richard's time reverse Gift was the opposite of Ghost's, who could see the future. They were connected by blood—that's why only Richard could catch him. But he couldn't tell anyone, and not only because detectives weren't allowed to investigate the cases of their close relatives, but personal connections made people clumsy. Richard had a heart—the same naive belief Kyle Turner had had in his father. Some people could change, but not selfish narcissists and psychopaths.

"That's why you let him escape," Lana said.

He nodded. "Yes. I couldn't kill him."

She sighed. "I can imagine."

"He promised to stop, but he keeps killing innocent girls. I can't let him do it anymore. Lana, he's way too powerful. We must finish it."

"Maybe it shouldn't be *you* that stops him."

"No one but me can come close enough."

She nodded. "What's my part, then?"

Richard gave her the roll of paper. This precise handwriting could belong to an A student; it was weird that it had been written by the person who had killed twelve teenage girls.

Lana read the message.

I hope you've missed me, little brother.

So many years without seeing you has made me a different person. We made a deal, and I've kept my promise until now. But the world keeps changing, and our Gifts keep developing. Terrible things are coming.

I miss when we were young and naive—when we believed in happy endings. Things change so fast. You know that better than anyone.

I really need to see you, Rick. Our world is doomed, and I hope you make the right choice. I know that you care; you always have.

Don't look for me. I won't be around for a couple of weeks. But when the guardian woman reads this letter, I'll be close. By the way, they will accuse the guardian captain. The evening after the day in court, the chief will organize a huge ball to celebrate the victory.

I'll wait for you in the glade in the forest near the chief's house. Meet me there at eleven o'clock, and I'll tell you everything.

See you, Rick.

Lana put the letter away. "He's your elder brother, then."

Richard nodded.

She put her head on his chest. His heartbeat was intense, and his breathing was ragged.

"He's wrong. I'm not a guardian," Lana said.

"He probably meant that you're the guardian chief's daughter."

"Anyway. We don't have an upcoming ball."

"We just don't know about it yet."

Lana leaned back. "I would know about a ball in my house."

"I know it sounds unrealistic now, but just think—he knew about Turner two weeks before we caught him."

"Yeah. It would have been nice if he'd told us."

Richard sighed. "He's too cocky and selfish."

Lana shook her head. "Alright. But if we're really having a ball, I would love to dance with you."

Richard smiled. "I'm not a good dancer."

"I just want you to be there."

"I'll be there, but I'll have to meet him first. He's always right. It's funny. I wanted to leave town yesterday to avoid playing his game, but I stayed. Did he know that I would?"

Lana smiled. "I don't know what he knew, but I'm glad you stayed a bit longer."

He gave her a warm look. "Me too. But I must finish this."

She squeezed his hand. "I'm afraid for you, Richard. Are you sure you won't need my help?"

He shook his head. "Just concentrate on the hearing for now, okay?"

She sighed. "I don't know what to say on the chair of truth."

Richard put his hand on her shoulder. "Just say what you need to. Even if they don't accuse him of Bella's murder, his destiny has already been decided. Turner did enough to spend the rest of his life in prison."

Lana nodded. "I really want to trust you."

"From now on, I want you to trust yourself."

Lana moved closer and kissed his lips. He smelled of coffee and morning dew.

He hugged her shoulders. She wished the courtroom would burn in hell with the judges and lawyers. Richard was right; Turner's fate had already been decided. If only she knew what *her* destiny was.

Chapter 40. The Court

Lana walked through the aisle of the courtroom. Heavy purple curtains covered the windows, and not a single sun ray broke into the room of justice. Candlelight illuminated the benches and a copper statue of a woman which stood in the corner of the room, looking straight forward and holding a wide plate in her hands. The chair of truth stood below her. If someone lied, her eyes would turn red. The irony was that everyone had their own truth.

The dark wooden seats were half empty, but they were slowly filling up with people. Elisa sat in the front row and stared at the statue; she twirled a golden lock of hair with her fingers.

Lana sat next to her. "This statue is gorgeous, don't you think?" she asked.

Elisa lowered her hand. "You're here!"

"Of course. Are you ready for the questions?"

"Ready."

Lana glanced across the room. Charles stood near the curtain-covered window and talked with a lawyer, a tall, red-haired man in a white cloak. Defense lawyers always tried to mitigate or impede punishments, ruining guardians' hard work, but today, the guardians had strong evidence.

"The prosecutor will interview you first," Lana said. "Then it will be Turner's lawyer's turn."

Elisa nodded.

Lana looked back at Charles. Something in him had changed. In the soft light of the candles, his face seemed dark; even his wide smile was dull. This Charles wasn't the same man who had impressed her and made her heart jump when she was young. Now he was just another man in the room, a shadow from her past.

Elisa touched her shoulder. "Is that him?"

Lana blinked. "Who?"

Elisa glanced at Charles. "That guy. Didn't you work with him on my mother's case?"

"Yes."

Elisa sneered. "How can you stand him now? After everything he's done?"

Lana raised her eyebrows. "What do you mean?"

"Before you left Triville, you said you would never forgive him for his neglect, and you would always hate him because he betrayed you."

That affair seemed to be part of another life or a bad dream. Now the bright morning light broke through the darkness, and the night was over. She wanted to live her life and stop looking back.

Lana sighed. "You know, it took me a long time, but I've realized that whatever I do, I can't change the past. Holding on to it hurt me more and more, like I was drowning . . . until I let it all go."

Elisa twirled her hair again. "It's not easy to let go."

"I know he caused me a lot of pain, but, you know, I relied on him too much for things he couldn't change. Now I know how foolish it all was."

"So that's how your love ended?"

"No, even after everything he did, I couldn't stop loving him. That's why I was so angry. It took me time to let him go, but only after I forgave myself for being so stupid."

Elisa's eyes gleamed. "At least you were together. I wish Julia could love me in the same way, but she never will. But that saved my life. If she loved me, I would be dead now. I'll never forget it."

Lana smiled. "You'll never stop loving her, but the connection will weaken with time. After a year, she will become a warm memory you can keep with you. Trust me, when the time comes, you'll meet the right person."

"I don't think so."

"After I broke up with Charles, it was a torture to see his face every day and to hear his voice. So, I left town, and it helped me heal my wounds."

Elisa nodded. "Out of sight, out of mind."

"Exactly. It's not fast, but it works."

The door opened, and the room quietened. The judge, a short gray-haired man in a silver gown, came into the room. The violet star on his chest glittered in the candlelight. He walked to the statue of justice and bowed, then he looked across the room.

"I greet you today, my dear friends," he said. "The deep sorrow that connects all of us today will never be forgotten." He put his palms together, and the bright violet energy of his Light leaked from his fingers. He formed his Light into a ball the size of a human head, and the room brightened. He looked at the statue. "Today justice will triumph."

He placed his Light on the plate in the statue's hands, and her eyes shone in the violet flame. The judge walked to his chair, a throne with a tall carved back, fixed his gown, and took a seat.

The bailiff gave him a yellow folder; the judge opened it and nodded.

"The hearing is called to order!" The judge raised his plump hand, and the curtains opened. Bright daylight filled the room, and Lana had to squint her eyes.

The judge dropped his hand and looked at the guardian to his left. "Please bring the suspect into the room."

The door opened, and two guardians accompanied George Turner inside. His hands were locked in blocking cuffs. His emaciated face was pale; dark circles were under his tired eyes. He seemed to lean away from people's glances, and he avoided looking anywhere but his feet.

Lana's heart sank. George Turner had been a brave guardian and her father's colleague. She'd known him since she was a little girl, and her mind refused to believe what he had become. She couldn't stop staring at him.

It was easier to call him a murderer when she'd prepared the paperwork. She had even shot him with a paralyzing spell when her life was in danger, but it was excruciating to see him like this. Lana's lips trembled. *He killed Rose and Rebecca. He almost killed Elisa and me; he deserves the worst.*

People around started to whistle and curse. Magic was forbidden in the courtroom, but it couldn't stop their hatred. The guardians who held Turner crossed the room and pushed him in a tall metal cage in the corner of the room. The metal door closed after him with a loud clank.

The rods of the cage blocked magic, and suspects couldn't create any spells inside—even if they managed to get rid of their cuffs. But the metal barrier also saved suspects from the enraged families and friends of their victims.

"Today, we are here to reach a verdict," the judge said. "George Turner has been blamed for four cold-blooded murders. He is also blamed for the severe injuries that could have led to the death of a fifteen-year-old girl, who is currently present."

Elisa took Lana's hand.

"Show them what you're worth," Lana whispered.

The judge sat down. "And now, I ask the prosecution to start the hearing."

Chapter 41. Confession

A middle-aged man in a black gown walked to the center of the room. He put his arm on his chest and introduced himself. "My name is Mark Lougheed, and I am the prosecutor in today's trial." He paused, then took a small notebook from his pocket and glanced at it. "The prosecution calls the witness, Miss Elisa Palmer."

Elisa stood up and walked to the chair of truth with confidence. She sat and gave Turner a sharp look.

The prosecutor walked to Elisa's side. "Please see the only victim who survived in a brutal series of murders made by this guardian's hand."

Elisa nodded.

"Miss Palmer, can you please tell us what happened that evening?"

"That evening, I went to see Kyle," she replied.

"Kyle Turner is the son of our suspect, George Turner," the prosecutor said. He looked at Elisa. "And Kyle is your schoolmate, correct?"

Elisa glanced at Kyle, who sat in the middle of the room, holding Julia's hand. Elisa narrowed her eyes. "Yes, he is my schoolmate."

"And how long have you known George Turner?"

"Since first grade, I believe."

The eyes of the statue of justice shone with calm violet light, and Elisa took a sigh of relief.

"All right," the prosecutor said. "Please go on."

Elisa sighed. "That evening, I went to visit Kyle, but he wasn't at home. Captain Turner opened the door and invited me in for a cup of tea."

"Did you agree right away?"

Elisa shook her head. "I refused at first, but he insisted. He asked me to tell him about Rose . . . to help him with the investigation. Then I went in."

The prosecutor smiled and looked at the judge. "Your Honor, I ask you to note that our suspect manipulated the victim, and he used their acquaintance for his dark purpose."

The judge frowned and wrote something down.

A lawyer in a white cloak stood up. "Objection! Your Honor, this is not proof of his manipulation."

The judge looked at the prosecutor. "Please explain how the suspect manipulated the victim."

"The suspect knew about the murders, and he used the witness's emotional connection with his victim to convince her to come into his house. Then he gave her sleeping potion." The prosecutor pointed at the cage. "This proves he is at fault!"

The judge nodded. "Objection overruled. Please, go on."

The lawyer in the white cloak sat down, his cheeks burning red.

The prosecutor continued. "Miss Palmer, please tell us what happened next."

"Then I sat at the table, and we started drinking tea. Captain Turner showed me some magic tricks with his Telekinesis Gift—he made spoons fly over the table while he served me." Elisa paused and looked at Turner. "Then he said he killed his daughter. I wanted to leave, but I felt weird and fainted."

"And where did you wake up?"

Elisa's voice started trembling. "It was somewhere in a forest. My hands and feet were tied, and I was at a tree . . ." She took a deep breath. "Then I saw him again."

"How did you feel?"

"Shitty," she said.

The judge knocked on his armrest. "Miss Palmer, please respect the court!"

Elisa nodded. "I'm sorry, Your Honor."

The prosecutor looked at her. "So, you saw the suspect in the morning. What did he do and say?"

"He said he killed Rose and his daughter, and he told me how he did it." Elisa paused. "Then he cut my face and promised to kill me."

"And how did things go after his . . . confession?" The prosecutor glanced at the judge, who remained silent.

Elisa blushed. "I asked him to untie me from the tree. My hands were tied with a blocking rope, but I managed to injure Captain Turner, and I ran away."

"How did you make him untie you?" the prosecutor asked.

"I said I wanted to earn his trust."

"Did he try to rape you?"

Elisa nodded.

"Please answer the question with words."

Elisa gave him a sharp look. "Yes!"

"And how far did it go?"

Elisa paused. "He kissed me, then he lay on the ground, and I went on top. . . . Then I stabbed a fork in his cock!" She looked at Turner, her eyes flashing with anger. "I hope you won't be able to use it anymore!"

Murmuring laughter rolled across the room.

The judge rapped his armrest. "Order, please!"

The crowd became silent.

"Those are all of my questions," the prosecutor said. "Your Honor, please note that our suspect confessed to two murders, and he also tried to rape the witness." He bowed and took his place.

Turner sat on the floor of his cage and squeezed his dirty shirt in his thin hands. He didn't dare raise his eyes. Everyone burned him with their judging gazes.

When the first part of the testimony was over, the judge glanced at the lawyer in white. "Does the defense have any questions?" he asked.

"Yes, Your Honor." The tall lawyer in the white cloak stood up. He introduced himself as Mr. Spence and walked to Elisa. "Miss Palmer, please tell us about your relationship with Kyle Turner."

Elisa lowered her eyes. "We're friends."

The statue of justice over Elisa's head changed. The Light ball in her hands trembled, and her eyes became red. Elisa glanced back and bit her lip.

"Please note that this is the first lie from the witness," Mr. Spence said, grinning. He took a small notebook from his pocket with a brown leather cover.

Elisa's heart sank. It was Kyle's diary. *What else has the bastard written about me?*

Mr. Spence gave the notebook to the judge. "According to this document, Elisa and Kyle had several dates, kissed, and were . . . very close."

Elisa clenched her teeth.

"Kyle was your boyfriend. Is it true?" Mr. Spence asked.

"Yes, but not anymore," Elisa said. "We broke up."

"Why did you break up?"

Elisa looked from Kyle to the lawyer. "He tried to rape me."

"Can you guide us through the events?"

"It happened just before we found Bella in the glade. He kissed me, and then . . . he started touching me, and I ran away."

"Miss Palmer, I have a question." He narrowed his eyes. "When you kissed Mr. Turner, did you give him any reason to move further along?"

Elisa's cheeks turned scarlet, making her scar almost invisible.

The prosecutor stood up. "Your Honor, objection! This question has no relation to the murders."

The judge nodded. "Sustained. Mr. Spence, please ask questions relating only to the case."

Mr. Spence took two steps and turned to face Elisa. "Have you talked with Kyle since then?"

"No."

"Then why did you decide to go to his house that evening?"

Elisa sighed. Lana had warned her that these questions would be tricky; she had to be careful—not to lie, but to tell just enough. She looked back to the lawyer. "He started dating my friend Julia, and I was afraid for her. I went to see if he was home."

"And did the suspect ever try to rape you before that accident?"

Elisa squirmed under the lawyer's gaze. "No."

"After Mr. Turner untied you from the tree, why did he think you consented?"

Elisa gasped. "Because I suggested it. But I was only trying to escape!"

The lawyer looked at the judge. "Your Honor, harassment is doubtful; the witness offered herself."

Elisa opened her mouth and inhaled stifling air. She'd used humiliation as a tactic before. On the day Bella disappeared, she'd made the stupid joke with the flower garland and asked Kyle to help. She just wanted Julia to see Kyle's bad side; Bella was just a pawn. But it was terrible to sit like this under their gazes. How could she have done the same thing to Bella?

The only thing she wanted was to run from this terrible room—to stop breathing the same air as them and to avoid seeing their stupid faces. She wanted to find the fastest horse and ride as far as she could from this cursed town.

The judge looked at the defense lawyer. "Sustained. Mr. Spence, do you have questions about the other murders?"

The lawyer leaned over Elisa; the strong smell of sweat wafted from his gown.

Elisa wrinkled her nose.

"What did the suspect say about Bella's murder?" the lawyer asked.

A heavy silence hung in the room. All eyes were on Elisa—Lana, Kyle, Julia, her classmates, teachers—everyone.

Elisa lowered her eyes. "I'm not sure. I don't remember."

"So, he didn't confess to the first murder?"

"He didn't tell me about it," Elisa said.

"Please answer the question directly."

"No. He did *not* confess."

The lawyer smiled and looked at the judge. "No further questions. Thank you."

Chapter 42. Broken Heroes

Elisa returned to the bench and sat beside Lana, shivering. She looked down at her polished black shoes and breathed deeply. Blood pulsed in her temples.

Lana touched her arm. "He was just trying to mitigate the punishment."

Elisa nodded. "I know. But I hate how everyone looked at me."

"They won't remember it forever."

Now, Kyle was sitting in the chair of truth. He answered a number of tricky questions that the prosecutor asked him, then Mr. Spence stood up.

"Kyle, where were you the night of Bella's murder?" he asked.

"At home. As I already said, I woke up with the sunrise, and my father wasn't home."

"And you found him in the old barn close to your home?"

"Yes."

"Was he drunk?"

Kyle wiped sweat from his forehead with his sleeve. "He was. He could hardly walk."

"Does your father drink often?"

"Yes. Since my sister passed away, he's been drinking almost every weekend."

The lawyer narrowed his eyes. "Is it unusual for him to drink at the bar before coming home?"

"No."

"Does he come home every night he drinks?"

Kyle sighed. "No. Sometimes he walks in the forest to get sober."

The lawyer glanced at the cage with the suspect, then he turned to Kyle. "I have a question for you, Kyle. What would you estimate his chances are of committing murder while he was that drunk?"

The prosecutor stood up. "Objection, Your Honor! The boy is not competent enough to answer this question."

"Sustained. Mr. Spence, please ask the next question."

The lawyer frowned. "How was your father's condition after the night of Rose's murder?"

Kyle glanced at his father. "He came home by noon. He was sober."

Mr. Spence nodded and looked at the judge. "Please note that our suspect could have committed Rose's murder, but he was too drunk to kill another victim."

The judge put his palm on the file. "I am taking note of everything, Mr. Spence. I will be paying attention until the end of the hearing. Do you have any other questions?"

"No," he said.

The judge knocked the armrest. "Break for intermission."

* * *

Kyle stepped out onto the sunny courtyard. He shaded his eyes with his hand and looked around—the yard was overcrowded. There were so many faces. Some of them, he hardly knew, but others were too familiar—teachers from his school and guardians. One of them noticed Kyle and pointed at him, and the other guardians started discussing something with wide hand gestures, snickering.

"Come on, you can't be that stupid!" Kyle said, shaking his head. He walked down the narrow path that led around the building. He reached the backyard, where someone's quiet sobbing made him slow his steps. Kyle approached the bush and moved a branch away to see who was hiding there.

Elisa sat on a bench with her face in her hands, and her shoulders were shaking.

Behind him, the courtyard was crowded with gossipers who had come to stare at the "fake Ghost." He hadn't wanted to be there; he could only imagine what it must have been like for her. She'd probably run from the courtroom as soon as the judge's mouth closed.

Kyle walked out from the bushes and sat on the edge of the bench. Elisa's shoulders kept shaking, and he stretched out his hand and touched her hair. Light and soft, it shone between his fingers. Elisa raised her head. Tears glittered in her wide eyes, and she was smiling.

"Are you laughing?" Kyle asked.

Elisa burst into sonorous laughter.

"What's so funny?"

"I . . . I just . . ." she waved her hand and covered her mouth, but she couldn't stop. Tears rolled down her cheeks.

Kyle stared at her. Rebecca had reacted like this when she'd returned three years ago—when she lost her magic. No, Elisa wasn't crying with joy; she was having a tantrum. There was a thin red line on her cheek, a mark that George had left on her pretty face. Some wounds never healed—not even with magic.

"I know that wasn't easy for you," Kyle said.

Elisa shook her head.

"But it wasn't easy for me either."

"Oh, poor boy." Elisa touched his chin with her soft hand. "Sorry, by touching your face in the bushes, I've probably given you permission to rape me. For the sake of justice, will you forgive me?"

Kyle shook his head. "Elisa, please. Stop talking nonsense!"

"So, you won't forgive me?" She blinked. Then she wiped her eyes and laughed again.

"Elisa—"

She raised her hand. "Oh, I'm sorry. . . . Of course. You can rape me if you want. . . ." She glanced around. "Maybe someone else would like to join you? Maybe your daddy? He didn't finish with me. Well, I think I may have damaged him, but you know what? Bring someone else. There are lots of sick shit heads around here."

He took her wrists and pulled Elisa closer to him.

She stopped breathing.

"I'm not like my father," he said.

"No?" She rounded her eyes. "'Because I thought—"

"No."

"Really?" She narrowed her eyes. "Oh, maybe I gave you a reason to try to rape me, then. You're kind of normal in that sense. Is that what you mean?"

He lowered his eyes. "Listen, what I did . . . *tried* to do . . . it was awful, and I apologize." He released her wrists, and Elisa placed her hands on her lap. He looked up, and the bright summer sun warmed his face. The trees above them shivered, listening. How could such a beautiful day be so terrible?

"Listen, I was wrong," he said. "I thought I was privileged, being a guardian's son. But it wasn't right. We all make mistakes, and I'm ready to learn from mine. Today, when I looked at George in that cage, I only wished for one thing—not to become like him. I promise, from now on, I won't hurt anyone."

Elisa snorted with disgust. The gray bricks of the building wall were cracked from time and wind. How many soon-to-be murderers had sat here and sworn they would never cross the line? Probably many, and she bet George Turner was one of them.

Elisa faced Kyle. "Empty promises. What's actually going to stop you from doing more horrible things?"

He shook his head. "I'm not promising you. I'm promising myself. I didn't understand the impact of what I did; I was selfish and stupid. But now, I know what choice I have to make, and I'm choosing not to be a coward, like my father, who hid his hatred for the world under his guardian uniform."

The pink scar shone on his neck from the day she bit him. Elisa sighed. This terrible investigation had left a mark on all of them.

"I'm sorry. For everything," Kyle said.

"You spied on us—me and Julia. You lied to us."

"I did, but I'm not anymore. She knows everything, and I'll never let her down."

Elisa raised his eyebrows. "Really?"

He nodded.

"Then, Kyle Turner, I'll make you a promise too," she said.

"What's that?"

"I swear that if you hurt Julia in any way, I will find you wherever you are, and I *will* make you pay for it."

He smiled. "Sustained."

Chapter 43. The Bottom Line

Lana stood at the window. People walked around the courtyard, talking and laughing. The sun made the colors brighter and warmed the air. When she'd come back home to find out the truth about Rebecca's death, she couldn't have imagined it would lead her here. This case was a complete disaster, but at least it would be over soon.

Someone's hand touched her shoulder, and Lana turned back.

Julia smiled. "Hey."

Lana hugged her. "I'm so glad to see you."

"Did you see Kyle or Elisa?" Julia asked.

"No. I think they both walked out."

"Oh, no. I hope they don't kill each other."

Lana smiled. "Don't worry, they'll find a way to work it out."

"Why are you so sure?"

"Because they both love you," Lana said. "I mean, not in the same way, of course, but . . ."

Julia frowned. "What do you mean?"

Lana looked around for a different subject. Mrs. Sullivan stood at the nearby window. The green yard reflected in her big round glasses.

"That woman is everywhere," Lana said. "Why can't she leave us alone?"

Julia turned her head. Mrs. Sullivan noticed their interest and came closer. Her big yellow eyes were sad.

"Mrs. Sullivan." Lana mustered a smile.

The woman nodded. "I'm so sorry, Lana. I was supposed to talk to you when I saw you last time, but I never could."

Lana narrowed her eyes. "Why?"

"You've been busy."

Lana crossed her arms. "I'm sorry, but school is over now. You can spy on someone else."

Mrs. Sullivan sighed. "Sometimes, we have to pretend to get what we want. Isn't that right?"

"What do you mean?"

Mrs. Sullivan took off her glasses and wiped them. "The best way to push them into the witch's hands was to feign ignorance. The guardians never suspected me."

Julia widened her eyes. "There were rumors about Mercy House in school. All this time, it was . . . you?"

The teacher nodded. "Yes. I knew Rebecca. I brought her here to Triville."

"And you let her own father kill her?"

Mrs. Sullivan lowered her eyes. "If only I had known about the danger she was in. Rebecca was so afraid to see her father again, and she asked me to cover for her in case something happened. She told me to deliver you a message."

"She did? What message?"

The teacher fiddled with the hem of her black dress. "Three years ago, I joined a group of women in Middle Lake City. I volunteered to bring Rebecca home. Everyone thought we would stop the Mercy sorority from taking the girls' magic away."

Lana sighed. "I didn't know that Becca had *you* by her side."

"Yes, I tried to help her. The girl was in despair. She said that no one would believe her about Mercy House, and she was right. We wanted to do something about the facility, and before we came to Triville, we made a deal with the forest witch. Rebecca asked her to take girls with destructive Gifts and hide them from the Gift Hunter—to teach them how to control their powers. We were supposed to warn the witch about the guardians' activities, so she could stay safe."

Lana leaned over the windowsill, and the warm wind touched her neck. Meredith had never told her anything about Mrs. Sullivan. Maybe she hadn't trusted Lana.

"Mrs. Sullivan, I'm so sorry for everything," Julia said.

The teacher's eyes welled. "You did very well, Julia. We all did."

"After Becca died, you kept helping the girls," Lana said.

Mrs. Sullivan nodded. "When Rebecca passed away, Meredith and I started working together. I was waiting for you to join us."

"It took me a long time to come home. I was so scared, and I wasn't ready."

"Don't regret anything; you caught her murderer. And for me, it was a fine three years."

"Thank you for that. I think Becca would be proud of you."

Mrs. Sullivan smiled. "I know. But now that everything is over, I have to leave."

"I wish I knew you more," Lana said.

Mrs. Sullivan put her hand on Lana's shoulder. "I saved eight of them. Some of the girls came to me to confess. They felt too ashamed to speak with guardians or their parents. Some of them hated me, but I made sure they were warned about the witch, and they managed to find their way to her themselves. Maybe I'll hear from them someday."

Lana nodded. "It'll never be over. But I'll do everything I can to help these girls. They can't keep living in fear."

Mrs. Sullivan put her finger to her lips.

Lana glanced back. Her father stood behind her.

"What are you ladies talking about?" he asked.

Lana shrugged. "We were just discussing the case. How are you?"

He nodded. "Not bad. They said Turner will be sentenced soon."

"The poor man!" Mrs. Sullivan cried in a trembling voice. "I can't believe how he's ruined the guardian code. Terrible, terrible things are going on!"

Lana widened her eyes. The teacher played her part well. Lana clasped her shoulder. "I'm so sorry you have to leave Triville, but don't worry. The guardians will keep this town safe."

Mrs. Sullivan hugged her. "Thank you, sweetheart."

Her father shook his head and walked away. Mrs. Sullivan took off her glasses and wiped sweat away from her face that wasn't actually there.

Julia smiled. "You're a good actress."

She nodded. "I read a lot of classic books for my performances—that's why I make a good literature teacher. Good stories can always teach you something."

Lana nodded. "I know, I read a lot of beautiful stories too. Unfortunately, none of them tell the truth about Mercy House."

Julia shifted her gaze from Lana to the teacher. "You're an actress. If you tell this story to everyone, they'll see the truth."

"People only see what they want to see," Lana said, "and seeing is believing."

Mrs. Sullivan smiled. "Actually, she's right, Lana. As people say, words speak to the mind, and art speaks to the heart. Art is the best form of truth telling."

Lana sighed. "But it could be dangerous."

"Not after this case. Now people are starting to doubt the Mercy House, and it's the perfect time to open a new show. We can tell everyone about what happened to Rebecca."

Julia hugged her teacher. "Show them everything."

"I will," Mrs. Sullivan said.

The intermission ended, and people started to return inside. They gave Lana curious glances as they walked past, and she turned to the window. It was her turn to sit on the chair of truth next, and she had no idea what she was going to say. Lana put her palm on her chest to feel her beating heart. If thoughts could be transmitted to another person, hopefully, someone in this room would have a big enough heart to hear her.

Chapter 44. The Price of Justice

The statue of justice held the violet Light ball. Her shining eyes looked down at the room where town dwellers were filing in. People walked in and took their places at the benches; their quiet chatter filled the room. When the judge arrived and took his place, he announced that the hearing had begun.

After the announcement, Lana sat in the chair of truth and looked around. Almost the whole town was present. People whispered to each other. George Turner was in his cage, his hands squeezing the rods.

The prosecutor approached Lana and started his examination.

"Miss Morris," he said in a low voice. "You took part in the investigation, and you're a mind reader. Correct?"

Lana nodded. "Yes."

"Did you read the suspect?"

"Yes, I did."

The prosecutor glanced at the judge, then back to her. "Can you please share your observations with the court?"

"Sure. At first, I saw Turner poison Elisa and tie her up. Then I saw Rose. He used a sleeping potion and carried her into the forest, and . . ." She looked across the room; the crowd held its collective breath. "And then he committed his crime."

"Did you see anything else?"

Lana lowered her eyes. When she'd been in Turner's memories, she'd felt that he didn't want to kill his daughter—he'd chosen to obey his duty. All of his subsequent choices were in protest to a system that worked against people instead of protecting them.

Lana's heart pounded.

Here's what I've learned. The truth isn't ugly. Cowardice is.

Julia was right. Turner was a coward. He had decided to obey the system, instead of fighting for his daughter's life. Turner didn't have enough guts to protect her.

But his daughter was different. She had died, but her tragedy had inspired Mrs. Sullivan, Elisa, and even Lana herself when she'd returned to Triville. This is what Richard told her, *Rebecca's case can change everything.*

Lana sighed. "Yes, I saw Rebecca, the first victim. I knew her before I met her in Mercy House where her powers were taken away against her will. She escaped and came back home to find shelter. When I read Turner, I saw him killing his own daughter in a barn. He made it look like a suicide."

A murmur rolled through the room.

"Death to the murderer!" someone screamed.

Lana looked across the room—people looked anxious. Her father, sitting at the back of the room, nodded when their eyes met.

The judge knocked on his armrest. It took several minutes before the crowd quieted.

The prosecutor approached Lana and continued. "Miss Morris, did you see how the suspect killed Bella?"

"No, I didn't see the murder itself. I checked his memory of that night, but everything was blurry."

"But you saw something?"

"He walked along a dark street, and lights flashed before his eyes, but I didn't see Bella in his memories."

"You did not *see,* or he did not *kill* her?"

Lana lowered her eyes. "I'm not sure. I didn't see him killing her."

The prosecutor walked to the judge and whispered something in his ear. Then, the judge clasped his hands. "The court calls the expert, Lieutenant Charles Braun."

Charles stood up; his blue eyes were filled with confidence.

Of course. Who else among the guardians knew about her Gift so well?

The prosecutor looked at him. "Lieutenant Braun, please clarify your specialization."

Charles looked across the room. "I'm a Gift Reader. I can feel what kind of Gift a person has, and I see how it works. When we have seasonal training, I help new guardians discover their hidden powers and help develop them."

The prosecutor nodded. "Lieutenant Braun, please describe to us how the Mind Reading Gift works."

"A mind reader is able to catch imaginary fears or shards of a person's real memories, such as images and their connected emotions. A mind reader sees the same things in the same way as his opponent."

The prosecutor shook his head. His long black hair rustled and lay back to rest on his shoulders. "Is there any reason why a mind reader wouldn't be able to see a particular memory?"

"It can happen if the person being read doesn't remember the events. A forgetfulness potion could be used, or there could be memory loss from alcohol or drugs."

The prosecutor nodded, and Charles sat on his bench. Lana moved in her chair; sweat rolling down her back, moistening her undershirt.

"And now, tell us, Miss Morris, could it be that the suspect was so drunk that his memories were blocked, and he didn't remember what he'd done?"

Lana inhaled dry air. In the cage, Turner's eyes shone with hatred—the same look he gave her when he tried to kill her. Lana shifted her gaze back to the prosecutor. "Yes, I'm pretty sure his memory of that night is blocked."

The prosecutor smiled. "Your Honor, the absence of memory doesn't prove the innocence of the suspect."

Lana stood up and looked at the stand. What irony, calling it the chair of truth. Truth was never enough; everyone had their own ideas that could be understood in different ways. Ghost, Turner, and even she believed in things without knowing if they were right.

Well, she'd told them everything she knew, and the weight of the final decision lay on the judge's shoulders. Lana sighed and walked back to her bench.

* * *

The room of justice was enlivened as one expert testified, and another sat on the chair of truth. The statue of justice looked down at them, grinning.

Then, the judge stood up. "Thank you everyone who came today to help us find justice. I listened to everyone carefully, and now, I give a chance to the suspect to say his final word."

Turner rose from his knees and looked straight at Lana. "You're right; this system has destroyed way too many lives."

Lana flinched. She never expected him to talk like this. Not after everything he'd done.

Turner scoffed. "As a guardian, I had one purpose—to protect the people in this town and to protect my family. For the last six years, I was a Gift Hunter, and I did my job well. It was easy—I followed orders and sent girls with destructive Gifts to Mercy House. There weren't too many of them—four or five a year. All of them were scared, and if they panicked, I used a sleeping potion to knock them out. It wasn't hard to do, and I never questioned my duty. Until my own my daughter's Gift was revealed."

"It happened all of a sudden, but I was the one who had to take care of her." Turner's voice trembled. "If you think it was easy to send her away, you're wrong. I was never the same again. Everything started to fall apart.

"After two weeks, Becca came back, and she told me about Mercy sorority. I didn't want to kill her. I went to the chief to ask for help, but he said it had to be done, one way or another. He said that my whole family might die in an accident; there could be a fire in the house. I had a choice—Becca, or all of us. How could I choose between my two kids? But at least I could save one. And so, I did."

He looked at the chief. "Morris, you knew that something was wrong with the previous chief. That's why we all supported you after he left his post. But you're just the same—stupidly following these fucking rules. Nothing will ever change here."

The judge knocked his armrest and Turner sat on the floor, hugging his head.

* * *

When the crowd calmed down, Mr. Spence told the court his legal opinion. He insisted that the fact of Bella's murder was not confirmed, and that Elisa was the victim of her own recklessness. Then the prosecutor stood up; he concluded that Turner's guilt was fully proven and accused him of all four cold-blooded murders, including the forest witch.

At the end, the judge stood in front of the room. "After listening to all the evidence and considering all sides, the court finds George Turner guilty of three murders, with an effort to commit a fourth. The court does not consider the death of the witch to be a crime; her death was a result of her illegal activities. The court finds George Turner guilty of malfeasance and defaming the guardian code. I hereby sentence him to sixty years of imprisonment on Death Island. Carry out the sentence immediately!"

The room erupted in loud whistles and applause. Turner sat on his knees and stared at the judge. Lana sighed. *This* game was over, but it wasn't the end. Not for the real Ghost, and not for her.

* * *

Lana stood in the half-empty courtyard. People walked away, discussing the latest news and laughing. In the afternoon sky, stubborn sunrays fell on the earth like shining ladders.

Her father approached, his eyes shining with kindness. "You did a good job today."

"I just told them what I was supposed to say," she said.

He smiled. "You did much more. You helped catch a serial killer and saved Elisa's life. I underestimated you, Lana."

She shrugged. "It's fine."

He touched his mustache. "I think I found an interesting solution for how to rebuild our team."

"What's that?"

"When we hire someone, we never know who they will become, because becoming a guardian takes more than just two years of study in the academy. But today, the solution hit me in the face. We already have someone competent enough; we can forgo the traditional qualifications."

Lana widened her eyes. "You can really do that? I can't believe it! This can't be my old-fashioned father, protecting our sacred traditions."

"Traditions change when they need to."

"What do you mean? Are you going to hire a person who didn't study in the academy?"

He smiled. "Yes, and I think you know who I'm thinking of."

Lana paused. In the morning Richard said that her father was about to do something about the destructive powers in girls, and now he was speaking in riddles. Interesting, what could they do, unless . . . they hired someone who went through Rebecca's case personally. This young man might be sent to Mercy House to educate the girls, instead of taking their magic away. And to do so, he didn't need to be a guardian.

"Kyle Turner, of course!" Lana said.

He raised his eyebrows. "Why him?"

Lana's eyes sparkled. "He's a fine young man. He helped us with this case from the very beginning. Kyle knew about his father, and he did what he needed to do when it mattered."

He chuckled. "Oh, Lana. You never cease to amaze me."

"I just want the best for this town. Just talk to him. You'll see."

He looked intrigued. "I will. You know what? We should have a ball tomorrow at our house."

"A *ball?*"

"Yes. Let's celebrate the closure of this case. I'll announce the new guardian there."

Lana shifted her gaze at the sky. The clouds rolled over the sun's rays, and the horizon took on a red shade.

Ghost hadn't lied about the ball. He'd *really* seen it. That meant Richard would meet him tomorrow, face-to-face, and whoever the murderer was, they would catch him soon.

Chapter 45. The End is a New Beginning

Elisa stood in front of a big house, playing with the cool silk hem of her ballgown. In the tall windows, silhouettes of people twirled and danced. The light sounds of a violin reached her ears. Her dress was long and blue, the color of the night sky, and it fit her perfectly. It had belonged to her mother.

Elisa walked to the wide veranda, and the double door flew open before her. In the bright light of the chandeliers, people were dancing and laughing. The ladies with smiles on their faces, and men in gorgeous suits—they were exactly like she'd imagined them. Servants in black and white slid behind, holding trays of champagne glasses and appetizers.

She took a deep breath and entered the hall; the smell of adulthood was in the air. The sadness of her last schooldays vanished in the room's brightness. This didn't look like any of the dull parties she'd been to in the small school hall. Here, the colors were deeper, the air in the room more fragrant.

"Elisa!" Julia said.

Elisa turned her head and stopped breathing for a moment. Julia wore a long silver dress that sparkled in the lights of the chandeliers, and her lovely hair was decorated with elegant pins. A beautiful necklace shone on her neck, a silver heart with a tiny diamond that sparkled as she moved.

"Julia, is that really you?" Elisa smiled.

Julia spun around to show off her dress, and Elisa clapped her hands.

"I can't believe we're here!" Julia said.

"But we are, my dear. We really are." Elisa took Julia's hands, and they twisted in a dance. They moved around the hall with grace, their sonorous laughter making smiles appear on people's faces. Leaving their past behind them, they were embraced by joy and freedom. A new page of their lives turned, and their real journeys began.

* * *

After the dance, Julia walked onto the balcony, and the fresh night air cooled her flushed cheeks. Elisa followed her. They sat on a bench, and Julia looked up. Millions of stars covered the velvet sky like shining diamonds. The stars glittered, twinkled, and teased her. Her rare Gift opened so many possibilities. She was free to go to any corner of the world. She could even save people's lives. But the world was too big. She explored the stars, trying to read the answer among them.

"I'm so happy about your Gift," Elisa said.

"Thanks. I hope to see yours soon."

Elisa sighed. "I'm afraid of what it might be. Who will I become after everything I've gone through?"

Julia looked up. "You can worry about that, but your Gift is just the beginning. I have no idea what to do next."

Elisa's eyes sparkled. "You know what? No one has any damn idea what to make of their lives. We can only listen to our hearts and follow them."

"And what is your heart telling you?"

Elisa sighed. "To let my past go. I want to explore the world— to see different cities and kingdoms. To learn more about people, places, and life itself."

Julia raised her eyebrows. "Are you leaving Triville?"

"I think so."

Julia went numb. A lonely tear rolled down her cheek.

Elisa wiped her face. "I want it more than anything. I'm scared, but at the same time, it's so exciting."

"I thought nothing scared you."

"Trust me, lots of things do. I have no idea what I'll do if my Gift isn't proper. It's made me arrogant and cynical. It's time to face my fears and find out who I really am."

"You're a wonderful person and my best friend," Julia said. "You're the strongest person I've ever known."

"Thank you. Yes, I have some strengths, and that's why my Gift will be powerful, but I've learned one thing—our Gifts don't define us. We do. Whatever it is, I want to learn how to use it to help others."

Julia smiled through her tears and hugged Elisa. "Then I can only wish you good luck. I love you so much."

Elisa breathed in the smell of Julia's hair and closed her eyes. "I love you too, Julia," she whispered.

They sat in silence for a while. The music in the hall picked up, starting the fun. But Julia wanted to stay outside just a bit longer. The night was so beautiful and warm.

"You know what?" Elisa asked. "Let's make a promise to each other."

"A promise?"

"Yes. Let's promise that wherever we are, we will always support each other. No matter what."

"Of course," Julia said. She took her diamond necklace and gave it to Elisa. "Here, I want you to have it."

It shimmered in Elisa's hands, reflecting the light coming out from the window. "I can't. It's too expensive."

"My mother gave it to me to find my true love. I think you need it more. I hope you'll find someone you love and give it to her."

Elisa's heart sank. *To her.* She squeezed the pendant in her palm. "You know."

"I know. And I want you to be happy."

Elisa looked up. "That's impossible," she whispered.

"When there's love, everything is possible." Julia took her hand. "Now, let's go and enjoy the rest of the evening."

They walked back into the gorgeousness of the ball where the violins sang, and people danced. When the door closed behind them, the bushes under the balcony rustled. A shadow separated from the wall and walked through the dark yard.

* * *

Kyle stood by a pillar in the hall, holding a glass of champagne in his hand. The balcony door flew wide open. Julia ran to him and kissed his cheek.

Elisa came after her and smiled. "You two are a beautiful couple."

Kyle fixed his tie. "Yes, we are."

Elisa nodded. "Kyle, what are you gonna do next? Actually, I can guess—become a guardian?"

He shook his head. "I think I saw enough. All these investigations, criminals, and murders . . . it's just not for me."

Kyle's face was calm. Julia never talked about the future with him, because it was clear their paths would split. She could never muster the courage to ask which guardian academy he would choose.

"What will you do, then?" Elisa asked.

"Start a dragon farm."

Julia widened her eyes. "Dragons? They're too wild and free to be pets. And rare—people are lucky to see them once in their lifetimes."

Elisa chuckled. "The dragons just avoid people, but I've read there are plenty of them in the North. Do you want me to steal a couple of their eggs for you?"

Kyle crossed his arms. "You can laugh now, but I think I've found a solution. Humans have been trying to tame dragons since the dawn of time, and few people have managed to do it—brave kings, powerful magicians, and great warriors."

Julia shook her head. "Kyle, history knows no more than ten people who have done it, and all of them had a huge amount of power. I really like you, but . . . are you really comparing yourself to Emperor Archibald the Greatest? He conquered these lands."

"He was wise and kind—a person who *really* cared about his people. A person who had a great heart and who knew the true power of love," he replied.

Elisa chuckled. "It's all about love, then."

Kyle smiled. "Love is worth nothing without respect. All ten people who tamed the dragons treated them with dignity—that was the key to the dragons' hearts. Each dragon is an amazing, intellectual creature. Their wise masters never suppressed them; they looked to them as equals, and that's why they managed to establish such deep connections. The baby dragons they raised became strong and loyal to their masters."

Elisa sighed. "Love really changes people."

"It does." Kyle took Julia's hand. "Would you like to do it with me? We can start raising dragons here in Triville."

Julia blushed. He stood so close, and her heart belonged to him; it beat in unison with his. Her home was here. "Of course," she said.

Chapter 46. The Acolyte

Lana stood in front of a tall mirror. Her tight green dress made her look even slimmer than usual. She turned around and touched her curled hair. The woman in the mirror was beautiful.

Music and laughter sounded from the hall. People celebrated life, but little did they know a threat was awaiting outside their little cozy world. And Richard . . . he was in the forest nearby, and she couldn't even go there and help him—it was his own battle. Lana turned in front of the mirror one more time, sighed, and went down the stairs to the big, bright hall.

Candlelight supplemented by a soft shine of night flowers moved across the pillars. Musicians in the corner played violins. The gentle music flew over the hall and mixed with laughter and clinking champagne glasses.

Three friends stood at the pillar and laughed. Elisa, Julia, and Kyle—they were so grown up in their ballgowns and suits.

Lana approached them. "Girls, you're so beautiful," she said.

Elisa's eyes glittered. "Lana, look at you! You're hard to recognize in that beautiful dress. You look gorgeous."

Lana smiled. "Thank you." She gazed over them. "I'm so proud of all of you. You've all been through a lot, but you handled it because you looked out for one another. Never forget that."

Elisa chuckled. "It would be kind of hard to forget. But thank you—for everything."

Julia stepped forward and hugged Lana.

Lana wiped her eyes. "Okay, this is getting too touching now."

"It's okay," Julia said, laughing. "Tears mean that you really care."

"Oh, Julia. You've always been so kind and compassionate. You have an amazing, rare Gift, and all the doors are open for you. Where would you like to go?"

Julia glanced at Kyle. "Actually, I want to stay here. This is my home—where I grew up. Of course, if people really need me, I'll go to them. But I want to come back home where my heart is."

Lana nodded. "Just remember to stay balanced. Help other people, but don't forget about yourself."

Elisa grinned. "Thanks, Mommy."

Lana took Elisa's hands. "And you. Your Gift has not been revealed yet, but it will be. When I look at you, I see myself. You're so brave and always step up for the people you love."

"I have a good teacher," Elisa said. "I've decided to travel until summer ends. I want to see the world."

"That's what I did when I was your age, and it was a wonderful journey. I hope you find the answers to all your questions," Lana said. Then she shifted her gaze to Kyle. "Thank you for being brave and helping with the investigation."

Kyle shrugged. "No problem. I just did what I had to do."

"You'll make a good guardian," Lana said.

Elisa glanced at Kyle. "You didn't tell her?"

Kyle shook his head.

Lana raised her eyebrows. "What happened? I thought you talked with the chief."

He nodded. "I did."

Julia gave her an intrigued look. "Don't worry, Lana. You'll like it."

Lana frowned. Their faces were sly, and sparkles gleamed in their eyes. A loud ringing sound made her turn around.

The red-haired guardian whose name she always forgot stood in the center of the hall and held a bell in his hand. "Ladies and gentlemen, my name is John Fleming. Let's welcome the host of tonight's event and the chief of Triville Guardian House . . . Bernard Morris!"

The room erupted in applause. Lana clasped her hands and smiled. Her father walked down the ladder in his white parade uniform. Golden dragon embroidery shone on his shoulder. He held a roll of paper in one hand. He came to the center of the hall and looked around. The audience quietened; all eyes were on him.

"Dear guests," he said. "Thank you for joining us tonight. As you know, we are celebrating the end of a difficult time. We lost several young lives, and we will always remember them. Let's pay our respects to them with a minute of silence."

Lana put her palm on her chest. Of course, it wasn't the end—not for her. Her father looked at her, and Lana lowered her eyes.

After the minute was over, her father continued. "Life never stays calm. And we, the guardians, are here to protect you from evil. Little did I know, this evil was hidden in one of my closest colleagues. It's made me doubt everything I've come to know and all the choices I've made.

"Who can be a guardian? Is this just a person who is good at detective work? Maybe a strong mage? No. It's obviously not enough. What I've learned is that being a guardian means *caring* about people. A guardian sincerely wishes to make this world a little bit better.

"Our team is going through many changes. With that in mind, I would like to announce a new guardian acolyte. After successfully completing six months of training, this person will move on to complete the exams in the Santos Guardian Academy and join our ranks."

Lana glanced at Kyle; he stood nearby with a wide smile on his face.

The chief unrolled the paper. "So, ladies and gentlemen, let's welcome our brand-new guardian acolyte." He smiled and looked around the crowd.

Everyone held their breath.

"Lana Morris!" he said.

The sound of applause deafened her.

Lana stood in shock, trying to understand why her father had pronounced her name in the middle of the ceremony. Elisa poked her shoulder. "Go to him!"

Lana slowly walked to the center of the hall. Her father smiled and gave her the roll of paper.

"Why do you want *me* to announce his name?" she whispered.

He laughed and put his warm palm on her shoulder. "It's *you*, Lana. You're a guardian acolyte now."

She glanced at the roll in her hands. The letters blurred before her eyes, but she could read the name on the bottom—it was hers.

She raised her eyes. "I don't deserve it," she whispered.

Her father looked at the crowd. "Do you think she deserves it?"

The crowd applauded and whistled. Lana held his arm to keep her balance.

"Indeed, you do," he said. His voice was confident and calm. "People rely on you, Lana."

She hugged him. "Thank you," she said.

* * *

The lights dimmed, and the time for the traditional dance arrived. Beautiful and frail violin music flew across the hall. People around her twisted in a dance. They laughed and discussed their future plans. With the familiar steps, their lives seemed to become old and familiar. Their worlds became safe and comfortable again.

Lana and her father moved across the hall with the others. They followed the same steps they had during her first ball, the same steps they had learned from previous generations. Lana's silk dress reflected the light of a thousand candles.

The old traditions were beautiful, but time never stopped. It brought new changes, mostly sad ones, but sometimes, life surprised her with unexpected gifts. Lana turned around on the dance floor and took her father's hand.

People rely on you, Lana.

She would do her best not to let him down.

Among all the faces in the hall, she wished to see the one with dark green eyes, but she couldn't find him. Lana glanced at her time crystal; it was bright red. It was midnight, and Richard was late.

Her father touched her shoulder. "You look too anxious for my new acolyte. Are you all right?"

"Yes. There have been too many emotions today."

"I can imagine. Don't worry, you'll get used to it."

Late—it was too late. Ghost's second prediction had come true: she'd become a "guardian woman." Richard could be in grave danger.

"Today two of your dreams came true," her father said.

Lana looked at him. "Two? Being a guardian is all I dreamed about."

"You wished for the Santos guardian to leave town."

She frowned in confusion. "You think Richard left?'

Her father shrugged. "This morning, I sent a letter to Santos. Then he left. He has other . . . responsibilities to attend to."

Lana sighed. "Father, I'll be a guardian soon. I know about your plan."

He furrowed his brows. "What plan?"

Lana moved closer. "The *real* murderer, Ghost. He was the one who killed Bella, and now Richard is catching him."

Her father twirled her in a dance and laughed. "You've always had a good sense of humor, Lana."

Lana gave him a puzzled look.

"There is no Ghost, and there never was," he said. "I mean, not here in Triville."

"What do you mean? You sent us to the witch's house to catch him."

Her father looked around and lowered his voice. "Well, I actually wanted Richard to catch the witch, but by then, it was too late."

She shook her head. "But the ball—Ghost predicted it!"

"I planned the celebration several days after we caught Turner. You just missed the meeting. Wasn't it a good surprise?"

Lana stopped breathing. "Richard was there," she said.

Her father nodded. "Yes, he was."

"He knew about your plans for me."

Her father shook his head. "Actually, I decided this yesterday. Nobody knew but Kyle."

Lana nodded.

"Then it was a lucky guess," she said.

The music died, and they stopped moving. Lana took a bow, then she turned around and walked through the crowd of people, quickening her steps. She pushed a woman, and the woman spilled a glass of champagne on the floor. Lana didn't even notice.

Blood pulsed in her head. *Seeing is believing.* But what did *she* see? A guardian she'd fallen in love with. He had known the prediction would come true because he'd had more information than she did. Lana ran to the entrance and pushed through the heavy doors.

Chapter 47. Ghost

The fresh evening air hit Lana in the face as she ran along the veranda. She leaned on the railing, and a scream burst from her mouth. Slowly, she slid to the wooden floor. A light wind cooled her hot shoulders and burning cheeks.

Lana squeezed the hem of her dress. Illusions and mind games—it was so easy to believe them and so easy to get lost in fears and doubts.

It was good that Richard had run from town; otherwise, she might have killed him with her own hands. He was a liar—she'd always known he was. The last time she saw him was when she found the discrepancies between the two cases, so even his last words to her had been a lie.

Lana bit her lip. Richard was a liar, but no one could lie 100 percent of the time. In some moments, he had been truthful. *But when?*

On the night when Bella was murdered, Richard was under arrest —the affair with his ex-chief's wife. He couldn't have killed Bella, then. And he hadn't killed the witch either because, as the report had said, Meredith had died on the same day. Richard wasn't a murderer. But who was he?

That morning, when she'd woken up in the forest, Richard had changed his attitude toward her. And then . . . then, he slept with her and showed her Ghost's letter to gain her trust. Emotions had blinded her and made her rely on him. He had known the judge would find George Turner guilty anyway. But it also meant that no one would search for the *real* murderer.

Lana gasped. The picture was bright and clear, but she had to think like a guardian. Despite everything, there still was one discrepancy left—his Gift. He'd stopped time for her; she'd *seen* it.

He really loved her, then. There was still a weak piece of hope left. Lana rubbed her temples. If he'd lied about his agreement with the chief, he might have lied about his brother too.

But why would he do that? Maybe he wanted to buy more time to escape, but that didn't make any sense either. He could have left as soon as the investigation was over. Richard hadn't needed to show her the letter, but he had. So maybe the letter was real.

When the guardian woman reads this letter, Ghost had said. Then, she was supposed to read it, and it meant something. Was she just a pawn in Ghost's game?

Lana turned her face toward the dark yard where the bushes shivered in the night wind. Her heart pounded at the bottom of her belly. *The glade.* If Ghost existed, he was waiting for Richard in the forest glade near the house. There was only one way to find out what happened to him and figure out the truth.

Lana stood up and approached the stairs that led to the front yard. She took a step down, and then another one. The night was still; a violin cried somewhere behind the house's doors. Then someone's quiet steps waked by the yard, and Lana rushed down.

The darkness wrapped around her, and the night shielded her from the little cozy world of her house—from all the guests and the guardians.

A silhouette split away from the tree trunk and walked toward her. She squinted; the man was wearing black clothes and a hat. His green eyes shone in the dark.

Lana froze. A looming threat pierced her heart, but she couldn't move.

The man approached and removed his hat. She recognized his unshaven cheeks and his wonderfully familiar face.

"Richard!" she said.

"Lana," he replied, smiling.

"You came."

"I did."

She stepped back. "You scared me. I thought you left—or worse."

He chuckled. "How could I leave without seeing you again?"

"I have so much to tell you—"

"Later." His face became serious. "I need your help."

Lana paused. "Is Ghost dead?"

He shook his head. "No, he's very much alive. It would be great if you could read him."

She nodded. "Of course."

He smiled and walked toward the forest, then he looked back and beckoned her. "Do you trust me?" he asked.

"Yes." Lana took a deep breath and followed.

* * *

In the forest, summer night colored the nature. The green moss on the trees glowed, and the flowers shone with red, blue, and yellow shades. The plants lit up the narrow trail, and the leaves shivered above their heads. An eagle owl hooted somewhere in the branches, and Lana flinched.

"Where are we going?" she asked.

"To the glade, sweetheart."

Lana scowled. Something was wrong with him. She had too many questions for him, like what this sudden change in his mannerisms was about, but the most important one was about Ghost.

"How did you catch him?" Lana asked.

He turned to face her. "You'll see everything soon. I promise." He quickened his pace, and Lana had to run after him.

Finally, the trail led them to the glade, and they stood under the serene shine of the stars. The glade was covered with night chamomiles; the flowers shone with charming yellow and white lights, and little fireflies slowly hovered among the plants.

"Isn't it beautiful?" he asked.

"It is, but—"

He raised his arm. "Oh, please, don't ruin the moment. Time admires patience."

He took her hand and kissed her fingers.

"Do you feel anything?" he asked.

She gave him a puzzled look. "What should I feel?"

He laughed. "This will be harder than I thought—but it'll be more interesting. All right, I assume I owe you a dance."

He pulled her closer, and they moved around the glade. The flowers shone under their feet, the tree leaves rustled, and the warm, tender night embraced them. He'd even lied about his dancing skills—he wasn't a bad dancer. Now, when they moved under the light of the shimmering stars, Lana obeyed his confidence, his strength. His hand wrapped around her back, and his lips moved close. She closed her eyes and kissed him.

An acidic taste of fir and tobacco opened her mind. She could read him—his every memory and thought. She dived deep into his consciousness. In a summer forest, he played a game with a boy with the same face and the same sonorous laugh. Then, there was a carousel of glades—and the girls from the red folder.

All of them, the twelve girls, stood around her in the glade with knives in their bellies, looking at her in silence. But they weren't scared—they were under hypnosis.

Bella stood at her left, and she stared at Lana with her big brown eyes. "Will you teach me?" Bella asked.

His roaring laughter made the victims blurry. His mind led her to the moment of Bella's funeral. Town dwellers in gray clothes stood at the blossoming orchard. They cast their Lights into the gray sky and looked up. But one of them looked straight at her. It was her own face.

Lana opened her eyes widely and stepped back. "Ghost! It was you who I saw on the funeral. You're the murderer!"

He slowly raised his hands and applauded, the sound loud in the night glade. Her heart sank. When Richard had said he had an elder brother, he never said that he was a twin. Had he done it on purpose?

"Where is Richard?" Lana asked.

He shrugged. "He'll be here soon, don't worry."

"How do you know?"

"Oh, it's easy when you have a Time Prediction Gift. You'll see how much fun it is." He pulled his hand up and held up one finger. "One: she takes two steps back."

Her instincts screamed to run away, but she was too afraid to expose her back to him. She stepped back with one foot, and then the other. *Another of his predictions have come true.* Lana froze. She placed her palms outward, and her time bracelet glowed pure white.

He put up the second finger and smiled. "Two: she decides to cast a spell—a fireball to ensure she kills him. And now, for the most intriguing part."

Lana narrowed her eyes and pushed energy to her hands. Several orange sparkles shone at her fingertips, and then they disappeared. Lana shook her hands, but nothing happened. Her magic had stopped working.

He came closer. "Three: she realizes she's in a magic trap," he whispered. He pointed up, at the tree branch above her head. A green net was hidden in the leaves, shining bright.

Lana moved forward, but her shoulder hit an invisible wall, and she fell to her knees.

Ghost sighed. "Well, that was interesting, but everything good goes away."

Lana sneered. "Oh, *now* I hear a familiar phrase."

He shrugged. "Well, we have different senses of humor. And not to brag, but mine is far superior." He looked around and raised his voice. "Am I right, Rick?"

Chapter 48. True Colors

Lana hit the invisible wall of the trap with her fist and clenched her teeth. Nothing could help her get out of this nightmare, except for Richard, and he wasn't here.

Ghost sighed. "I know, right? Our Ricky is shy today."

Lana gave him a sharp look. "Are you going to kill me?"

"Finally, a good question!" He walked across the glade and scratched his cheek. "You know, if I had met you several years ago, I probably would have. But now, it's not that easy."

Lana widened her eyes. "Why not? You killed twelve teenage girls without hesitation and who knows how many witnesses."

"You're so chatty. Well, let's talk, then. Anyway, we have time to kill." He sat on the ground in front of Lana and fixed his gaze on her. "You know, we're not actually very different. There's just been a little misunderstanding between us."

"Yeah, just a tiny bit."

He laughed. "I like good old sarcasm, but let's be serious for a moment. Tell me, why did you want to become a guardian?"

"To catch people like you, I guess."

He grinned. "You see, you and I want the same thing. To make this world a better place."

"By killing innocent people? I don't think so."

He shook his head. "You catch people after they commit crimes, but I do it *before*. That's the only difference."

"But the future is uncertain. There might be a chance they won't commit the crimes you see."

"Each one of these girls would become a powerful witch, and all witches disobey the law."

Lana paused. "You're not even giving them a chance."

He grinned. "I gave *you* a chance. Thanks to me, you'll become a guardian."

Lana frowned. "What?"

"You're welcome."

"How did you do that?"

He sighed. "Well, my Gift is a tricky and interesting thing. When I saw you at the witch's house, Lana, you were just a scared young woman looking for justice."

"It was *you*." Lana widened her eyes. "I saw you when I visited Meredith!"

"It was good you didn't see my face. Otherwise, it would have ruined everything." He laughed. "I followed your trace, and I met an interesting girl in the forest. I killed her to make you meet my brother, who shares the same passion for detective work. He did the rest."

"*Richard* helped me, not you!"

"The letter from me was the last step, and after that, your career was sealed."

Lana frowned in confusion. "The one you wrote to Richard. How did that help?"

"Lana, a letter could be easily overlooked as a small detail, but this one had great influence. When you read it, your inner spark of justice became a fire. People who listened to you in court felt it, and this affected his final decision."

Lana breathed out. "My father."

Ghost nodded. "There was actually a chain of events I started, but yes, he made the final decision about your future guardian career."

Lana shook her head. "Why did you bring me here, then?"

"I've told you that my Gift is a tricky thing. You were supposed to change the course of history—that's what I saw. But now things have changed too much. It's even worse than it might have been before."

"I don't understand."

He stood up and clenched his fists. "No one does! No matter what I do, everything falls apart. It's getting worse and worse. I don't ask for anyone to understand; I never have! I've tried to handle it on my own to prevent a doomed future—I'm the only one who can do this. But this world is determined to go to hell!"

He cast a fireball and shot the tree trunk behind her.

The spell burst behind her back, and she flinched. Here he was, the real Ghost, a mad murderer who struggled to carry the weight of his Gift. His green eyes shone brightly, vibrating the bracelet on Lana's hand. The time crystal glared white and grew hot—too hot. She took the bracelet off and threw it on the grass.

Ghost continued. "I see civil wars, catastrophes, and the inevitable war between Incapables and mages. I thought you could prevent this whole mess, but I was wrong. You're the *reason* everything started!"

Lana took a deep breath. He'd definitely lost his mind, but she kept listening to him. Hopefully someone at the house would notice her absence soon. "I would never let that happen," she said.

He gave her a sharp look, and she stepped back. Her spine touched one of the trap's invisible walls.

"I see your future with Richard now! I can't let you stay together."

"Are you going to kill him?"

Ghost's hoarse laughter cut through the night air. "No. What do you think of me? I'm not the kind of person who would kill his own brother."

Lana rolled her eyes. Time; she just needed to buy time. "Then what do you want?"

He moved closer. "All I need from my brother is for him to make the right choice."

"A choice?"

"Yes, a choice. Everything in life hinges on them. When our paths fork, everything changes. But it's not too late to change the ending."

A tree rustled behind her, and she glanced back, but she couldn't see anyone. The moss on the tree was dry, but not burnt, from his fireball spell.

Lana licked her lips. "It's not too late for *you* to change," she said.

He grinned. "Do you think so?"

Lana nodded.

"This proves that you know nothing. I see only three options for myself." He raised his hand, and a fireball flared up in his palm. "I could run away, but nothing would change." He looked at his fireball, and the flame reflected in his eyes. "So, there are just two choices left. Everything is in my brother's hands now, and the destiny of the world will be decided."

Lana gave him a puzzled look.

"The magic in the net above your head is tied to my blood and life energy. If Ricky leaves you to die here, the world will be saved. But to save you, he will have to kill me."

Her heart sank. Richard wouldn't be able to reverse time like he did with Turner. That's why Ghost had made this trap. Richard's Gift didn't work on blood relatives and the people he loved.

Ghost raised his hand. "So, what will you choose, Rick? The world, or the silly woman?"

He moved his hand, and a huge fireball hit the tree trunk behind Lana. The dry moss on it ignited, and heavy smoke wrapped around her body. Lana tried to move away, but the trap's walls held her in. Ghost stepped back and looked around.

Richard ran out from the tree trunk with a fireball in his hand. Lana closed her mouth and nose with her palms, but the smoke was too heavy, and she started choking. Through her stinging eyes, their two blurry silhouettes stood in front of each other. Their voices were loud, but their words were almost intelligible. Lana closed her eyes and fell to the ground.

* * *

Richard walked into the middle of the glade and raised his hand. A fireball flickered in his palm.

"I've heard you missed me, David," he said.

The man in front of him chuckled. "I'm glad you finally came out. Chatting with her exhausted me."

Richard narrowed his eyes. "Let her go."

"You've heard me, I can't."

Richard ran to Lana. She lay on the grass as thick smoke covered her body, and her thin hand covered her mouth. She gave him a blurred look. His hand touched the invisible wall that separated them. He knocked against it, but the trap was too strong. Lana was still alive, but for how long?

David approached. "Come on, we both failed at being guardians; we have nothing to lose."

"Take the damn trap off."

David grinned. "Or what?"

"Or I'll kill you."

"If you kill me here, the guardians will know everything, and you'll be screwed. You'll lose your career forever."

Richard gasped. "I don't care about it."

"You don't understand. I found them, Rick! The family of Incapables and the boy who will start the war! Come on, we need to stop them before it's too late."

"Again?" Richard scoffed. "You found a kid who *might* harm humanity? I'm tired of listening to this bullshit. You have to stop this."

David glanced at the burning tree. "Nothing is more important than your family. If you don't stop the Incapables, you'll lose everyone you love."

"I love *her*."

"This woman is a mess; she will ruin your life. Trust me—you have to let her go."

Richard shook his head, and a tear slid down his cheek. "Never." He threw his hand forward, and the fireball whistled as it flew.

David's eyes widened, and he looked down at his chest. An orange spot blazed on his jacket, and the heat enveloped his chest, not letting him take a breath. His heart made a final heavy beat and stopped.

He took several clumsy steps toward Lana and fell to the ground.

Chapter 49. No Lies

Lana opened her eyes. A man lay two steps from her. Chamomile flowers lit up his face and his shining green eyes. Then his sight became dull and empty.

The air around her started trembling. Lana pushed on the frail walls of the trap and fell to the grass, coughing. A pair of strong hands lifted her from the ground and pulled her aside. The tree was ablaze behind them. This man had the same face and the same eyes, but these eyes were full of anxiety.

Lana coughed. "You told me . . . he was your . . . elder brother!"

"Yes, five minutes older. That was a twin joke."

She wanted to object, but another heavy cough squeezed her lungs.

"I'm so sorry, Lana. For everything," he said.

She gave him a sharp look.

He touched her shoulders. "Damn, I couldn't make myself kill him. I just sat behind the tree and watched you. When he set it on fire, I was so scared."

Lana sighed. "I know. We always hope that people will change, but they never do. I'm so sorry you had to do that."

Richard shook his head. "I was at the fork, and I almost lost you. Maybe he was thinking about the future of the world, but he didn't know what love meant."

Lana smiled. "What does it mean for you?"

He kissed her forehead. "I promise, no more lies. I'll tell you everything."

* * *

They sat in the middle of the glade, surrounded by glowing chamomiles. The big tree blazed behind them, lighting up the glade and making the fireflies fly away. The night forest beside them shimmered with green.

Taking his jacket off, Richard placed it on Lana's shoulders. "When we were kids, David and I were inseparable. We used to live on a farm, and we played in the forest for days. We loved to climb the trees and read stories about heroes. We dreamed that we would change the world together after our Gifts were revealed."

Lana leaned on his shoulder. "That sounds like a good dream."

"It was, but then something happened. We were sitting at the table with our parents. It was fall, and our mother had baked a duck with red apples. She carried the dish and put it on the table, then David told her to be careful and to not break her glass. She turned to him and swung her hand. The glass in her hand fell on the floor and shattered. Water spilled everywhere.

"Mother went to the kitchen to grab a broom. I stared at the shards of glass, and then I felt something. I didn't want my mother to be upset. And then, I moved my hand. The shards jumped back together, and the water poured itself back in. The glass flew back onto the table—it was full again."

"And they all saw it?"

"Yes, my father sat at the table and looked at me, speechless. When my mother came back, she was surprised. David said that he'd already seen it happen."

"But how could _he_ have seen what happened to your mother? I mean, wasn't he limited by their blood connection?"

"His Gift is one of the most powerful ones—and the most dangerous. It doesn't have those blood limits. David saw all of our futures. It was excruciating for him. But he didn't understand that the things that were supposed to happen would happen anyway. If he interfered, events always had a worse outcome."

"What do you mean?"

"That glass. When our mother was washing the dishes, she broke it again. She cut her hand badly, and it took a long time for it to heal. I couldn't do anything about the cut because I couldn't affect the same situation twice. I realized it was a mistake to cheat time.

"However, David didn't learn this lesson. He was convinced that his Gift was given to him to prevent something. Then it worsened—our dad got sick, and David saw his death months in advance. Nothing we did helped, and he passed away that spring."

"I'm so sorry."

He caressed her head. "We all have limited time on this earth, and his time was up. Only human cruelty can be prevented—not the occasion."

"And then you became a guardian?"

"We both did. When school ended, we applied to the local Guardian Academy together. The exam committee confirmed that our Gifts were incredibly unique, and we were enrolled in a special program. We had to split apart because our Gifts worked against each other. Each time I went to move back time, David saw thousands of new possibilities. When we tried to use our powers together, it created an endless gallery of events—like when you put two mirrors in front of each other. So, I moved to the academy in Santos, and he studied in Esplendor. But he didn't graduate."

"Why?"

"Our teachers warned us about the impossibility of changing destiny. They said we could affect people and prevent crime, but natural events were not under human control—even with our Gifts. David didn't listen, of course. He didn't trust anyone after he started developing his Oracle Gift. He saw lies all around him, and he saw how people reacted and what they did long before he said or did anything.

"David told me that the committee wouldn't let him pass his examinations because his Gift was too dangerous. His magic was too powerful, and everyone knew it. They were planning to send him to Death Island, he said."

Lana widened her eyes. "Would they really do that?"

"I tried to stop him from having these depressing thoughts, and I told him that people deserved his trust." Richard sighed. "But he was too anxious, too caught up in the ideas that had already formed in his mind.

"When we came home from the winter holidays, David started telling me things that were supposed to happen. He told me about the upcoming war and about Incapable rebels. It sounded like nonsense, but I believed my brother, and I said that we would get help from our tutors."

"But he didn't trust them," Lana said.

"Exactly. I couldn't deter him anymore, and he left the academy without graduating. We lost Dave because he was smart enough to erase his traces. A year later, the first murder happened." Richard glanced back, where the flames devoured the tree. "And you know the rest."

Lana turned to the fire. With a loud crack, one of the branches fell and landed close to Ghost's body. She flinched.

"You don't have immunity from his Gift. You didn't tell anyone because he looks the same," Lana said.

Richard nodded. "I was too afraid they would lock me up somewhere to avoid the inconvenience. They probably would've thought that he would try to replace me and gain access to secret information. But time went by, and he kept killing. I couldn't prevent anything. If only I had told the truth as soon as I figured out that he was a murderer." Richard paused. "Anyway, soon the guardians will know everything. I've made my choice, Lana. For me, everything is over."

Lana stood up; the flames reflected on her face. "We can burn his body. Nobody would ever know or see his face."

"No."

"They will lock you up. You'll lose your job!"

He rose and took her hands. "Lana, you don't understand. Every Gift has a price to pay. We cannot use them to hide our mistakes. You heard what David said—whatever he did, he made it even worse. It was the same for me. But the truth is, to make a change, the first thing we need to do is to change *ourselves*. I realized this too late, but I did realize it eventually. I can't involve you in this."

Lana squeezed his hands. "Are you sure?"

He nodded. "Before I met you, I moved from one lie to another. I want to release myself from that cycle. If that means I'll never become a guardian again, I'm ready for it."

Lana glanced at Ghost's body. "What about him?"

"Even if we burn him, the guardians will take his blood and figure everything out. It's gone too far."

Lana sighed. She put her palms forward, and her yellow Light grew into a ball. Richard formed a blue Light ball with silver sparkles in his palms. They looked at each other and lifted their Lights up, and then they burst into the night sky with two loud bangs. The blue and yellow sparkles blinked and melted in the air.

Lana looked at him. "So, is this the end of us?"

He shook his head. "No. It's only the beginning, Lana. You'll become a guardian and make this world a better place."

She gave him a sad smile. "I'll do my best, but I can't catch all the criminals in the world. I won't change that much."

He touched her cheek. "You're a wonderful woman, Lana—the first female guardian. It means that you'll inspire girls with dangerous Gifts to become guardians themselves. This is how you'll end the mess of Mercy House."

Lana held her breath. Now everything made perfect sense. It was Ghost who wanted Mercy House to shut down, and he pushed Lana to become the guardian. Legalizing destructive Gifts in women was the only way to stop "powerful witches" that he hunted for. Thus,

Ghost made her meet his twin brother, knowing that Richard would see something in Lana and support her on her way.

The tears filled Lana's eyes. With his time prediction Gift, Ghost could have succeeded without killing Bella. But he was a maniac who manipulated them instead, and he ruined everything. Two girls and the witch perished because of him, and now, Richard sacrificed his career so Lana could continue changing this cruel system that ruined so many lives. He was a real guardian.

"I love you so much," she said.

"I love you too."

Richard leaned to her and kissed her wet lips. His warmth and the quiet glowing light of his love soothed her.

The heavy steps of guardians ruined the silence; they were close. Too close.

Richard leaned back. "I'll never forget you," he whispered.

Lana wiped her tears with her palms.

Then, the guardians came into the glade. There was a dozen of them. The chief stopped at Ghost's body and slowly raised his eyes at Richard.

His voice was stiff. "Lieutenant Laine, would you care to explain what the heck is going on?"

Richard approached him. "Chief, the mission is complete. Ghost is dead."

The chief gave Lana a worried look. "Did you know about it?"

Lana stepped forward, but Richard didn't let her speak.

"Lana didn't know anything. She was just bait," Richard said. "All the time, I hid the truth about my brother from everyone, disobeying the guardian code. I am ready to be punished."

The chief waved his hand, and two of the guardians approached Richard. They locked blocking cuffs on his wrists.

"Lieutenant Laine, by the name of the King, you are under arrest," the chief said.

The guardians took Richard away for interrogation. He gave Lana a sad smile, then his figure disappeared behind the glowing tree trunks.

The chief approached Lana and put his hands on her shoulders. "Are you all right?"

Lana nodded.

"Are you sure?"

"Yes." Lana sighed. "Richard had to kill his brother to save my life."

"Even if it's true, he hid the identity of a serial killer for years. I'm sorry, but it's over."

Lana gave him a sharp look. "Over? He just lied to save my reputation. I knew that Ghost was his brother, and I knew it for a while—"

"Stop it!" He shook her shoulders, and Lana went silent.

"Lana, you are still shocked, so I won't listen to you now. But tomorrow, when you bring your report, your every word will count. If you start protecting Richard Laine, it might cost you *your* career. Is that clear?"

Lana lowered her eyes. "Yes."

"Now, I'll ask someone to follow you home."

"Just give me a minute here," Lana said.

He nodded and his hands released her.

The guardians wrapped Ghost's body in a black cloak. His dull, lifeless eyes in his pale face made her heart sink. The branch on the ground was almost burnt out; only red charcoals remained. Her time crystal lay in the grass near the branch, and it shone a bright yellow. Lana picked it up and squeezed it in her hand.

She put her palm on her chest; her heart burned. Time was cruel. People said that it could heal the worst wounds of the soul, but time was never enough. Lana stared at the time crystal. There was only one power that healed all wounds—love. It took her a long time to understand its true strength. When it was free from expectations, love transformed into a blinding glare, and all the fears and doubts melted away. Love was the most powerful force, and it was stronger than all known Gifts. Even if it was a time Gift.

Lana smiled. Maybe Ghost predicted the end of Richard's career, but he never knew what people were capable of doing when they were in love. They could overcome their biggest fears and sacrifice themselves. She put her bracelet on her hand and walked to the edge of the glade, when her father was waiting for her under the tree. Tomorrow, he would need a report, and he would get to know the whole truth. Even if it meant the end of her own career.

Chapter 50. Winter Dream

Six months later

Twilight fell on Triville and colored the sky dark blue and indigo. A layer of snow covered the roofs, quiet streets, and valleys. The black walls of the Guardian House were stark in the snowy yard.

Lana sat at her desk, reading a letter. The candlelight lit up her room; there were several elegant bookshelves along the wall. Lana smiled and put the letter away. The last day of the year was almost done. It was the quiet time before the great New Year's celebration, and it seemed that all the criminals had decided to take a vacation too.

The door creaked open, and her father came in. He smiled.

Lana stood up. "Did you get my papers?"

He shook his head. "Not yet."

She sat back in her chair. "That's annoying. Could the academy just tell me whether I passed the exams or not?"

Her father sat on a chair in front of her. "I'm pretty sure you did. Just wait."

Lana sighed. "I can't wait. And nothing is certain! Richard was supposed to have an interrogation three days ago, and I haven't received any information from him since then. Do you know what's going on?"

He gave her a warm look. "Let's say, your report impressed the committee. Now, we can only hope he managed to save his career."

Lana's heart pounded. "What if he said something wrong, and they fired him?"

He smiled. "Trust your old father, this guy knows what to say."

"Of course."

"Lana, you should know that patient people eventually receive more." He looked at the paper on her desk. "I see you've received a letter."

Lana smiled. "Yes, Elisa wrote me. She just passed her first term in the academy in Middle Lake City."

He raised his eyebrows. "What's her Gift?"

"She shoots lightning."

Her father touched his mustache. "As the old saying goes, 'Everything happens at the right time.'"

"Yes. She might end up in a Mercy House."

"The facility is having a hard time right now. It will shut down soon."

"See, we did a good job."

He shook his head. "It's not just us. Yes, I wrote a petition to the King, but to my own surprise, all the guardian houses supported us, especially in Middle Lake City."

"Why are you surprised?"

"It's a capital, and they never cared about our small town. I just don't really understand why they stepped up."

Lana gave him a sly look. "Maybe Rebecca's story found a way into their hearts."

He narrowed his eyes. "You know something, don't you?"

Lana shrugged. "Some secrets are better left untold."

Her father smiled and put his hand on hers. "Lana, you've worked hard this year. I think you can go home early."

She looked around. "Well, I'm almost finished. I can wait for you."

"No need. Go for a walk; get some fresh air."

"It sounds like you want to get rid of me."

He chuckled. "You just look a bit tired."

"Then I will."

"Good."

When he left, Lana put her folders on the corner of her desk. It had been a good year. Who knew what the next one would bring?

* * *

Lana walked into the courtyard. White frost covered the tree branches, and the pale blue shine of tree trunks brightened the street. She inhaled the frosty air and stepped onto a squeaky snowy trail. She liked to walk home through this little park; the quiet flow of the river soothed her thoughts.

Time flew quickly, and it had made many changes to Triville. The dragon farm was now built, and two baby dragons could sometimes be seen flying in the skies over the forest. As it appeared, Elisa wasn't kidding about stealing the dragon's eggs, and with her new friend who had a Gift of invisibility, she stole them. Julia and Kyle had managed to tame the reptiles. Of course, accidents happened—that's how the old barn was burned to the ground in the fall. Otherwise, it had gone pretty well.

Lana touched the cold railing of the Bridge of Wishes. The time crystals glowed bright blue—exactly like his Light. But Richard was gone.

During all this time of his placement on Death Island, they wrote each other letters almost every week. Richard had promised to come during winter, no matter if he managed to keep his career or not. *Was it just another lie?*

Lana walked in the middle of the bridge and stopped. The dark waters of the river were confined under a solid layer of ice, and the moonlight lit up the smooth surface. The stars blinked above, charmed with the stillness of the night. They looked down at her from the depths of the enigmatic universe. The stars kept their secrets as quiet as the guardians who swore their oaths.

How many wishes had she made from here? How many times had she wished to become a guardian and change the world? Who could have known that this dream would come true? Now, when she looked at the stars, she had only one wish, but maybe it would never happen.

Her lips trembled. "I just want to see *him* again."

The sound of heavy footsteps in the snow broke the silence. Lana turned to the park, and her heart expanded as she saw a man in a guardian uniform. He looked at her with his warm green eyes and smiled.

His black glove touched the metal railing. "I never had a chance to see this bridge last time. Now I understand why people talk about it."

"Richard," she whispered.

He came closer to her. "Lana."

Her eyes widened at his uniform. "They didn't fire you."

"Well, this truth-telling thing actually works. After I came back from Death Island, I was interrogated. The committee let me keep my job after I told them everything."

Lana sighed. "Of course. You sacrificed your career to stop David."

He shook his head. "No, I was damn scared. I thought I would lose my job because of him. The committee appreciated my honesty."

"I just can't believe it!" she said. "It's really you."

Richard chuckled. "There was just the two of us. I don't have another twin."

Lana snickered. "That's good. I couldn't handle another one."

The frost covered his chin. More than anything, she wanted to touch him, to feel his cool stubble on her palm. But if she did, she would never be able to let him go.

"That's why you came later," she said.

"Oh, right!" Richard took out a paper roll from his pocket. It had a shining stamp on it. "I wanted to deliver this to you personally."

Lana broke the stamp and unrolled the paper. It was a letter from the Santos Guardian Academy. An image of a dragon was on top of the sheet, and its paws touched curving letters. She'd passed the exams, but that wasn't the only news. She'd gotten an offer to work in the Santos Guardian House. Lana read through the letter until she got to the name, but it wasn't hers.

Lana gave him a puzzled look. "Who is *Lana Laine*?"

"You."

She waved the roll in his face. "No, they got my last name wrong. Wait—this is *your* last name. Didn't you notice? Why didn't you tell them?"

He took her hand. "Oh, I did."

She narrowed her eyes. "This isn't right. We need to fix it."

"Of course we need to." He got down on one knee. "So, Lana, will you marry me, and we can fix this mess together?"

She stood motionless, the light frost pinching her wet cheeks. Her words stuck somewhere in her chest.

Richard squeezed her hand. "Of course, we can just change the name back. It won't take long."

She shook her head. "Please don't. I agree."

"Agree with the marriage part, or the fixing-the-last-name part?"

Lana pulled on his hand, and he stood up. "With the marriage part, of course," she said.

He kissed her, and the warmth of his love melted all of her anxiety away.

Richard wiped her cheek. "If I could turn time back for you, I would do it in a less awkward way."

"I wouldn't let you erase it from our history."

He smiled. "I missed you so much."

They walked down the bridge. The winter forest glowed with blue lights. Everything was quiet, except for the snow crumpling under their feet.

"My father will be surprised to see you," Lana said.

"I saw him today. He already knows."

She pushed his shoulder. "You guys are unbelievable!"

He laughed.

Epilogue

The moonlight lit up the high wooden walls, hiding a small village from the forest. Tiny houses with snowy roofs were huddled together on the cold ground. Windows with black curtains hardly let out any light.

A boy, twelve years old with bright blue eyes, climbed up on his windowsill. He carried a thick book in his hands. Wood crackled in the fireplace, and its warm yellow light lit up the room. He opened the book in the middle and looked at the picture of a mage who held a fireball in his hand. The boy put his palm on the picture, and his heart fluttered.

He moved his hand to the cold window and shifted the curtain. The stars decorated the dark sky, shining like millions of fresh dew droplets. They were exactly the same as they had been the night he'd held the fireball in his hands. *Magic.* It was warm—almost hot. And it was powerful.

"Eric, how many times have I told you about the light?" His mother's voice was close.

Eric moved the curtain back. His mother wore a simple polka-dot dress and an old blue apron that was faded with time. Her blue eyes were tired.

"Mom, can I ask you a question?"

She came closer. "Of course, you can."

He glanced at the book. "Why are some people free, while others have to hide or serve?"

She took the book from his hands and put it on the windowsill. She glanced at her hand, her fingertips scarred from old burns, and put it on her chest. "My little boy, you're almost an adult now. I wish I had an answer for you, but I don't. Life isn't fair."

He took her hand. He'd seen her scars many times and had felt their roughness whenever she touched him.

"I swear, I'll make it fair," he said.

She released her hand. A shadow of fear appeared in her eyes. "Eric, don't even think about doing anything. Mages are strong and powerful, and they can kill you with a single flick if they want to."

He nodded. "I know."

She petted his head. "You'll turn thirteen soon. I know it's scary to leave your home to become a servant in Middle Lake City. If you want, you can stay in the village for a little longer. It's okay to be scared."

Eric shook his head. "I'm not scared." On the windowsill, the flames from the fireplace gleamed on the book's cover. The decision that had grown in him was now ripe and ready to be released from the depths of his heart. "I'll become a servant this spring," he said.

She smiled and kissed his forehead. "My brave boy," she whispered. "Now go to bed."

When she walked away, Eric took the book and approached the fireplace. The flame danced among the logs, teasing him with its warmth and impossible touch. He opened the book in the middle where the picture was and threw it in the fire.

The blaze reflected in his wide eyes. The flame ate the book with greed; it devoured the pages and converted them to ash. Eric grinned and walked to his bed. He wrapped himself in his warm blanket and closed his eyes. Winter was almost over, and very soon, the injustices of this world would burn in hell with all the mages.

About the Author

LUBOV LEONOVA was born in Vladivostok, Russia. After completing her BA in English translation, she immigrated to British Columbia, Canada. While obtaining her Linguistics Certificate from Douglas College, she volunteered in a support group for women who had experienced trauma and domestic violence. This experience inspired her to write "Two Worlds," a series of fantasy novels with feminist themes. Today Lubov is a blogger and a fantasy fiction writer. She lives in New Brunswick with her husband and her bunny, George.